ACCIDENTAL TRYST

NATASHA BOYD

DATE DUE

ACCIDENTAL TRYST

218419

PINXIS

ACCIDENTAL TRYST

TRYSTAN

Charleston Airport
    I slide my fingers under the rim of my starched shirt collar as I walk off the plane in Charleston, South Carolina. The reason I'm here now makes my collar and tie feel like they're choking me.

I'd been hoping to at least stop by my hotel to check in, drop my bag, and connect to my scheduled meeting back in New York. But my flight had been delayed so I need to connect into my meeting from here.

I set my laptop bag on the bar height workstation at the gate across the concourse from my arrival gate and plug in my dead cell phone. Might as well get some work done before my call. Seems like everyone has the same idea. Almost every charging outlet is taken, but I don't have time to find somewhere quiet.

A hint of sugar and flowers wafts through the air, and I'm jostled as some chick next to me digs around in her oversized purse. Women and their massive purses. I shake my head almost involuntarily. Why so much stuff?

My phone buzzes as soon as it's got juice, and I answer.

"Trystan? It's Mac. When are you back?"

"Best case, by tonight, worst case I'll be back Friday."

"Are you sure there's not something you're not telling me?" Mac asks.

I frown. "What do you mean?"

"Rumor has it Carson is offering more. A lot more."

Bloody hell. "I'll grind his fucking nuts," I snap, momentarily forgetting I'm in public. The pressure of my current situation has apparently caught up with me.

"He doesn't have any fucking nuts or he'd up his game." Mac laughs, but he sounds nervous. "It isn't the first time he's done this. But I can trust you, right, Trystan?"

I'd never shaft Mac. We've been doing business for years, and I owe him.

"It's a good offer," Mac adds. "He knows it. We know it."

Yeah. Of course I know it. But I'm just over people being greedy motherfuckers. Where's the honor? The fucking decency? I'm strung tight today and can't check my irritation anymore. "If you see him before I do, tell him to shove his offer up his—"

Now I definitely feel censure emanating from the floral hippie chick with the oversized purse. I turn and catch her blue eyes. "His arse," I finish.

"That's my boy," says Mac.

She's cute. But hippies don't really do it for me, no matter how pretty they are. There's a higher chance of underarm hair, coconut oil, and quinoa for breakfast.

I shudder.

Been there. Tapped that.

"Exactly what I thought you'd say," Mac says. "Or hoping anyway."

Hippie Chick scowls at me and wanders away. I follow her arse, the shape of two full moons visible against the fabric of her long patterned skirt. Probably got legs like tree-trunks. Yes, I'm an asshole, but I prefer a delicate calf. Fuck it, why do I even care? Because her hair is my weakness. Red. No, ginger. No, freaking rose gold and wavy.

What is wrong with me? I shake it off and snatch my gaze away.

"Trystan? You still there?"

"Yeah, I am. Sorry."

Mac sighs. "Look, you good to get on the call with the bank in five minutes? They have some follow-ups from the meeting this morning. And try not to sound like you're holding this deal together like MacGyver with a handful of paper clips." He laughs. "I know it's a bad week."

"Ha. I'm going to take a leak, then I'll call in."

I tap the end button and breathe out a long, slow breath. Immediately, I pull up my Spark app. I'm going to need to get laid if there's a rat's hell chance of surviving the tension of the next few days. The app is location based, so it's useless to pull it up here at the airport. I may be an asshole, but I'm not going to have a quickie right before or after the funeral. Or in a freaking airport bathroom. That's beneath even me. Still, it's worth a look to get my mind back to neutral. Maybe Hippie Chick is on Spark. Wouldn't that be a bloody laugh? With that in mind, I quickly tap through to see if anyone is around me. No joy. Not in this terminal anyway. My phone battery is still so low. I set it down, leaving it charging. I hate to do it, but I've got a long day ahead. I grab my laptop bag though and head to the men's room across the way before the conference call starts.

I wash my hands and then splash water on my face, running my hands over my rough chin. I look up and stare myself in the face. I have my mother's eyes, and my grandmother deserves to see them today. To see the eyes of the daughter she turned her back on. I blow out a breath and drag my damp fingers through my short, dark brown hair.

Game time.

Minutes to spare. I stalk back to the work area. Luckily the spot next to my phone is still open. I unzip my laptop and power it up. I open my email for the dial-in number my assistant, Dorothy, sent me for the conference line. I'm late. Grabbing my charging cell phone, I jam the on button with my thumb and keep it there to fingerprint identify my code. Except there's no code. The screen opens to an array of icons. I wonder if the last update undid my security code. It's probably time to upgrade the entire device, I've been meaning to. I make a mental note to have Dorothy order me the latest iPhone. I hurriedly press the green phone icon and keyboard so I can type in the number.

There's a beep prompt for the conference pin, and I enter it and take a breath.

The call with the bank drags on for almost two hours while they go through our balance sheets line by line. After finally hearing the beep that they've disconnected, MacMillen stays on the conference line. "That went well. I think we're a go."

I exhale in relief, knowing I've spent years building to a point where I could sell. "I'm headed to the funeral. So I hope you don't mind if we talk while I walk?" I glance at my watch. Shit. I'm going to be late to the funeral too.

"No problem. Listen, I forgot it was today, I should have rescheduled the bank. I'm sorry. Will you make it?"

I stalk down the concourse toward the exit and baggage claim. "I think so." I squint at the people milling about at the bottom of the escalator and spot a uniformed girl in a knee length skirt and baggy suit jacket leaning against a pillar. She's scrolling through a phone with one hand and half-heartedly holding a scrawled sign that reads *Montgomery* with the other. Her mousy hair is scraped back into a ponytail so tight, it looks painful. Dressing up for work doesn't seem natural to her.

"Look, I just want to say something to you, Tryst," Mac says in my ear, his age and weariness echoing through his tone. "I know what you're walking away from by ignoring Carson's offer."

"I know you do." I stand in front of the girl. A teenager. Jesus, can't people employ grown-ups these days?

She looks up. Her eyes register me, and her pale skin turns puce. "Sorry," she mumbles. "Are you—?"

I point at my name she holds and nod, jerking my head toward the exit, hoping we can get going. I motion I only have my roller bag.

"I wouldn't blame you," Mac says as I stride out the airport terminal into the muggy Lowcountry air and follow the girl to the limousine waiting area. I hope she's old enough to drive. The phone beeps with an incoming call, I look down but don't recognize the New York number. "I've taught you to look out for yourself, after all," MacMillen continues as I put the phone back to my ear. "That's a lot of money. Money going directly to you. You haven't fought this long and this hard to walk away from what you're worth. And you are worth it. Every penny, and more. I wouldn't blame you," he repeats.

I slide into the back of a dark Escalade, the air-conditioning cuts on, and I take a deep breath. "Yeah," I say. "But *I'd* blame me." I stick a finger in the knot of my tie, yank it loose and undo the top button of my shirt. I cover the phone briefly as I tell the driver to take me to the church instead of the hotel. "And today, of all days," I continue on my call, "I don't need to beat myself up any more. You're a mentor but also a father figure to me. The only other person who might have been even *close* is lying cold and about to be buried. This company represents everything I had to overcome. I've built it stone by stone, and there's only one person I'd trust enough to do what needs to be done. That's you."

The phone beeps again. Same number. I frown, but Mac is talking.

"I'm proud of you, son. Not sure how that family of yours produced you, but I'm glad they did."

"Thanks, Mac," I say sincerely, slightly embarrassed by his pride and faith in me. "I'll talk to you soon."

"Okay. And good luck today. Remember, you succeeded in spite of them. You don't need anything from them. And you don't owe them a damned thing."

"Thank you. Later." I clear the roughness from my voice and end the call.

A voicemail beeps through. Make that two.

I look down, remembering the apps all being rearranged, then I notice the perfect screen. No crack.

My stomach sinks. *Shit.*

I go to the voicemail page and see the caller list, and it truly sinks in that this is not my phone.

David

David

David

David

David

Followed by two voicemails from the number in New York. I tap the first one to listen.

2

EMMY

"*I*'ll grind his fucking nuts," the deep voice next to me growled.

I flinched despite the noise of the busy airport terminal and surreptitiously glanced sideways to the figure sitting next to me at the workstation on his phone.

Who spoke like that to people? And loudly, in public, where everyone could overhear? And his cologne . . . I sniffed, we were close enough after all . . . nice, spicy. It made me think of old leather and rough-hewn wood. The antithesis to his sharp, tailored suit. But there was far too much of the scent. My nose tickled.

His free hand, closest to me, poked out of a dark suit jacket and crisp white cuff and was curled in a fist. A stainless steel watch was barely visible. The skin was tanned and lightly sprinkled with dark hair. My stomach did a little jig. A *very* little jig. It was a purely Pavlovian response. See potentially sexy forearms, have physical reaction.

Probably a vain, stuck up, custom fancy suit-wearing, heavy cologne-wearing, Wall Street douche-wagon. With a small penis.

"Yeah. Tell him to shove his offer up his-" His head jerked

toward me, and I looked up into sharp gray eyes set in tanned skin. "His arse," he finished, eyes pinning mine.

Ah, so he was British. They always were a bit uncouth.

My mouth dried out.

I quickly turned my back.

I had yet to be introduced to the legendary British charm. The only Brits I knew sang loud rugby songs at bars, got shit-faced, and always overstayed last call. Though my college bartending days were far behind me. I'd slogged my way into my executive marketing position and wouldn't pull another pint of Guinness if Jamie Fraser himself was lying naked on the bar in front of me with his mouth open.

I wrinkled my nose and decided to remove myself from the suit monkey's caustic aura. It reminded me I needed to go buy some earbuds for my flight, so I could drown out any other potential idiots. Even if they were too handsome for their own good. Especially if they were.

My phone still needed to charge, so I left it plugged into the worktop where it shared an outlet with the British invasion of peace. As soon as I slipped off the stool, the suit with his broad back seemed to spread out into my newly vacated space, not even noticing I'd left, just that he had more elbow room. Giving in to an eye-roll, I shifted my carry-on bag more securely on my shoulder and headed toward the newsstand.

I browsed the books, picked up a Snickers and selected a bright pink pair of earbuds. My flight was about to be called. Finally. It had been delayed three hours, so I'd gone over and made myself comfortable at the gate opposite that didn't have a flight leaving for a few hours.

Glancing down at my watch, I figured I still had—

Oh, shit! It was past my boarding time. I'd completely lost track. I dumped the chocolate and the earbuds and dashed back the way I'd come. There was hardly anyone left at my gate, the attendant was talking into the speaker.

"Last call for New York, La Guardia," she intoned.

"I'm here," I screeched as I ran past her. "I'm just grabbing my phone. Please don't close the doors."

Shit. I angled to the other gate, thankfully noting asshole was nowhere to be seen.

"Ma'am," the gate attendant called from behind me. "I'll really need you to board now."

"I'm coming," I yelled over my shoulder and grappled with my phone and the cord, yanking it out and wrapping it around my phone as I raced back across, dodging passengers and almost wiping out over a toddler in a stroller.

"Jeez, watch it, lady," the angry mom snapped at me.

My bag slipped down my arm. Gah. "Sorry," I yelped and made it toward the sour-faced woman at the door to the gang-way. Great. Hours to relax, and now I was stressed and damp with sweat. Why was I always so bad with time? I just couldn't figure it out like most people. Thank God for electronic calendars, alerts, and reminders nowadays. It was the only way I could function in my job.

"Thank you," I gasped as I took back my ticket and hustled down to the plane. Unfortunately my cheap airline didn't have assigned seats, so I was liable to be sandwiched into a middle seat at the back. And darn, now I needed to pee. Why hadn't I peed during all that time I had?

My cheeks flamed as I entered and shouldered my way down the narrow aisle avoiding the passengers' irritated glares at the latecomer. To top it off I was accidentally bumping people's arms as I moved along with my unwieldy carry-on that for some reason now wouldn't stay on my shoulder.

"Sorry. Sorry. Sorry," I mumbled as I headed toward the back of the plane looking for a free seat. I finally spotted one in the second to last row between a large man who was already passed out and snoring loudly, and a skinny, teenaged boy on the aisle who was fidgeting nervously and glancing frantically between me and the seat next to him.

As I approached, his face matched and surpassed mine in probable color. He looked like he was going to die of embarrassment if I sat next to him, but I had no other option. I glanced down to make sure my top wasn't gaping and bra straps weren't showing. No need to send this clearly hormonal teenager into an apoplexy.

"Sorry," I said again, for what felt like the millionth time and looked meaningfully at the seat next to him. The boy half grunted, half mumbled, and leapt up out of his seat so I could squeeze past him.

"Ma'am, I'll need you to stow your carry-on under the seat in front of you and fasten your seat belt. The aircraft is about to leave the gate."

I scowled at the flight attendant as I wedged myself into the seat and stuffed my bag between my feet. What did she think I was trying to do, exactly? Her eyes widened under my glare. Oops. Probably not good to piss off the person who was in charge of your comfort for the next hour or so. Gah, I needed to pee so bad. There was no way to do that now.

"I'll need you to put your phone on Airplane Mode too," she said, looking at my phone still clutched in my hand. Oh yeah, I was still holding it, the white cord wrapped around it. I looked closer. I may have scratched the screen somehow. Or was that a crack? My stomach sank as I thought about the cost of having the screen replaced. About as much as this airline ticket had cost. Exactly what I didn't need. Hopefully it was just a crack that wouldn't get worse.

I stuck the phone between my legs and fumbled for the seat belt, elbowing the large man next to me. "Sorry," I said yet again. He didn't even move. Thank goodness for small mercies.

Clipping the metal buckle together, I dug out the phone from between my legs. I wouldn't have time to text David to let him know I was on the plane and about to be out of contact. Dammit. He would worry like crazy.

The plane shuddered, jerked, and began a slow roll away from the gate. Wow, I really did cut it fine. Didn't they normally have ten minutes between closing the doors and leaving the gate? I must have really been late. Late and lucky. The flight attendant was still waiting, staring pointedly at me.

I depressed the home button and went to swipe up and select Airplane Mode when everything in me simply froze in confusion. I stared down at the foreign picture in front of me.

A screensaver of a bridge.

A long, beautiful suspension bridge I'd seen before. The beautiful, graceful, and delicate looking Verrazano Bridge that connected Staten Island to Brooklyn. The sky was red behind it. Gorgeous.

Had I accidentally saved a random picture as my screensaver? Maybe. I was a little distracted sometimes. And very under pressure at work.

"Ma'am. Airplane Mode."

"Got it." I swiped up and hit the small airplane icon and then gave her a tight smile.

She smiled back thinly. "Thank you."

My eyes went back to the phone in my hand as she moved off into the galley. The case, plain black, was mine. Right? The cord? The same. Standard. The crack—unfamiliar. With sinking dread, I pressed the home button again and then swiped right across the screen to open phone access.

A keypad appeared.

My heart pounded, and my stomach sank.

I never used a code.

Stupid, I know. But . . . oh shit.

This was not my phone.

* * *

THIRTY THOUSAND FEET Above Sea Level

"Is this like a Jedi mind trick or did you forget your passcode?"

I jerked in surprise at the voice right by my ear. "Shit." I expelled a breath. And looked over to the kid on my left. "What?"

"You've been staring at the phone lock screen for twenty-five minutes. Are you trying to unlock it with your mind?"

I looked down at *his* phone that was in the middle of some game with little villages and people.

"You were distracting me from my raid," he said when I didn't answer, pulling his large earphones back to hang around his neck. "I kept thinking, if she's going to pull off this Jedi shit I don't want to miss it."

"Your language."

He shrugged. "Sorry to offend."

"Not offended. But don't your parents tell you not to swear?"

"I'm fifteen. And if they gave a shit they probably would. But they're too busy fighting over me and swearing at each *other*."

"I'm sorry," I said, looking around. "Are they on board?"

"No. My mom lives in Charleston. My dad lives in New York."

"So you're heading to your dad's. Where do you go to school?"

"I homeschool. After social services got on our case about all my missed days, it seemed like a better option, you know? Anyway, school is overrated. So why are you staring at your phone like you've never seen it before."

I pursed my lips, then blew a small breath out the side of my mouth. "That's coz I haven't," I mumbled.

"Sorry?"

"It's not my phone." I winced.

There was no response. After a few seconds I glanced up to see the kid staring at me, an assessing look on his face. Now that I was looking at him, his eyes did seem a little more mature than a fifteen-year-old's should. Maybe going through a family breakup would do that to you. I wondered if I'd looked the same.

"You steal it?" he asked.

"No. Jeez. No. I took it by accident."

"Uh huh."

I tried to explain to him what happened.

He shook his head. "That's one I haven't heard before. And I've heard a lot."

"I bet you have."

The drinks cart was four rows away. Was it too early to have a cocktail? I shook my head. How could I be so stupid? My whole life was on that phone. My calendar, my appointments, every meeting. Call in numbers for conference calls. My photos. *Gah!* My photos.

"So you lost your phone. And now you have someone else's. Did you at least back yours up to the cloud?"

My chest grew tighter and my nose stung. I could not lose control of my emotions right now. My eyes prickled. I blew out a breath. "Shit," I said. "'Scuse *my* language." It was no use, tears spilled over. "Dammit."

"So, I'm assuming . . . no?"

I shook my head vigorously. I'd been meaning to, of course.

"So you need your phone back. Any chance the person whose phone you have, has yours? Maybe they took yours first, that's why you thought that was yours."

A spark of hope flared. "Maybe."

"So just call your number when you land."

I nodded. "I can't be without a phone." I thought of work and my annoying boss, Steven. I thought of David. My stomach clenched with anxiety again, my breathing became shallow. God, even if I could get into this phone I wouldn't be able to access our annoying POP server work email. Not that I could remember the password for that anyway. "I just can't."

"I feel you." He shuddered. "But use this one until you get yours back. At least you can use the GPS and browser and shit and make a phone call if you need to. There, see? Problem solved."

I held it up where the lock screen still showed number circles. "Duh."

The kid shrugged. "I can bypass that for you."

I frowned. "What? Really?"

"Sure. It'll cost you, but sure."

"Cost me?"

The kid winked.

"If you're going to ask me to flash you, I'd rather be without a phone."

His shoulders slumped. "Damn. And you're so hot too."

I snorted an unexpected laugh. "Um, thanks . . .?"

"Your loss."

"Yours apparently."

"It was worth a try." He tilted his head toward the flight attendant and her cart. "You could buy me a screwdriver, and we'll call it even."

"You're fifteen," I hissed. "I'm not committing a crime just to get into someone's phone."

"Bitcoin?"

"Is that a question?"

"I guess not." Again he shrugged. "As I said, I can do it. But if you don't really need a phone . . . then whatevs." He slipped his massive earphones back over his ears and closed his eyes, chin bopping.

I squeezed the phone in my hand. "Fine." I sighed.

3

EMMY

oncourse B, La Guardia Airport
       Two hours later

"This will never be discussed, is that clear?" I scowled.

"Yes, ma'am. Do you want my number?"

"No!" I thought of my phone issues and general computer issues. "Yes. Maybe. And don't call me ma'am. It makes me feel ancient."

The kid grinned. His braces had blue elastics.

"As long as you know I will never, *ever* do that again," I reiterated and winced. "But maybe I can call you to ask questions?" God, I sounded pathetic.

He nodded and handed me a business card.

"You have a business card?" I looked down.

"Sure. I'm a YouTuber when I'm not mining bitcoin. Gotta have those for cons and shit."

"Cons?"

"Conferences? Conventions?"

This day was shaping up to be the most surreal of my twenty-eight-year-long life. I read his name. "Xanderr? What kind of a name is that?"

"It's my YouTuber name. You can call me Al."

"As in the Paul Simon song?" What the hell was I going to do? I couldn't call anyone. All my phone numbers were in my contacts. I couldn't remember a single one.

"As in short for Alex? Alexander? My real name." He raised his eyebrows. "Who's Paul Simon?"

"Never mind." I shook my head. "Sure, sorry."

"Well, I don't tell anyone my real name. But I like you, Mad Emmy."

"Just Emmy." I glanced at the phone in my hand. It was now unlocked with the passcode disabled.

"Cool. So, I gotta jet, yeah?" He pulled on a cherry red cap with the peak as straight as a ruler and yanked it sideways on his head. "Good luck with the owner of that phone. My spidey senses say you're gonna need it."

"Thank you, I think."

Al gave me a peace sign and turned, lumbering away down the concourse with his pants hanging low and his high tops undone.

I grinned at his retreating figure in spite of my dilemma.

Al had put the phone back on Airplane Mode after unlocking it so I could think about what to do. As long as it was on Airplane Mode it couldn't be tracked. Not sure what that accomplished for me except the owner of the phone wouldn't immediately assume it had been stolen and cancel it. He might think it was in his luggage somewhere.

Who was I kidding?

I glanced around the busy concourse. I needed a pay phone, but of course those probably didn't exist anymore.

A twenty-minute walk turned up nothing, so I ended up using the phone at the information desk. I typed in the digits for my own number. My fingers were sweaty. Why was I so nervous? It was an honest mistake.

My call connected and began to ring, making my heart

pound. Not straight to voicemail. So my phone was on. Maybe no one had taken mine, and it was still sitting there at the charging station.

No, I would have seen it. The only way I could have taken the wrong one was if it was the only one there. Finally my voicemail clicked on, and I heard my voice asking the caller to leave a message.

It beeped. "Um . . ." I was leaving myself a message. Seriously? "Um . . . This is my phone."

I glanced up at the information agent, an older African-American gentleman who was looking at me askance. "I mean . . . I'm calling my own phone to leave a message in case you, whoever you are, took it, or whatever. Um . . . God, this is stupid," I finished on a mumble and thrust the mouthpiece toward the information agent. His name tag read *Phillip.*

Phillip took it slowly and hung it up, his eyebrows raised. "Sounds like you got yourself into a bit of a pickle. Why don't you go on into the wireless store over there and get you a new one. They can keep your number these days, you know."

"I know. But I can't." My shoulders slumped. "I can't afford it right now, and anyway all my contacts and photos and all that stuff is on my phone, not backed up and . . ."

A thought struck me. Oh shit! I leaned across the counter and grabbed the phone set back and with shaking fingers dialed my number again. It rang, and I drummed my fingers impatiently.

"Please don't cancel your phone," I blurted as soon as I heard the beep. "Listen . . . I can't be without a phone and . . . I may have yours? I mean if you took mine, then I'm pretty sure I took yours. By accident. Please. I know you don't know me." My mind raced to come up with a solution. "I'm in New York now. I don't know where you live or where you were going, but if there's a chance you were arriving in Charleston, I'll be back there in three days. We could meet and swap phones back?" I blew out a breath. "I . . . please?" Swallowing, my cheeks beating with heat from my predicament, I tried again. "If . . . you don't mind I can make a couple of calls with your phone and you can use mine, I would be forever grateful. It's just . . . if you get a call or a text message from someone called David, can you pretend to be me? I mean on text, not on a call obviously, and say . . . oh jeez. God, I'm babbling. Can you just call me back if you get this? On this number, I'll wait a little while."

Phillip raised his eyebrows at me again but shrugged.

"Or on your phone," I continued. "Which I'm pretty sure I have. And I'm sure you want it back. Okay . . . okay, bye."

I handed the phone back.

"Well," said Phillip. "That was awkward."

I leaned down and banged my head with a solid *thunk* on the counter.

Mortified. That's what I was. Mortified and hopeless. What the hell was I going to do? I took a few steps and leaned my back against a pillar then slowly sank down to the ground. I needed to sit for a few minutes and think.

* * *

"Miss?" I jumped and turned my head to see Phillip. "Phone call for you, I think."

"You think?"

"You didn't leave him your name, so I'm assuming the red-haired hippie girl is you?"

"I'm not a hippy!" I snorted indignantly, getting up. "Wait, how the hell does he know what I look like?"

Phillip shrugged. "I suggest you ask him. And I suggest you hurry. He doesn't sound like the most patient person."

I followed Phillip to the counter. He handed me the phone while attending to another customer.

Taking it, I took a deep breath and held it to my ear. I heard muffled talking, as if his hand was covering the microphone. A man and a woman's voice.

I cleared my throat. "H-Hello?"

"Hold on," I heard through the muffled sound. Then, "Thank Christ," a male voice said loudly.

I jerked the phone away as my eardrum sang.

"Who is this?" the voice barked.

What the hell?

I cautiously brought the phone back to my ear. "If you can refrain from yelling—"

"Sorry. I'm sorry. Who is this, please?" The male voice had a British flatness to the enunciation and sounded as if the act of apologizing caused him immense pain. A vision of slate gray eyes and strong hands flashed in my mind. *Oh, no.*

At least he immediately apologized, which was unexpected. Also his accent was not purely British. He'd been in America for a while by the sound of it

"Hello? Hello? *Christ,*" he snapped. "Hello?"

"Yes. Yes, I'm here."

"Do you have my phone?"

"Do you have mine?" I asked, indignance crawling up my throat.

There was a long sigh, and I realized my error.

"Of course you do," I mumbled, embarrassed at my stupidity. "That's why . . . you, uh, got my message and called me here, on this phone."

"Riiiight. So I don't mean to be an arse, but what the hell is going on?"

I pulled his phone out of my purse. "It's still on Airplane Mode. I'll turn that off if you want to call it and check. But I'm assuming it's yours. And I'm sorry. I was late for my flight, so I only realized once I was on the plane with no time to come back."

"Uh huh." He sounded anything but understanding. "Turn Airplane Mode off. I'll send myself a text."

I tapped the airplane symbol and watched service bars come back to life. "So can I ask how on earth you managed to take my phone?" I couldn't help asking.

"Took *your* phone? Lady, I picked up the only phone left charging, which I assumed was mine since it was where I plugged it in. So if anyone took the wrong phone first it was you."

The phone in my hand beeped. I looked down.

UNKNOWN NUMBER: *Who the hell doesn't recognize their own cell phone?*

MY MOUTH DROPPED OPEN.

I ANGRILY TYPED BACK: *Spoiled, suit-wearing monkeys who think screens magically fix themselves.*

A PUFF OF AIR, suspiciously like a short laugh sounded over the line. "Great point," he said, his voice a purr. "My apologies."

"Accepted. And . . . I'm sorry too," I said gruffly.

"Listen, we need to make a plan. I'm . . . I'm late." Feminine laughter sounded in the background again. "And for some lunatic reason you all but begged me not to cancel my phone." Clearly he was late for a date of some kind. An irrational feeling of jealousy made me frown as I wondered what type of woman this enigmatic, apologetic, temper-filled, silver-eyed, man was attracted to. Then I shook my head.

"I know, I'm sorry. I can't be left without a phone. I'm in New York City. I can't afford a new phone right now, and I didn't back mine up to the cloud. I'm home in three days, then I can mail your phone to you, and you can do the same?"

"Three days? You must be out of your mind. I'm in the middle of a deal to sell my business."

"Where are you?" I pressed on, determined to make this work. "I mean what city?"

"Charleston, South Carolina."

"That's where I live!"

"Yeah, well, you're not here now, are you, and I don't plan on staying here longer than I have to." He followed this statement with an inhalation of breath that sounded as if he'd surprised himself with his admission.

"What's wrong with Charleston?"

"It's fine. Nothing. So-"

"For real. Be specific. Why don't you like Charleston?" Stunning architecture, restaurants to die for, beaches . . . he obviously didn't appreciate the same things I did.

"That's a question I don't even discuss with my shrink."

"You have a shrink?"

"No. But I probably should have one, given that I'm sharing my secrets with a virtual stranger."

I laughed unexpectedly. "By the way, I am *not* a hippie." I looked up at Phillip who was regarding me with one eyebrow raised.

"He told you that?"

"He did tell me, and I did *not* appreciate it."

"So what's your name, Hippie Chick?"

"Emmy," I answered automatically, surprised he wasn't hurriedly ending the call for his busy schedule as he'd been ready to do moments before. "And yours?"

"Emmy," he repeated, my name sounding like caramel. "Short for?"

"Not even my shrink knows that."

He laughed, deep and smoky, and my blood warmed.

"You don't have a shrink," he said.

"I could have a shrink," I answered indignantly, though God knew why. I was smirking as we bantered. Holy shit, were we . . . *flirting?*

21

"You don't," he answered smoothly. "Besides, now that I have your phone, I could probably find out more about you than anyone alive. Even your shrink."

My stomach dropped. "You wouldn't."

"Why? What are you hiding?"

I swallowed, my cheeks hot. I looked down at his phone. "I guess since I have yours, I could do the same."

"Good luck with that, I have a code. A security detail you probably should have had on yours too."

"Good thing I bypassed that code then, isn't it?"

"That's funny."

"And serious." I opened his phone and mulled his apps. "Ugh." I couldn't help the grunt of disgust. "You have a smorgasbord of dating apps. Figures."

"Lucky guess, Hippie Chick."

"Emmy," I corrected, but somehow I wasn't as annoyed as I'd expected. I pulled open a stock ticker app to prove to him I was looking at his phone. "Why are you watching Delta Industries? Own shares of them, do you? Whoa, quite a lot of shares by the looks of it."

"Mother fucker. You're serious."

I bobbed my head back at his tone. "You have a foul mouth."

"Who the hell *are* you? Is this a joke?" His voice was cold. Memories of his ice-chip eyes and growl like a biting arctic wind at the airport flooded back to me.

"Excuse me?" I was genuinely confused. "Listen, Dr. Jekyll, I'm not sure what crawled inside your bespoke suit and into your crack, but you have my phone too!"

"You've bypassed my security code. So either you're a hacker holding my phone hostage, and probably employed by my competitor in the midst of a multimillion-dollar deal, or you're lying. And you're not lying, are you?"

I swallowed. I guess I hadn't really thought the whole code breaking someone's phone thing through.

"Consider that phone burned," he said and the line went dead.

I stood for a few seconds then pulled the white handset from my ear. And stared at it like I expected it to apologize. Then I handed it back to Phillip. My blood pressure rose with my anger, but I had no direction for it. He hadn't even told me his name. As if it would help me somehow, I went to his email. If I was in trouble I may as well earn it.

A ton of emails from someone called Carson. Whatever. I wasn't going to read them. I just needed my nemesis' name.

Tmontgomery @ and some long ass, important sounding extension. I didn't even look to see what the T stood for. I selected and copied.

New email.

To: tmontgomery
From: tmontgomery

MR. MONTGOMERY,

YOU ARE A GRADE A PRICK. *Now I am in your email (you asked for it). If you cancel your phone I will leak all of your financial information.*

REGARDS,
Hippie Chick

I HIT SEND. Then immediately felt the kind of remorse one feels after doing something really, really bad. Or really, really stupid. Immediately, I pulled up the text app and found the message he'd sent from my number.

SORRY ABOUT THE EMAIL. *Please, please, don't cancel your phone. I'm in New York. As it is I haven't even left the airport yet. I need to get a cab out to Far Rockaway and need access to a phone for safety reasons, and I can't afford a new one right now. I'll bring it back to you, I swear. I'll explain how I got into your phone as long as you don't cancel it.*

DOTS CAME up to show he was typing a response. Then they disappeared.

I held my breath, but nothing happened.

"Shit," I said.

"Are you quite done here?" I looked up to see Phillip again. "It's probably time you moved on," he said. "I think you're scaring people away."

I pouted at him. "Offense taken," I responded and hefted up my purse. "But thanks for the use of the phone."

He nodded and turned to a lady who was holding an armful of enormous Toblerone bars, wandering toward the information desk and looking really lost.

"*She* doesn't look scared," I told him.

"Bye." He widened his eyes and wiggled his fingers at me.

"Fine." I rolled my eyes, headed toward baggage claim to get my bag, then out to the taxi stand.

I clutched Suit Monkey's phone in my hand the whole time. It was warm and noisy outside, with cars honking to get the attention of their waiting passengers. The line for taxis moved fast. My cab driver was monosyllabic, and as I sat in the backseat, I decided to at least add my number into the phone as a contact. I started typing my name, but then if he texted or called me and my own name popped up it would be weird.

I decided on

First Name: *Suit*

Last Name: *Monkey*
Company: *who has Emmy's phone held hostage*
Address: *Douchbag Industries*
Save. For some reason that made me feel better.

Then I called ahead while I still had use of a phone that hadn't been disconnected.

4

EMMY

I should have flown into JFK, it would have been better than having to drive through Manhattan to get to my destination. Phone calls made, I unlocked the phone again and looked at the dating apps and couldn't help shaking my head. What world did we live in? I'd taken the leap a couple of years ago to dip my toe in the cesspool, and it was as murky and gross as I'd imagined. This guy didn't seem to mind though, if anything he had memberships to every type of dating site I'd heard of and some I hadn't. I wondered if he was on the site for married people wanting to have affairs too. That would tell me a lot about him.

Who *was* T Montgomery? I went back to his email.

The senders were repeats—some guy named Trent, about five from someone named "Mac" MacMillen, more from Carson, all interspersed with emails from a person named Dorothy. I opened one from Dorothy this morning that was marked as already read:

RECEPTION *after the funeral address is 17 Laurens Street, Charleston. I've already informed the car service. Home of Alston Family (presume friends of your late grandfather). They've also requested your presence at the reading of the will after the reception. Address of law office attached. Good luck today.*

I DIDN'T KNOW this man, even his name yet, but all of a sudden his gruff demeanor and snappy attitude seemed different in the context of him attending the funeral of a family member.

Before I could talk myself out of it, I opened the text box again.

YOU NEVER TOLD *me your name*

THE RESPONSE CAME IMMEDIATELY.

SUIT MONKEY: *I'm surprised you haven't ferreted it out of my phone.*

I WANTED *you to tell me. And by the way I'm not a hacker.*

SUIT MONKEY: *I know.*

YOU KNOW? *I'm kind of offended you don't think I'm capable of being a hacker. You have to admit bypassing your code was pretty awesome.*

SUIT MONKEY: *Honey, you have zero security on your phone. Interesting photos btw. I don't think you fit the profile.*

I'M NOT sure there is a hacker profile. And STOP GOING THROUGH MY PHOTOS. Or I'll go through yours.

SUIT MONKEY: *Fine. Are you a hacker?*

No. So anyway—your name?

SUIT MONKEY: *It's not a good time. I'm about to walk into a church.*

THAT MAKES it the perfect time!

SUIT MONKEY: *Um. There is so much wrong with that statement. But I'll bite. How so?*

I'M ASSUMING since you are going to a church in the middle of the week in the middle of the day, that you aren't there for any of life's happy occasions.

SUIT MONKEY: *Astute.*

FAMILY MEMBER? Friend? Or both?

SUIT MONKEY: *Family member.*

NOT BOTH. Interesting.

So DO you hate your name? Is that why you won't tell me? Is it weird?

SUIT MONKEY: *Weirder than the fact you are texting me when you know I'm heading into a funeral? Thanks for the condolences, by the way.*

SUIT MONKEY: *And no, I don't hate my name.*

*:: drums fingers :: Do you **want** me to go through your emails?*

THERE WAS A LONG PAUSE.

SUIT MONKEY: *Trystan Montgomery. And like that would stop you.*

TRYSTAN.

SUIT MONKEY: *Yes.*

WOW.

SUIT MONKEY: *Wow?*

THAT'S MY FAVORITE NAME.

ANOTHER LONG PAUSE.

SUIT MONKEY: *So you're not a hacker but . . . are you a hooker?*

ARE YOU SERIOUS RIGHT NOW?

THERE WAS NO RESPONSE. I looked out the window as we crossed the bridge into the city, the driver weaving in and out of traffic and lurching to a stop periodically when he misjudged the distance between cars. I was starting to get motion sickness.

I looked down at the phone in my hand and wondered how many times David was blowing up my phone that was probably in Trystan's pocket. Trystan. It fit. Somehow. And spoke to me in a strange punch to the chest. Sighing, I opened the screen on Trystan's phone again.

BY THE WAY, the wake is at 17 Laurens Street, your driver has the details. And Dorothy says you are also requested to attend the reading of the will. If you decide not to accept any inheritance money due to your pride or whatever, feel free to put it in my name: Emmaline Angelique Dubois. Social Security number XXX-XX-XXXX (now you can get your background checkers on me).

SUIT MONKEY: *Definitely not a hacker. Maybe we should have a session on online safety. Never send personal information via insecure channels. French? You don't sound French.*

STOP TEXTING ME. You're at a funeral. It's rude.

SUIT MONKEY: *Luckily the only person who I'd be worried about disrespecting is dead.*
Suit Monkey: *Who's David?*

5

TRYSTAN

*E*ven though I'm in the air-conditioned back seat, sweat is beading at my temple. I have to get myself under control. I pinch the bridge of my nose and squeeze my eyes closed. The car stops, engine running, outside Grace Cathedral. I want to be pissed at Emmy or whoever she is for breaking into my phone, but I'm reluctantly impressed. More pressing though is the reality of where I am.

"All right?" my driver asks, staring at me through the reflection of the rearview mirror.

I blow out a breath. "Yeah. Are you okay with waiting?"

"Your dime. Your time." She shrugs.

I look out the tinted windows at the parked cars and the people milling around the entrance. I don't recognize anyone. Not surprising as I haven't had anything to do with this family since I was a child. Not by choice back then. But by choice now.

The phone on the seat next to me buzzes. I expect it be yet another call or voicemail from "David." Boyfriend? Jealous husband? Hacker contact? Who am I kidding? Emmy is no more a hacker than I'm the prodigal son. I don't know what possessed me to suddenly accuse her. I guess I felt uncomfortable with our instant and surprising intimacy, and her admission she'd broken into my phone gave me a perfect out that I grabbed with both hands. I look at the phone, stalling for time before I have to get out and walk into that church. She's in New York. In my city. And I'm in hers.

As soon as most of the people congregating outside have moved into the church, I do my top button back up, pull my tie back to my neck, and step out of the vehicle.

* * *

ON MY WAY toward the entrance of Grace Cathedral, I see my cousin Beau. At least I think it's Beau.

"Trystan?"

"Yeah, Beau. Wow. Look at you." He's grown up and thinned out. I can't help smiling at his warm brown eyes that remind me of happier times in my distant childhood.

"Me? What about you?" His eyes rake over my suit, the Patek Filipe on my wrist and down to my Gucci loafers. "Something tells me this is your normal dress code, and you're not just dressed up of the funeral. Unlike me. I'm normally in shorts and Dockers." He tugs at his collar. "I'm dying in this suit."

It's a little ill-fitting, but I don't comment on it. "You're looking good though."

"Yeah, no longer the chubby kid. Damn, I'm glad you're here. I was hoping you'd come."

"I didn't want to."

"Probably not, but I've been following your successes, and I was hoping you'd come down and rub their faces in it."

I bob my head back, surprised.

"What? You think I didn't think they were fucking psycho for throwing you guys out?"

I swallow and grab the back of my neck. "No, I just, uh, didn't think you knew. We were kids."

"Well, I didn't for years, I just thought you and your mom moved. I was bummed."

"We did move."

"I mean, moved by choice. But then, well, I overheard some shit growing up. If it's any consolation, they fought about it until the end. And I'm sorry about your mother."

Scowling, I let the words roll over me, unsure how they make me feel.

"Come on," says Beau, oblivious to my discomfort. "Let's get you inside. I have to help carry the coffin. Just waiting on the hearse to arrive." He grimaces.

"I can see myself in. I'm not sitting up front with her."

Beau hesitates. "You sure?"

I nod once. Decisively. "Let's catch up after the service."

The phone in my pocket buzzes again once more. I pull it out. *Emmy: I'm sorry for your loss.*

I quickly type out *That makes one of us*, then I delete it and write a simple *Thank you.* Just then the hearse pulls up.

I tense, watching, sizing up the suited men who come to help bear the coffin. In a parallel life perhaps I'd be one of the six.

With Beau is his father, my uncle; he's smaller than I remember. In my memories he's large and mean. Now he looks older, flaccid and unkempt. Weak.

I blow out a breath and hurry toward the entrance, watching as they and four other men ease the coffin of glossy dark wood out of the hearse and heft it up to their shoulders.

Some last stragglers scurry inside to get their seats. I follow them in.

* * *

STANDING IN THE DIM, cool church at the back, I feel none of the expected emotions. Not that I know what I should be feeling. My eyes glide down each row, noting coiffed hair and black hats, until I get to the front. The stiff neck and shoulders of the Montgomery matriarch holds her head high. Her gray hair is tied tight in an elegant chignon. I presume the small hat she wears hangs a tasteful veil over her eyes.

I do feel a spark of something then. The prick of a little boy's fear rushing back at me through the years as if I hadn't grown up the last two decades. The dread of being a disappointment. The shame of it. The utterly helpless feeling of how I couldn't change to be what they wanted so they could love me. But with all these emotions, anger emerges too. Anger at how one woman could so utterly destroy lives she didn't feel worthy of fitting into to her social order. And hatred. With every fiber of my being, I hate Isabel Montgomery.

Maybe I really should consider a shrink.

I don't know what makes me do it. But I pull the phone out of my pocket.

TALK TO ME, I type. *I need a distraction. Is Trystan really your favorite name?*

I SLINK into a pew at the back, nodding to an elderly couple I don't recognize. She hands me a hymnal. "Thanks," I whisper, and she nods, facing forward again. As soon as I look down at the phone, though, I feel her staring daggers at the side of my face. I look up and stare right back at her until she drops her eyes and looks forward. Her husband glances at me, and I nod, looking away.

EMMY: *It really is. Tristan was a knight of Author's roundtable. But mostly, it reminds me of a movie I adore. Stardust. Have you seen it?*

ME: *I don't watch a lot of movies. Don't have a whole lot of time.*

EMMY: *Well, if you ever find yourself at a loose end with two hours free, I highly recommend it. There's comedy, romance, murder, family feuds, gay pirates, and witchcraft.*

ME: *That sounds like something I'd avoid at all costs. There's enough of that in real life.*

EMMY: *Color me intrigued with your life! Which part, the murder, the gay pirates, or the witchcraft?*
 Emmy: *Hold up. My cab just pulled up at my destination. Bit of a dodgy neighborhood so have to keep my wits about me. Text u later.*

IT BOTHERS me Emmy is not safe. She has my phone, of course I want her to be safe. I want my phone back.

Sighing, annoyed that I no longer have her texting as a distraction, I put my phone away just as Beau and the other pallbearers turn from the front to find their places. My gaze tracks down the aisle toward them and passes Isabel Montgomery again. She turns her head then and looks right at me as if she'd known exactly where I was sitting. The years have taken their toll. She looks weary, and so, so sad.

Something heavy and uncomfortable turns over inside me.

I blink and look away.

6

TRYSTAN

*W*e sing hymns, ones I'm yanking the tunes for from the bottom of my childhood memories. Because of course I haven't been in church since I left this cradle of the South.

People I don't know eulogize about what a wonderful man my grandfather was. I try not to focus too hard on why we're here, but the long buried anger is clawing its way out of me. I loved him. But, no, he wasn't a wonderful man. He wasn't strong enough to stand up to his dragon wife. He wasn't strong enough to stop his daughter and grandson being kicked out. Perhaps he did give away lots of money to charities, but what does that really mean? I let out a harsh breath and pinch the bridge of my nose. Does it make you a better person if you give money to your church but don't take care of the emotional well-being of your own flesh and blood? My hand itches to go to my pocket to grab the phone and distract myself, instead I start running through the financials of my deal with MacMillen to keep my mood neutral. I think about my call with Mac, and how he reminded me I built my company from nothing. Nothing. I don't want anything from this family. They didn't want me, and now I've been fine without them. Whatever last ditch attempt my grandfather has made by including me in the will, I don't want. I promise myself I'll sign whatever it is over to my cousin Beau if he wants it.

This thought steels my resolve to pay my respects and then get the hell out of this town.

Finally the six pallbearers return to the front of the cathedral and heave the weight of the solid wood casket onto their shoulders again and walk solemnly down the aisle.

Maybe the best thing that ever happened to me was this family excommunicating my mother and me. Perhaps I wouldn't have had the same appetite and ambition without their cold shoulders. Maybe I'd be a plump, weak man like my uncle. He passes me then, glancing to the side as if he hears my thoughts. His eyes, so much like my mother's, reveal no recognition. He flicks them forward again. Following behind is Isabel Montgomery, and then a few others I don't recognize, but who seem to be important to the family. I should have slipped out before the recessional. Now I have to leave the church while people mill around outside exchanging solemn talk about how fitting the eulogy was and hope no one recognizes me.

IF YOU WERE STUCK *in a church and there were angry villagers outside, how would you escape?*

EMMY: *That's happened to me before. It's best to stay inside.*

I LET out a bark of laughter, drawing the censured looks of a few last funeral attendees as they file past.

WHAT DID you do to make the villagers angry? I ask, buying into her make-believe for a moment.

EMMY: *That's a story for another day. But if Father Pete is still there, tell him Emmy says hello and ask him for a shot of fortifying Irish Whiskey. He keeps some in the sacristy.*

MY GOD, this girl. If you take out the fact she stole my phone, she's a sparkling, fresh mountain brook on an otherwise shit-filled sewer of a day. I look up. The priest is at the doors of the church accepting thanks for his thoughtful sermon and wishing the last people well. I have no idea if it's Father Pete or if she just made that up. As much as a shot of alcohol right now would be welcome, I don't need to see my family with whiskey on my breath. I stand and make my way to the exit. I shake the priest's hand and then step into the bright South Carolina sun so I can head to the reading of the will.

* * *

THE LAW OFFICES OF RAVENEL & Maybank is on the first floor of the historic Sassaportas building overlooking King Street. Out the window of the reception area I can see all the brand name stores interspersed with Crogan's Jewel Box (the family jeweler) on down to Berlin's where even my twelve-year-old self remembers my grandfather used to buy all of his suits. I'm early, hoping to get my part done and dusted and not have to sit with Isabel Montgomery and have her flick her eyes over me again.

Unfortunately, the receptionist with the tight bun who introduces herself as Daisy informs me Mr. Ravenel, the family executor, is still on his way back from the reception. I park myself in a corner armchair and lament the fact I didn't bring my laptop in from the car so I can do some work. Pulling out Emmy's phone, I try and log into my email through a browser and can't remember the password because our IT guy makes me change it every month. My inability to get work done starts to make my skin crawl. Deciding I'll just call Dorothy, my assistant, I then freeze when I realize I don't have my own assistant's number memorized. *Jesus.* I know I know it. But I'm so agitated now I can't get my mind to bring it up. I loosen my tie and blink hard.

"Sir, can I get you anything?" The receptionist's voice makes my eyes snap open, and I become aware I've been sighing and shifting and generally climbing out of my skin. It crosses my mind I'm showing symptoms of a digital withdrawal.

"I'm fine. Thank you."

"Water?" she presses, looking at me like I might lose my shit, and she's legitimately concerned she'll have to witness a grown man cry. If only she knew my agitation came from annoyance rather than grief.

She stands and moves around the desk toward the spring water dispenser in the corner, and I become aware of her tight black skirt suit and really long legs. She's cute too, in that librarian way. I let my eyes linger on her while she's not looking. It's inappropriate, I know, but I'd give my left nut for a distraction. Any distraction. She bends to retrieve a paper cup, and I suddenly veer from inappropriate to downright pervy. God, I'm going to miss my dating apps for the next couple of days. I have to catch a flight out of here tonight, get my phone back, and return to my life. Dragging my eyes away, I search the reading material on the table next to me for something to read. *Golf Digest, Golf Digest, Good Housekeeping,* and *Golf Digest.*

The receptionist clears her throat, and I look up to her holding out a cup of water with a smirk playing around her mouth. I glance back at the water machine and note the reflective plastic. Normally, not one to embarrass easily, I feel heat claw its way up my neck. "Thank you," I mumble, taking the water.

"Daisy," she says.

"What?"

"My name? It's Daisy."

"Yes, sorry. Thanks, Daisy."

No problem," she says huskily. Then she lays a hand on my shoulder. "Do you, uh, need to talk?" she asks and bites her bottom lip. "Maybe we could go out later?"

I stare at her a beat before the absurdity of her question hits me, and I snort out a laugh.

"No. But thank you." Is she seriously picking me up after a funeral? Talk about taking advantage of a situation. I'm reluctantly impressed.

She frowns, confused but not offended, then turns around to walk to the desk.

Sighing I pull out the phone again and text Emmy.

ANY CHANCE *you can look up Dorothy's number and send it to me?*

TWO SECONDS LATER, the phone vibrates, and I see a contact come in a text. I dial Dorothy's number and check in on my messages and see about her cancelling the hotel and getting me on a flight out of here tonight. No point sticking around any longer than I have to. Then the door to the office suite opens and a tall, lanky, gray-haired man in a navy pinstriped suit enters.

"Mr. Montgomery, I presume?" He extends a hand, a fascinated look on his face. "We were wondering if you'd show up. Your grandfather always loved to have the last word. I'm sure he thanks you for indulging him."

I stand and accept his firm handshake. "Mr. Ravenel. Let's get this over with."

* * *

MR. RAVENEL STANDS at the door to his office ushering everyone in and indicating they should join me around the conference room table. I have already picked the prized seat halfway down with my back to the bright window when everyone else arrives.

Isabel Montgomery enters.

I stand, my insides rigid. My mother's years of schooling on manners are ingrained.

My grandmother has removed her hat, her gray hair is twisted against the back of her head, and her mourning attire of a black dress and small fitted jacket screams haut-couture. There was a time I wouldn't have recognized the lines in a well-made piece of clothing, but I do now. I've been relentless in my pursuit of only the best.

Her eyes are small and hard but somehow resigned. "Trystan." She nods.

"Isabel," I return. If she was expecting me to call her grand-mother, she doesn't show her surprise. "I'm sorry for your loss."

Beau enters next, nodding at me with a small grin followed by my uncle and a young woman I don't recognize. Wait.

"Suzy?" I ask, struck with a memory of my small toe-headed cousin who followed her older brother, Beau, and me around like a shadow. I'm instantly transported back, and her soft brown eyes light up.

She could always get a smile out of me. Now is no different. I'd purposefully made myself forget Suzy and Beau, but looking at them now together, I can't understand why, for all the warm memories are right there to be picked over. Perhaps because they're interspersed with painful ones. I mentally slam the lid on the box closed.

Suzy smiles and leans over to shake my hand, giving it a squeeze. "Yep."

"Robert." I greet my uncle next, and he shakes my hand. I feel shaken and off base. I know I should have been prepared to be with these people again, but I'm not sure anything could have gotten me ready. My inner coldness toward Isabel Montgomery is only intensified in this situation.

Isabel sits at the head of the table where Mr. Ravenel has laid out a thick folder. The man quickly moves the folder to another place as if that had been his intention all along.

Then an older couple are shown in who look vaguely familiar. They're introduced as Magda and Jeremy, and I seem to remember Magda was the housekeeper and Jeremy took care of the maintenance at the Montgomery homes both in town and their country home out at Awendaw. If I remember rightly, it was a beautiful old plantation house.

"Shall we get this over with," Isabel says.

"Please," I agree. Sitting in this stifling room with people I never thought I'd have to think about ever again, much less see, is making my teeth ache. I work on my granite boardroom face. If I can stare down tight-fisted bankers and greedy venture capitalists, I can handle one old woman.

Mr. Ravenel shifts.

The sooner I can sign whatever needs to be signed, the better. Whatever token of affection my grandfather has left me to show he didn't forget my mother and me after all will be too little too late. I don't plan on leaving these offices with anything other than what I walked in with. I wouldn't even be here in the first place if I hadn't made a promise to my mother several years ago to come if I was called. But now that promise is kept, and this will be the last time I ever interact with them. I drum my fingers on the polished mahogany conference table as everyone is offered water and coffee.

"As you all know, my friend, the late Wilson Robert Beauregard Montgomery, the third, made me executor of his last will and testament. He also asked that it be read in a formal gathering of those named herein. And in two parts. Let's begin," Mr. Ravenel adds finally.

7

TRYSTAN

"*T*o the keepers of our home and our family's well-being, Magda and Jeremy, I hereby bequeath ten percent voting ownership of Montgomery Homes & Facilities—"

An audible intake of breath comes from my Uncle Robert, but Mr. Ravenel continues as Magda and Jeremy sit wide-eyed, "to be held by them, or either one of them by survivorship, until their death."

Magda makes the sign of the cross, a gesture of her Catholic upbringing, and squeezes Jeremy's hand.

"At which time the shares are to pass to my grandson, Trystan Montgomery."

Holy shit. What?

"What?" Isabel Montgomery explodes.

Uncle Robert pushes back from the table. "Outrageous." His arm sweeps out, motioning to Magda, Jeremy, and me. "It's bad enough he's given away some of the family business to Magda and Jeremy. But to include Trystan? What the hell does he know about running our operations here? None. Do you know why?" He leans forward and looks right at me. "Because you've never fucking been here."

My face could win a best sphinx-like impression award. I'm stone cold reactionless, if you don't count my heel bouncing a mile-a-fucking-minute under the table. But he can't see that. I clear my throat instead of reaching across the table and choking him with his own tie. "That's because, Robert, long before I stopped giving a shit, I was never fucking welcome." I don't add that I don't fucking want it either. It's like an insulting afterthought. Like *I'm* an insulting afterthought. I hate it. Let them sweat. I'll see about speaking with Magda and Jeremy afterwards. I can always put something in place for it to go to one of their heirs or to Beau and Suzy.

Isabel Montgomery lays her hand on Robert's arm. "Sit down, dear. We'll work something out with Magda and Jeremy. I'm sure at this time in their lives, they would rather not worry about the burden of Montgomery Facilities. Isn't that right, Magda?" She turns to her former housekeeper.

Magda doesn't answer, and I silently applaud her. I have a feeling Isabel Montgomery will try to pay her off for a paltry amount. I wonder what the valuation of Montgomery Homes & Facilities is. It was spun off from the main Montgomery Real Estate holdings, which had dwindled to just a few properties after the last real estate crisis.

"To my grandson, Wilson Robert Beauregard Montgomery, the fourth, or "Beau," I leave my boat, the berth at Charleston City Marina, the berth at Breach Inlet, the large warehouse property located on James Island, and the commercial waterfront lot on Shem Creek."

Beau looks like someone sucked the air out of his chest. He turns a funny shade of pink, and not breathing, collapses his head into his hands. I frown, glancing at the others. Only Suzy is smiling. Isabel and Uncle Robert look confused. And then I remember Beau and me during the summers and his obsession with the antique wooden boat being restored in a workshop next to the marina. So my grandfather had been paying attention. He's just given Beau everything he needs to start a boat building business, including warehouse space in which to work. I hope he has capital saved up. He's going to need it.

Suzy takes his hand and gives it a squeeze, accompanying it with a reassuring smile for her brother. She is so happy for him.

This final action of my grandfather, giving Beau his greatest wish, satisfies me in a way I can't explain, and I find myself reassessing my grandfather. I'd certainly kept my distance. Anger had made that easy. Now, I'm wondering if I'd let him say his piece whether he would have apologized for his part in abandoning my mother and me. But even as I think it, I know I wouldn't have listened. It's Isabel who I can't stand, and more than that, I can't stand that my grandfather was so weak to her will.

Mr. Ravenel continues with instructions for Suzy to receive ownership of the warehouse factory buildings on East Bay Street, and for Uncle Robert and Isabel to have fifty-fifty ownership of the remaining portfolio of Montgomery holdings after the aforementioned properties that have been given to Beau and Suzy are transferred. I can't imagine what would be left in the portfolio. Perhaps just the family home on East Battery. Of course that's worth several million. And the country house.

Looking up, I see Robert is also clearly perturbed by my grandfather splitting up all of the family assets. Isabel's mouth has grown so pinched I fear it may disappear into her face. This reaction alone makes it worth coming here.

The phone in my pocket sends a double vibration informing me of an incoming text. It takes all my will power not to have a look. I tell myself it's not because I want to see what Emmy will text next but that I have a huge business deal back home in New York hanging on tenterhooks.

Mr. Ravenel drones on, and I wonder if now that my part has been addressed as the remainder-man of Magda and Jeremey's gift, I can slide out of here. I'd rather not be around for the fake

46

pleasantries after the meeting, but I know I probably have to sign something. Then I can get on a plane home to New York.

Suddenly everyone is staring at me with varying expressions of shock. There's complete silence.

"What?" I turn to Mr. Ravenel who is looking at me quizzically. I replay the last few words he said that I was hearing and recording, but not really following, a skill learned from being double and triple booked for meetings for the last several years as I built my business at breakneck speed.

Then I swallow. I'm not sure but I think he just said that . . . my brain started recording it the minute I heard my name mentioned.

"Would you mind repeating that part?" I ask, my voice sounding strangled even to my own ears.

Mr. Ravenel stares at me a beat longer and then looks down at his pages.

"'To my grandson, Trystan Montgomery, the son of my beloved though estranged daughter, Savannah, may God rest her soul, I leave my remaining voting stock of Montgomery Homes & Facilities, Limited and also hereby name him as my successor to the position of CEO and Chairman of the Board.'"

Fuck me.

8

EMMY

"*We*'re here," the cab driver said as we lurched to a stop, and I looked out the window at the bleak surroundings. Gray buildings, rusty wrought iron railings and sidewalks with trash blown up into the corners like cobwebs. I swiped my almost maxed-out credit card and signed the receipt.

I needed to ask Suit Monkey to forward my confirmation email from Airbnb to his phone so I could double check the address of where I was supposed to be staying after I visited David. I pulled out the phone just as it buzzed with a text from himself, asking me to forward him his assistant's contact info. I quickly looked up "Dorothy (Assistant)"in his address book, finding her between "Debbie (don't answer unless you're in a dry spell)" and "Dude from Vale (with the ski pass hookup)." I scrunched up my nose, forwarded Dorothy's contact to my own phone number, then climbed out of the cab.

I took my wheelie bag from the cabbie and hefted my purse onto my shoulder. I pulled my cardigan closer around myself to ward off the late spring chill. Gray afternoon clouds had rolled in. I'd have to text Suit Monkey later.

I was late. David was probably going out of his mind waiting for me. David whom I hardly ever saw because he was here in this rundown part of New York, and I was in sunny South Carolina. If only I could figure out a way to get him there. Hopefully I could get some advice from the administrative offices or the social workers at his facility while I was here.

An orderly was sitting on the steps, smoking. His short dreads bobbed as he listened to whatever was piping through the earbuds nestled in his ears. I'd know that figure anywhere.

The orderly looked up and caught me smiling. "Emmy girl, is that you?"

"Sure is."

D'Andre stood, his six-foot-five frame blocking the view up to the front door as he reached out a fist.

I bumped it with my own. "Who are you listening to these days," I asked.

"Logic," he replied, and he reached for my bag. "He's a genius."

"I'll take your word for it. And you still working on your own lyrics?"

"Sure am. Started a YouTube channel."

"Huh. That's the second person today."

"Rappin on YouTube?"

"No, at least, I don't think so. Just gaming or something. Anyway, how's David?"

"He's been going out of his mind waiting for you. And man, trying to tell him not to call you?" D'Andre shook his head. "That was not fun. What happened to your phone anyhow?"

"Long story. Accidentally switched phones with a total stranger. But the bottom line is I won't have access to that number for at least the next few days. I'll give you the number I'm using, but you'll have to monitor him, he can't keep using it after I get my phone back. The man on the other end is a self-important one-percenter." A funny one who I'd enjoyed bantering with, but still . . .

The thought of Trystan Montgomery in his busy suit-wearing

life having to deal with David's calls every day could be quite entertaining. It would drive him crazy. I smiled to myself. If it wouldn't upset and confuse David, I'd totally let it happen.

"Intriguing." D'Andre grinned, and we headed up the stone stairs and into the bright fluorescent-bulb-lit lobby.

"Irritating, more like." I huffed then arranged to keep my suitcase in the office while I visited with David.

* * *

DAVID WAS SITTING in the chair by the window in his small room when I entered. If he sat in one certain spot, he could see down the street, between the buildings and to the water of Rockaway Inlet that led out to the Atlantic Ocean.

"This isn't Manhattan," David said as I entered. "I was told I'd be staying in New York."

"It *is* New York," I said softly so as not to startle him. His gray hair was clipped short, thanks to D'Andre I was sure. Haircuts weren't administered nearly as neatly or as often as I knew David was used to even though I kept his account stocked with funds for all the extras like haircuts and adult diapers. He turned toward me, his eyes not lighting with recognition. I never knew what I would get when I visited him.

"No. It's not. That is *not* the Hudson River, I'll tell you that much."

"You're right, we're not in Manhattan, but we're just outside. We're near JFK airport."

David nodded, his eyebrows rising. "That's very useful. Noisy, I bet. But probably smart given all the traveling I have to do this coming year."

I smiled and perched on the end of his hospital bed so I could face him in the chair. "Traveling? Where are you headed?"

David grunted. "My job takes me all over. You have to keep an eye on the Far East manufacturers, you know? My clients would skin me alive if I hadn't personally visited and approved of all their investments."

"Huh." I nodded. "You have a very important job."

"It's a big responsibility managing other people's money. They have to have the utmost trust in you." A shadow passed over his rheumy eyes.

I swallowed, hoping his mind wouldn't serve up the reality of his situation and what had happened to him and his business. "So, what's the food like at this hotel?" I asked, buying into his odd reality.

David's eyebrows rose. "Oh well." He smiled. "It's the best of course. Normally I avoid hotel restaurants, but this one is pretty good. And it's very entertaining. There's a Chinese family that runs it. Their kids are a hoot. The two daughters are acrobats. They do an incredible show where they hang from the ceiling during dinner."

"Wow," I deadpanned. "Talk about dinner theater!"

"Right? I wish you could see it. Maybe you'll stay for dinner." David looked at me, and like a curtain slowly being peeled open to reveal the day, his gaze sharpened, and he came back. "Emmy! It's so great to see you. Why didn't you say something. Always sneaking in like this, trying to surprise an old man." He grinned.

"Hey, David." I stood and walked over to him so I could lean down and give him a hug. I squeezed his bony shoulders and pressed my cheek to his papery one. "Great to see you too."

"Well, you're a sight for sore eyes. Look at you. Your new fella must be treating you well. When can I meet him?"

"Wait, what?"

"Now, now, Emmy. You don't need to be shy. I'm happy for you."

I swallowed thickly. I'd really been hoping we could talk properly today, but now I was starring in his elaborate made-up world. Goodness knew what would come out next.

I peered closely at him.

"What?" he asked.

I only saw his keen intelligence and mischief dancing behind his eyes. No confusion.

"Nothing. You missed a spot shaving, by the way," I redirected our topic.

"Did not."

I shrugged. "Did too."

He rubbed a hand over his jaw, and I felt a twinge of guilt.

I knew full well it was D'Andre who shaved him. The facility didn't allow anyone scissors, razors, or even nail clippers after Mrs. McClatchkey nipped her husband repeatedly on the arm with hers.

"So how's my little shoebox in the Village?"

I took a breath, bracing myself for telling him the same news again for the first time. "You remember we had to sell it, right?" Eight years ago when our whole world fell apart.

"We did?" His eyebrows dropped down heavily. "Maybe I remember that."

"And you live here now."

"And where are *you* living?"

"Charleston, South Carolina. Where I went to college? Remember how much you loved the history and the restaurants when you came to visit?"

"So you're not living in New York? No wonder I haven't seen you. Why didn't you tell me?" The hurt was unmistakable.

I reached for his bony hand and squeezed. It was cool to the touch. In the past, I'd remind him his memory wasn't working right, but sometimes that just angered him. Of course guilt still choked me because he was right. I hadn't been up to see him enough. There simply wasn't much I could do about it. "I come as often as I can. You know that."

David looked away toward the window, giving me the silent treatment.

I waited. I thought of changing the subject again, but I simply couldn't think of what else to talk about.

"I always wanted you to find love, but now I feel jealous of this new fella who's taking up all your time."

I let out a surprised snort of laughter. "I don't have a fellow, David."

He looked at me. "Why would you hide it from me? If you moved away to be with a fella—"

"I'm not hiding anything." I frowned.

"Well, then who's this Trystan man answering your phone?"

I froze.

"Knock, knock." The voice came from the doorway.

I dragged my eyes away from David and looked up to see D'Andre at the door.

"The administrator needs to see you in the business office, if you have a moment," D'Andre said.

I stood, rubbing my hands down my skirt. "Sure."

* * *

"Miss Dubois." The administrator greeted me and held out her hand. "Penny Smith, I'm the one you speak to on the phone."

"Oh, right." I shook her hand. "It's great to put a face with a voice."

"Likewise. I appreciate you coming during the week when I have regular office hours."

"I'm glad I could make it. Normally it's impossible for me to take time off work during the week, but I finally have some vacation time."

"And you spent it coming to see David. He's your uncle?" She motioned for me to take a seat in the worn chair in front of a desk covered with piles of paperwork.

"Um. Yes. Well, a foster uncle. My late foster mother's brother. It's complicated."

"Well, in my experience real family hasn't much to do with blood ties. He's lucky to have you. Looks like you fostered each other. Does he have any other family?"

"Neither of us do. I . . . I think this is in his medical file, isn't it?"

"We have a lot of patients, and I wanted to hear it from you."

I cleared my throat. "So you needed to see me for something specific?"

Penny sighed and shifted uncomfortably, her eyes flicking down to a folder in front of her. "Well, yes. So, I'm sure you've noticed his dementia is getting worse. We are getting close to a point where we won't have the resources to give him what he needs at this facility. How is it going with finding a facility closer to you in South Carolina?"

I clasped my hands together on my lap, squeezing my fingers together. "Not well. I've looked into all the places I know who have Alzheimer's care, and we're . . . well, we're waiting. *I'm* waiting. There's a waiting list that may take over a year."

Penny nodded. "I've been in contact with the Medicaid planner you found to evaluate the eligibility requirements between New York and South Carolina. I think you might be able to make the case for him to get Medicaid assistance there. But because of the change of state you'd need to cancel his eligibility here, and then reapply in South Carolina, so there may be a period where you'd have to pay out of pocket."

"And hope he gets approved. That might be almost impossible." *Completely impossible.*

"Keeping him in New York may be the easiest option as far as funding goes," Penny continued, her eyes bleeding sympathy. "But as long as he doesn't see you frequently he deteriorates. And of course, a move to another facility will further affect him. Adversely. Although that might be unavoidable at this point."

The lump in my throat had grown so much it had sunk into a boulder in my chest. "So my choices are move him closer to me, but risk losing coverage that he desperately needs, or keep him in New York, but he'd have to leave this facility anyway?"

"I'm afraid so, yes."

I willed myself not to cry. "H-how long do I have until you can't keep him anymore?"

She let out a long breath. "As the dementia grows, the more he fights and argues with the staff. Unfortunately, recently he has gotten physical at times."

"What?" The thought of David becoming violent was as alien as Trystan Montgomery turning out to be a virgin. I wrapped my hands around my waist. Where in the Sam Hell had that thought come from? "My God. I'm so sorry. Are . . . are you sure? I mean, David isn't . . . I mean he's *never* been violent. Ever."

"It often happens with dementia patients. Bizarrely, it's sometimes in their moments of extreme lucidity that it happens. They 'wake up' as it were and don't understand why they're here, where they are, or why they don't recognize anyone. Often times they might try to leave and have to be restrained. And they get quite belligerent with people trying to stop them. We've put an ankle bracelet on David, and it sets off the sensors by the exit several times a week. He's been trying to walk out of here pretty consistently."

I tried to wrap my mind around what she was telling me. I'd thought he could stay here indefinitely until I figured out a way to get him closer to me. But now that was off the table too. "Are . . . are there any facilities you recommend for someone like David. I mean, if he stays in New York State?"

Penny pursed her lips. "We've put some calls in, but are you sure that's what you want to do? I think seeing you more often would be better for him."

My nose stung, and I lost the battle against tears as my eyes filled. "No. Of course I'm not sure. I don't know what to do."

"Is there anyone you know who might be able to pull some strings to get him into an affordable place closer to you? Oftentimes, if you know someone, they might be able to put in a good word, bump him up the list."

"But I can't risk him losing coverage if I move him to South Carolina. I can't afford to pay for it out of pocket. It's an impossible position."

"I know," Penny said gently. She grabbed the box of tissues next to her and held them out to me. "That's why I was hoping you'd know of any other family members or relatives of David's who might be able to share the burden with you. I'm sorry you are on your own with this. But whatever you decide, he'll have to leave this facility before the end of next month."

9

EMMY

*O*utside the overcast clouds threatened rain. It was early evening when I finally said goodbye to David, having left him eating a plate of meatloaf, mash potatoes, and beige broccoli. I wished I could sign him out and take him for a meal at one of the old expensive steak houses he used to frequent in the city. Smith & Wollensky's perhaps. I blinked back more tears from my swollen eyes. I'd told David I had allergies when I came back from talking to Penny.

I'd finally remembered to text Trystan to send me the confirmation email I got from Airbnb to *his* email but I still hadn't heard back from him. God, this was getting complicated.

I walked along the narrow sidewalk. Within minutes I felt I could wipe a layer of grime from my skin and see it. The smell of the halal grill on the corner sent the pungent scent of roasting meat and strong spices wafting out to mix with the exhaust or honking rush-hour taxis and stagnant drains.

Finally, after a twenty-minute walk, I found the right address. I squinted at the dirty numbers on a brick pillar next to a rickety looking metal stairway that looked like it descended into the bowels of hell.

I looked down into the gloom. Were those eyes peering back up at me?

"You better be a cat down there and not a rat," I whisper shouted. My spidey senses were zinging off the charts as I stood on the sidewalk debating what to do.

I was a headline: *Single girl books "room" in New York for two nights at low, low price.* What did I expect? I guess I expected Lady Luck to give a shit, but she'd been on an extended smoke break since this morning when my flight was delayed, I lost my phone, and the news about David's eviction had been dumped on me.

I pulled out Trystan's phone to see if he'd emailed the confirmation and mulled my options for a few more minutes. Knock on the door and risk meeting a serial killer or double check the address? Double checking seemed like the smart decision. I opened a new text message to Suit Monkey.

Hi, me again. I know you're busy. Sorry. I'm standing outside this Airbnb, or what I remember the address to be, and I feel like if I go inside, I may never come out alive. It has to be the wrong address. Will you check in my email and forward it to your email so I can see the address? Please, please, please.

After I hit send, I waited and pretended to be on the phone so no one would talk to me. Pedestrians passed by periodically, groups of men with beards and hats, walking to the synagogue I'd passed. The building above the basement apartment looked as derelict as its foundation. The windows were dirty, the first-floor ones barred, and a few newspapers piled up outside the main entrance at ground level. In fact, on closer inspection it looked to be the remains of someone's bed for the night. Panic began to churn my insides. I'd prepaid for the Airbnb, and there definitely wasn't enough room in my budget for an additional hotel bill.

I stared down at the phone in my hand, willing Trystan to text back. As I watched, the battery bar ticked down to nineteen percent. I needed to plug it in. I was going to have to call him.

* * *

My call went straight to voicemail. "Hi, you've reached Emmy's phone—" I mashed the end button. Does anyone ever like the sound of their own voice?

He was either on the phone already or the battery had died.

It was five thirty. Surely he was done with his reading of the will or whatever by now. I hated that I was having to bother him on what was clearly a difficult day.

No.

Screw it.

This was an emergency.

I dialed again.

Straight to voicemail.

I dialed again.

And again.

And again.

"What?" Trystan's voice barked.

"Oh, hi. This is—"

"Emmy, I know."

"Oh." I swallowed quickly while I gathered my scattered thoughts and recovered from his abrupt tone. "Um."

"What do you want?" he snapped.

Oh my God. Was this guy for real? "For you not to act like an asshole for a start."

"Excuse me?"

"You heard me. I phoned you bec—"

"Seven times. You called *seven* times."

"And you ignored it *seven* times!"

"Because I'm in the middle of something."

59

"And I'm in the *middle* of nowhere with a suitcase and no information about where I'm staying tonight. You know why?" I ploughed on. "Because some asshole took my phone." He hissed but I talked right over it. "And now said asshole won't even answer it to help me figure out where I am supposed to sleep for the night. This . . . is . . . an . . . emergency," I enunciated. My heart beat in my ears, my hands shook, and my face throbbed. All the tears I'd only recently been able to stuff back inside me came back, rising like a tide, and I was mortified to realize my voice had begun wobbling on the last word.

There was silence and a muffled expletive on the other end and then nothing.

I frowned and pulled the phone from my ear. Did he . . .?

"Ugh!" I squealed loudly, almost throwing his phone to the sidewalk in despair and swiping the tears off my cheeks. He'd hung up on me. I couldn't believe this day.

Did you seriously just hang up on me?

Suit Monkey: *Keep your bloody knickers on. Information headed your way in a bit.*

I blew out a breath. *Thank you, I guess.*

How long is *this going to take you?* I texted again. *I'm standing on a street corner with my suitcase. Someone's going to think I'm a hooker looking for a commitment.*

Suit Monkey: *Just give me a fucking minute to locate it amongst all your junk mail from Cats R Us and Sewing Monthly. Jesus, you have a lot of shit in your inbox. How do you find anything?*

I USE THE SEARCH BAR, Genius.

SUIT MONKEY: *But, whyyyyyyy do you subscribe to these things?*

I ROLLED MY EYES, and a grin tugged at my mouth even though I was irritated with him.

SUIT MONKEY: *Never mind. Don't tell me.*
      Suit Monkey: Are you aware you have over 10,000 unread emails. You are a mess. HOW DO YOU LIVE?

I CLEAN THEM OUT PERIODICALLY.

SUIT MONKEY: *Are we talking periods like Ice Age to Information Age?*
      Suit Monkey: Is there anything else you need because I had a shitty day that won't be over for some time, and I can't be at your beck and call. And for the record, everything about you screams commitment.

MY GRIN EVAPORATED. Letting out a squeak of frustration, I gritted my teeth and hammered my message out with angry fingertips.

YES, actually. I NEED you to stop being so mean. I've also had a pretty shitty day. And your phone is literally the only thing I have to try and navigate my life right now. So please give me a tiny break. Forward the info to your inbox please.

SUIT MONKEY: *Fine. Try not to read the rest of my email. It's confidential.*

DON'T WORRY. I'm not interested in your self-importance. What did he do for a living that made him feel like he was king of the universe, anyway?

SUIT MONKEY: *And just text me if you need something. Don't psycho-call me seven times straight.*

AT LEAST MY first instincts about him at the airport had been correct. What a tool.

THEN YOU SHOULD ANSWER your texts, and I won't have to.

THREE DOTS APPEARED and then disappeared. I switched to his email and found the forwarded email for my reservation. I read the address with my jaw set grimly. I was at the right place. Of course I was. This day was just chucking it right at me.

I hit reply to the email then cc'd Trystan himself so he'd get it too when he logged on to his email on his laptop or whatever.

IF NO ONE ever hears from me again, this was my last known location.

I LOOKED UP, face tilted to the sky, as if for a response from God himself but ended up with a raindrop hitting me square on the eyeball.

"Dang it!"

I blinked rapidly, knowing I was about to cry all over again, and hurried toward the rickety metal steps.

I needed my phone back, and I needed to try and figure out a way to help David's predicament, which I wouldn't be able to do until I was back in Charleston in three days time. There was hardly anything I could do in this hamstrung position with no resources and no access to my email. I simply had to suck it up and get through it.

The stairs were old and rusty. A dank smell hung heavy in the air as I descended. The windows of the basement unit were so grimy I couldn't tell the color of the drapes pulled across them. Beige? Brown? The door, however, tucked into a small recess, was painted a cheery turquoise with a brushed brass knocker. I glanced down at the email and read the instructions. Turning around I looked for a combination lockbox hanging under the stairs.

The rain started coming in heavily, pooling on the concrete under my feet.

I followed all the prompts, and for the first time in the whole bizarre day, everything went smoothly. The key turned easily in the lock and the door clicked open.

EMMY

*T*he apartment was small but clean and freshly decorated, thank goodness.

I rolled out my yoga mat onto the clean tile floor, worked through twenty sequences of poses until my muscles were well-used and my skin was damp with sweat. Ending in Child's Pose, I finally allowed my mind to slip back into the day's problems, seeing them more clearly.

I would redouble my efforts to find David a bed at a facility near me, though it would have to be quite far outside of Charleston to be affordable. But that was doable. At least I could go and see him every weekend instead of once every month or two. The money I was spending on airfare and accommodation, though not much, could be redirected toward the shortfall in his care. I'd take a second job. I was already sewing little extras from custom orders that came in through the interior design store on King Street. Perhaps I could ask around and increase my load of orders. The small voice in my head calling me a ridiculous Pollyanna for thinking I could make enough to help was surprisingly quiet for the moment.

The other option was to try and get a job in New York.

I looked around me. As lovely as this small apartment was, clean, newly renovated and nicely decorated, it was, for all intents and purposes, an underground tomb. The square footage was smaller than that of my tiny carriage house in Charleston, the couch was actually the bed, and the rent would be at least five times more expensive. Not to mention the lack of charm on the streets outside. Though I'd gladly forgo charm in order to see David somewhere safe, permanent, and closer to me. Another siren blared along the street outside and I sighed. It had taken all my mental concentration to shut out the noises of the city as well as my own thoughts during my work out, now it was just getting annoying. I unfolded myself from Child's Pose to Dead Man's pose, breathing in through my nose and out through my mouth. My stomach growled and gnawed at my insides.

I showered and dressed quickly, then I grabbed Trystan's phone from where I'd been charging it. I'd have to see what was close by to eat. He'd had about ten dating app notifications and a ton of missed calls from various people. My curiosity got the better of me, and I scrolled the lock screen. That guy Mac called again, two from a Manhattan number, and a sprinkle of calls from various women's names. I wondered if he had a rotation of women to date or if they were family or friends.

Not that it was my business.

He was a good-looking guy. Really good-looking in a raw, sensual way.

My mind cast back to his strong forearms and his piercing gray eyes. Well-dressed. God, I really hoped he wasn't gay. All the good-looking men I met nowadays seemed to be. I hated that my gnawing stomach actually sank a little in disappointment at that thought—it would be a real loss for women everywhere. No, wait, the clues all said he was straight. Those gray eyes had been just a little too . . . hungry. After I found somewhere to eat, maybe I'd have a little peek at his dating apps to see if he was into girls or boys or both. Just out of curiosity, not because I was interested in him.

No.

I wouldn't.

That would be nosey. Snooping. A violation of privacy. It was none of my business. Besides, we lived in different cities. What would be the point? I swallowed, disappointed that my good side had won this round.

I opened his phone and looked for a restaurant app of some kind that was location-based. Nothing looked promising on the first page, and I did well to ignore the dating apps with notifications pending. There was a crypto-currency tracker, a foreign currency exchange app, a jogging app, chess (interesting), Words with Friends (obviously), all the social media apps (except Facebook which was a weird omission). "Ooooo," I cooed out loud. "A Kindle app." I'd be back to that later.

God, his text messages buzzing in every few minutes were getting annoying.

I kept searching, checking each folder I saw.

He was quite good at keeping his apps organized, unlike me. Then I saw Yelp. Ahhh. I pulled up a list of nearby restaurants looking for anything that had at least three stars and published their menus. Call me cautious, but I didn't feel like ending up getting sick on top of everything I had to deal with. On my own phone, I had a gluten-free restaurant tracker that listed restaurants that catered to special eaters like me, either with a gluten-free menu or easy to modify items. The most appealing place I could find was about a twenty-minute walk. A quick check behind the curtains and through the window thick with a coating of pollution showed me it was dark and still raining in sheets.

I looked around by the entry, but there was no umbrella.

I'd have to pop across the road to the little corner store I'd seen and at least buy some nuts and a piece of fruit if they had any.

I grabbed some cash, and the key, put my flip flops on, and opened the front door. I splashed through a disgusting two inches of water and climbed the slick steps. I was soaked in seconds. I shouldn't have bothered to shower after yoga.

Thank goodness the store was open, though tiny. I snagged two bananas, a small carton of Greek yoghurt, two bottles of water, and a bag of peanuts. Not exactly satisfying, but it would have to do for dinner and breakfast.

I splashed back across the road and descended into the small warm tomb. I stripped down and climbed back into a hot shower, then pulled on my favorite pineapple sleep shorts and a cami. Hanging my wet clothes up, I then settled in on the couch and ate a banana while trying to read my current book on my Kindle, a new series about hot astronauts by Brenna Aubrey. At least I didn't have to worry about work. I'd already put together our presentation deck for the pitch on Friday when I was back.

Trystan's phone buzzed again, and my eyes rolled as I saw yet another female name. *You busy tonight?*

The urge to respond on his behalf was overwhelming. But I forced my mind back to my book.

He definitely dated women. But there were a few texts from guys too. Hard to guess if they were romantic though. Maybe just one peek at his dating app profiles, I told myself as I opened his phone.

"Ugh, what are you doing?" I asked the empty room and put his phone down. What was wrong with me?

My book. I searched the page for where I was in the story. At least he had his laptop with him so he could get online, check emails, and even watch Netflix. Basically he could have a life. I had this huge pressing problem I needed to deal with and I could do nothing about it till I got home, had access to my computer, and got my phone back.

At the very least I could look at the list of nursing homes back in South Carolina and see if I'd missed one that might be farther out, more reasonable and also dealt with dementia. I opened his phone and went to the web browser. There were a few pages open already: ESPN, the New York Islanders homepage, and Ticketmaster. What was he buying tickets for, I wondered? I opened it and saw he was looking at dates for next year's Coldplay tour. Huh. Well, at least he had good taste in music.

I opened a new page and searched nursing homes in South Carolina. Somewhere no more than three hours away from Charleston. That way I might be able to get there and back in a day.

The phone buzzed in my hand and another text appeared at the top of the screen. Another woman. *I had fun the other night. Repeat?*

Ugh. He must be bored out of his mind having my phone. No one called me except my boss, David incessantly, Armand, and my good friend, Annie, of course. But Annie was a new mother, my godson was two months old, and she knew I was spending the next few days with David so I doubted she'd call.

I wondered if perhaps *I* should join some dating apps. I'd tried a few last year, but for some reason when people saw my profile picture something about it screamed dominatrix. There were so many weird messages with coded questions that I was too scared to google on my work laptop in case they were gross. I had to get Annie to decipher and research, and yes, they were gross. It made me never want to try online dating ever again. And you had to get past the fact most men used fake profile photos, one even used Chris Martin from Coldplay, I mean, please.

But even worse, most of the people who messaged me were open about the fact they had significant others, they were just looking to be spanked on their lunch breaks. It was hard to look at society the same way again. I gave a little shudder in remembrance.

Though looking at Trystan's phone, dating apps clearly

worked for some people. I hovered over an app called Whirl. It had 3 pending notifications.

I bit my lip. Was I really going to do this?

I dropped my thumb and touched the app. It opened.

I told myself I'd only have a quick look. I'd never seen this app; I just wanted to see what it was about. How it worked . . .

Whirl mail: 3

Whirl-o-meter: 15 people could be a good match

If I read a message, I was worried it would show up as "read" and he'd know I snooped. So I ignored the mail icon and clicked through to his profile.

Name: *Jeff*

Huh?

I grimaced. Gross. He was also one of the fake ones. Why couldn't people be honest on these dating apps? The photo was of him though, and holy shit he was hot. Whereas this morning I'd seen him in a suit, which he wore in way that suggested he'd never be caught dead without one, in his picture, he was wearing a soft flannel shirt and worn jeans. He was crouching down and had his arm slung around the neck of a red brown retriever with soulful brown eyes. Huh. I'd have never pegged him for an animal lover.

I zoomed in on his face. The jaw looked hard, his eyes crinkling against the sunlight looked blue not gray. I wondered if they were the type of blue eyes that changed to gray or green depending on the weather or his mood. He had been in an icy gray mood this morning. His hair, brown, was unruly but tamed, as if it had been windy that day, but he'd recently raked his fingers through it. My stomach clenched, and I was annoyed I found him so attractive.

Jeff. Ugh.

My eyes tracked on down the page. *Jeff* was thirty-one years old, loved his dog, hiked on the weekends, and was looking for someone fun and adventurous who didn't need a commitment.

Of course he was. *Adventurous* . . . was that like one of those terms people used to make something good out of something bad? I looked around . . . like a small, cozy, jewel-box apartment really meant one airless room so small you could simultaneously shower while watching a show from the living room and heating up dinner in the kitchen. Adventurous probably meant kinky. Not looking for a commitment might mean he already had one and was looking for a piece on the side. I'd ask my friend Annie when we next spoke. She'd actually met her baby daddy online. Granted, it was in a forum for Star Wars Live Action Role Players, but still.

At least, apart from his name, and maybe the dog, *Jeff's* profile was fairly honest.

Why didn't I get someone hot like Trystan connecting with my profile, I wondered.

Ugh.

I did *not* want to start crushing on the phone thief. So what if we had a bit of conversational chemistry earlier today, most of the time he was an asshole.

As if he'd heard my thoughts, the phone rang in my hand and *Suit Monkey* lit up the screen.

Shit.

I swallowed, my cheeks heating, like I'd been caught doing something I shouldn't. "He-hello?"

TRYSTAN

*S*tepping out of the law offices onto the sidewalk, I breathe in the heavy humid air. Christ, this place is warm. Why had I never remembered the humidity? I peel off my suit jacket and slip my fingers into my tie knot and yank it loose. I keep going and use two hands to pull it undone and then undo the top two buttons of my shirt. I need to breathe. Why does it feel like there's no air?

Not allowed to leave? Those were the exact wishes expressed by my late grandfather. Mr. Ravenel looked totally embarrassed reading my grandfather's controlling missive from beyond the grave. The last will and testament was clear, the rest of the instructions would be given tomorrow after everyone had had a chance to absorb the fact that a man who, for all intents and purposes, didn't give two shits about me had made me his successor. And in doing so had pitted me against a family who already hated me.

I cast my gaze around for the black SUV with my driver just as it pulls up from a few feet away. The driver hops out and opens the back door so I can throw myself into the dark cool interior of the back seat.

"Trystan." Beau's voice stops me.

I turn to him. "Did you know?"

The minuscule flick of his eyes to the side and back to me tells me all I need to know, even as he says, "No."

"Bullshit."

"Truly. I had an idea. Something he said to me once. But no, I didn't *know*." He puts air quotes around the last word.

I stare at him a few minutes, his friendly eyes set in his tanned skin. "You get what you wanted?" I ask, though I already know the answer.

Beau nods, grimacing slightly. "Grandmother might contest it. She thought she was getting everything. Or at least that she and my father were."

"It's good to see you," I tell him. "But I don't want anything to do with this family. I hope she leaves you alone, but she won't need to contest my portion, I have no intention of keeping it."

"That's what she's hoping." Beau shakes his head. "I hope you reconsider. I'd hate for her to have the last word after all she's done to you."

"Removing myself as quickly and completely from this family is my only concern."

A fleeting look of hurt passes through Beau's expression as I say this.

"I—" He starts then clears his throat. "Never mind. See you tomorrow, I guess. Where are you staying?"

"I don't know. I told my assistant to cancel my room at The Planter's Inn earlier, but now I'll have to have her remake the reservation."

Beau frowns. "Good luck. The Spoleto Festival's starting in a couple of days, there won't be a free bed in town."

"Hopefully, I'll be gone by then."

Beau's mouth straightens and then he nods. "See you, Trystan."

I watch him turn and walk away. No one else has come out of the offices yet. Isabel is probably already objecting.

My driver must have gotten back into the car while Beau and I talked. She climbs out again and reopens the back door.

Inside I'm enveloped in the cool blast of air conditioning, and I breathe deeply for what feels like the first time in several hours.

The driver climbs in the front seat. "Everything all right?" she asks.

"Yeah."

"Where to?"

"Just stay here for now." I pull out Emmy's phone and call Dorothy.

"Mr. Montgomery, I've cancelled your hotel reservations and booked you on an eight o'clock flight to La Guardia." Her tone is as confident and reassuring as ever.

"Change of plans. Again. It looks like I may have to stay here a few days after all."

* * *

DOROTHY MANAGES to work her magic and books me two nights at the hotel. I get checked in and plug in my laptop, jumping onto the hotel Wi-Fi. I have a deluge of emails about the deal. I quickly take care of all the ones waiting for responses, mostly from the bankers doing their last-minute double checks and due diligence and a couple from Mac. Then I see one unread one from myself with the subject line a reply to my forwarded Airbnb email.

If no one ever hears from me again, this was my last known location.

I stare at it a few seconds then reread it. I try to think back to the text I got from Emmy earlier. I thought she was being dramatic. She could just as easily have been legitimately nervous.

I search the address. It's out toward Long Island. I shake my head and stop myself shy of checking crime statistics for the area.

Why do I care? She is not my concern. I have enough going on, and now that I'm done dealing with work emails, the will and all the ramifications of it start ricocheting around in my head.

With that thought, I change into my workout gear and find the hotel gym. I spend the next ninety minutes overworking myself to sheer exhaustion in an attempt to quiet my mind. It doesn't work, and when I'm done I'm soaking with sweat, my lungs and heart are working overtime, and I'm filled with rage at Isabel Montgomery. Beau will be happy that I have, indeed, reconsidered. I won't be turning down my inheritance. Isabel can contest it if she wants to. What I *will* do, I think with cold resolve, is sell off the entire operation piece by piece and *then* walk away with the money.

I head back across the hotel courtyard, legs like jelly, and my body temperature finally matching the warm mugginess of downtown Charleston. The sun has set, but the heat remains. Lights have flickered on in the topical landscaping and the calming sound of trickling water comes from a fountain. The city has charm, I'll give it that.

I'm also filled with a bizarre sense of guilt that I've somehow misstepped. I think at first, it's to do with Beau. But then I realize it has nothing to do with my family and everything to do with Emmy. We'd been bantering earlier, had been . . . friendly. And then I all but yelled at her. I'll check in with her before I go to bed and make sure she's all right. I tell myself it's in my best interests to know where my phone is. My stomach chooses that moment to remind me I haven't eaten dinner, and I decide I'll call her under the guise of needing a restaurant recommendation.

As I take a hot shower, change and contemplate dinner, I find the silence of my evening disturbing, though not altogether unwelcome. If I had my phone it would be buzzing with texts and calls as it always does early evening in Manhattan with people looking to meet for drinks, dinner, or more. I'm rarely alone. And if I am, I usually rustle up a date from Tinder. Emmy's phone is silent. Even the calls from David have stopped. I wonder what she must be making of the incessant texts I receive in the evenings.

I scratch the back of my neck.

A quick glance tells me she has one dating app on her phone. I open it up and read the profile she put up there. The picture takes me by surprise. I remember her from this morning at the airport, or thought I did. I remember porcelain skin, wide eyes, gorgeous, wavy auburn hair. Girl next door maybe. Plain, but pretty too. What greets me is sooo not plain. Heavy eye makeup on eyes that look like they'd strike you dead, glossy red lips, hair straightened, a glass of champagne in her hand, and a black top or dress, I don't know. The picture is cut off around the waist. I see the photo is cropped from some kind of party. It's not that she's not beautiful, she is. Christ, she's stunning, it's like a punch in the gut. But the picture doesn't gel with the scattered girl in my mind's eye. The playful girl with the neurotic tendencies and the quick wit. Her comment earlier of seeming like a hooker looking for a commitment made me laugh out loud. Which was saying something considering I'd just left the meeting at the Ravenel Law Office. I tear my eyes away from the picture and scan her profile entries.

NAME: Emmaline
    Age: 28
    Location: Charleston, SC
    Looking for: Men
    Things to know: Be real, I don't like bullshit.

MY EYES WIDEN. I can only imagine the type of guys she attracted with this profile. Even *I* feel a little intimidated by this version of Emmy. Weirdly turned on, but intimidated nonetheless. Maybe she's into being the boss in the bedroom. I shrug. I gave up trying to understand human nature a long time ago. The message folder is full, but she hasn't responded to any in over a year. For some reason that makes me feel good. She must have notifications turned off. I open one of the messages, and after three words, I shudder and close it. Gross. I open another. *Jesus.* Who are these guys? After several more my stomach feels sour, and I wonder how women survive out in the dating world. If this is my competition, no wonder I do so well getting dates.

I need to give her some pointers. At the very least she has to use a fake name. If even one of those perverts has stalkerish tendencies, she wouldn't be hard to find. I remember how readily she gave me her name and social earlier and shake my head. That open, sweet, funny girl I texted with on my way to the funeral would get a date no problem. Of course she'd probably be screwed over too.

That thought brings me back to her predicament today.

I can't put off calling anymore, so I dial my number. I must still not be recovered from my intense work out because my palms feel sweaty.

TRYSTAN

*E*mmy answers right away like she was holding the phone. "He-hello?"

"Emmy, it's Trystan." I wince at the obviousness of my greeting and clear my throat. "Did you find the place you're staying?"

"Oh, yes. I did. Thank you," she adds after a pause as if it pained her to thank me.

"That's why I called." I clear my throat again. "Well, a few reasons actually."

"Oh?" she replies then stays silent. It's a technique I know well. I've perfected it in boardrooms—staying quiet while others fill the silence and hang themselves with their ill-timed words.

Maybe it's the picture on her dating profile, or maybe I'm emotionally drained from the day, but I'm suddenly nervous.

I take a breath. "Yeah. I wanted to apologize for how I was on the phone earlier. It was, uh, a bad time, not that it's any excuse. Clearly it was a bad time for you too."

"It was."

"Well, like I said. No excuse."

"And second? You said two reasons." I thought of her profile. *Be real, I hate bullshit.*

"Oh, right. Well firstly, do you accept my apology?"

"Did you apologize?"

"Didn't I?"

"You said you *wanted* to apologize."

I grin then purse my lips. "Precision of language. Okay, I apologize about the way I snapped at you on the phone when you called to ask for help."

"I accept your apology," she says. I don't know her, but I think I detect a smile in her tone.

"Great. Thank you, so what's the place like? You didn't sound too sure about it when you called."

"I wasn't. It looks like a derelict housing project from the outside, but surprisingly, though small, it's clean and modern inside. Cozy, almost. It's only for two nights."

"Right. So we need to figure out how to switch our phones back. I was supposed to fly back tonight or tomorrow at the latest. Now, I'm not so sure. I might still be here when you get back."

"Where are you staying?"

"The Planter's Inn? Do you know it?"

She whistles. "Nice."

"I need a recommendation for dinner. Just me," I tack on for no reason. "Close. I'm starving."

"The hotel has a restaurant, The Peninsula Grill, which is one of the top-rated restaurants in the city. I'd kill for their duck right now. You probably won't get a table, and the bar is small, but maybe they'll do room service."

"Awesome." I stand and head to my laptop so I can pull up their menu. "When will you be back?"

"I wish I could come back early, but I don't think I can change my flight."

"Why early?" I ask absently as I scan the menu

"Oh, uh, there's some things I need to take care of, and I can't do them without my phone and a computer, you know?"

"Yeah. I have my laptop, but I must say this whole phone swap thing has thrown me for a loop. Crazy how much we depend on them. Or how much I do. I'm in one of the biggest business deals of my life, and people can't get hold of me except by email."

"Is *that* why you get so many phone calls and texts?" she asks with a laugh in her tone. "From women?"

"You noticed that," I say sheepishly.

"Kind of hard not to. I'll be setting the Do Not Disturb later so I can get some sleep."

The duck on the menu does look amazing.

"Hey, can you hold on?" I ask. "Or," I scratch my chin, working my fingers over the end of a day's beard growth, "can I call you back in a few minutes,"

"Uh, sure."

"Be right back," I say and hang up. I dial the hotel restaurant and order the duck and a bottle of red wine.

Then I lean back in the desk chair, prop my feet on the work surface, and call Emmy back.

"Hey," she says breathlessly.

"Everything okay?"

"Yeah, I just went to see if it was still raining. Spoiler, it is."

"I just ordered the duck on your recommendation, it better be good."

"Oh, it is. You lucky beast. But best enjoyed with a glass of red wine."

"Ordered that too. What are you having?" I may not be able to distract myself with a date, so Emmy was going to have to play stand-in.

"Oh. Well, there's nothing nearby, and it's pouring rain. I went across the street earlier and got a banana and some nuts."

"Oh God. Now I feel bad." I laugh. "At least buy yourself a sandwich or pastry, surely they had something more substantial?"

"I can't eat gluten, so sandwiches are out I'm afraid."

I make a dramatic shocked sound. "No sandwiches? Bloody hell. What about a hamburger? You can't eat a hamburger? Stop. What is this horror?"

She laughs, a trickle of honey over the phone. "Well, some places do very good gluten-free buns, so I still get to enjoy them. And I eat my weight in fries." She groans. "Oh man. Now I'm starving. I'd kill for a burger."

"I'm guessing that's your favorite meal?"

"Hmm," she hums. "I don't have a favorite. That just happens to be what I'm craving."

"Everyone has a favorite."

"Not me. So tell me how a Suit Monkey living in New York with family slash not-friends in Charleston has some vague British accent going on?"

Her question stops me mid type in my search for burger places with gluten-free options that deliver in Far Rockaway, New York. "That's a little personal, don't you think?"

She snorts. "I told you about my gluten-free buns, that's pretty personal."

I laugh, and I hear her inhale lightly.

Pursing my lips, I continue my search, zeroing in on a place that looks perfect.

"True." I stall as I pick the toppings I think she'll like but request them on the side just in case. "So my mother fell in love with an Englishman who was in Charleston on business. He was in shipping or something. She got knocked up, and in true uptight Southern tradition was cast out. Followed him home."

"Wait, your family kicked her out?" Her voice lowers. "How old was she?"

I type in Emmy's address and pay for the burger plus gratuity. I tell myself it's simply an act of charity for someone who won't eat otherwise. I have the means, so why not? What's she asking? Oh, my mother. "She was nineteen, I think."

"Wow, I'm so sorry."

"Old enough to know better."

"Young enough to be taken advantage of by some British guy who should have kept his raincoat on, you mean?" She volleys the question back to me, and it occurs to me I might have been harboring some anger at my mother all this time, when it was my father who should have known better.

"I guess." I frown. "Kept his raincoat on?"

"Suited up? Used a pro . . . phyl . . . actic?" she enunciates. "A condom."

My mouth twists in amusement. "Yes, he should have. Must keep the general in combat uniform at all times."

"You call him the general?"

"God, stop it. It's fine for you to joke, but not me?"

"So you don't call him the general? That's a shame."

"What is it about you? We've discussed my mother and my penis, topics I don't believe there is a person alive with whom I would have this discussion."

There's a pause where I imagine her shrugging. "Maybe because we're strangers forced together under strange circumstances which gives us a level of intimacy but who have no judgments or preconceived notions about each other?"

"Ding, ding, ding, I beg to differ on the judgments. I believe you called me a . . . wait, let me find the exact wording, you put it in writing, ahh, here it is: a spoiled, suit-wearing monkey."

"Ah yes, I guess that's true. Well, you called me a mess. And a hippie chick. Why was that by the way?"

"The hot mess part?"

"You didn't say hot mess, you just said mess. *Totally* different connotation."

"I meant to say hot mess," I admit. Why not? "Case in point, thousands of unread emails, picking up the wrong phone etc. etc."

"You—"

"I know, I know. Apparently that was my fault. The hippie

81

part? The long hair and long flowy skirt, I guess. I don't really know."

"I always like to be comfortable when I travel."

"So you don't normally wear long flowy clothes?" I ask and then think of the fitted black top that could have been the top of a cocktail dress in her dating profile.

"Depends on my mood. I have to wear skirt suits at work, so I like to be in anything but when I get off."

My mind immediately goes where it shouldn't, and I press my lips tight to keep from reacting.

"Work, I mean," she adds, only confirming she went there too. "When I get off work. God."

"Of course," I deadpan, though it almost kills me. "I normally like to get out of my suit when I get off too."

"Stop it," she growls, and my smile spreads wider.

I cough. "So, what do you do that puts you in suits every day?"

"I work for an agency that does restaurant marketing. I could probably work from home, and work in jeans, but my boss is a sexist pig who likes the women at the office to show their legs and thinks sending us out to restaurants with our legs and figures on display will win us all the business."

She sounds sincere, and resigned. "Does it?" I ask because I'm curious, and she makes a sound of disgust like I should have sympathized with her and called her boss an asshole. He is, but I'm curious about her tone.

"Honestly, while there are some real assholes, most of my clients are female, gay, happily married, or all three. I could walk into a pitch in a bustier and high heels and we wouldn't win more work. I win because I'm really good at what I do."

The visual hits me in the gut, and blood rushes south. I'm not sure if I effectively cover up the breath I take, but there's a knock at the door right at the moment. "Room service," a voice calls.

"My duck is here, be right back." I don't wait for her to answer.

The waiter wheels a cart, dressed in a white linen tablecloth past me, across the wide plank walnut floors to the other side of the room by the windows.

"Thank you," I tell him, expecting him to leave so I can get back on the phone, but he reaches under the tablecloth and flips up a side, turning the cart into a table, then he rights a silver candle stick and lights the candle from a lighter he slips out of a pocket. Then he picks up the wine bottle and holds it out for me to inspect.

"Fine," I mutter with a nod. "Thank you. I can do it."

He continues on and cuts the foil, winds the corkscrew in, and pulls it with a flourish. He turns an upside-down wine glass onto its base, pours a small serving and looks at me expectantly. Ugh. I start forward impatiently. Swirling it once or twice I do the requisite sniff and sip. "Fine. Thank you."

He nods, then pours a glass, and finally whips off the cover of the plate. The aroma of roast meat, herbs, spices, and caramelized fruit wafts up, and my mouth waters. The waiter hands me a check, which I sign and add in a tip. Then he bows and takes his leave.

Finally.

I grab the phone, only to see it's off. Battery must have died. Emmy probably thinks I hung up on her. Damn. I plug it in. Her battery is for shit, I just charged it when I checked in a few hours ago.

I pull the desk chair to the temporary table and put the napkin on my lap. I stare at the delicious looking meal. In all the dinners I've had alone in my life, though I try to avoid them, I don't remember feeling *this* alone. Weird. I take a sip of the red wine. I chalk it up to the day I had where I had to face a family I'd rather forget I had. And not having my normal distractions around me. And then talking with Emmy. I enjoyed it, sure. But part of me feels stripped down. Like I lost something. I don't like it. It makes me nervous. The phone makes a sound that tells me it has turned back on. But I make no move to get it.

I think of her getting her burger, and I feel ill. Like I've done something I shouldn't. Laid expectations. I just bought her dinner. If we'd stayed on the phone, it would have felt like a date. As it is, the sheer fact that she'll be eating a meal I bought her while knowing I'm eating mine at the same time makes me feel like a line of intimacy has been irrevocably crossed. And if there's one rule I've had that has kept me in good stead, it's to avoid intimacy at all costs.

The duck is amazing. She was right about that. Her phone buzzes with a text, and another and another. I don't touch it or look at it. It never rings. And then it's quiet for the rest of the night. I pull my laptop back out and work till I can't keep my eyes open, then sleep solidly for six hours.

When I wake up, habit makes me pick up the phone.

Emmy: *Are you alive? Did the room service waiter kill you?*

Emmy: *Did the duck kill you?*

Emmy: *Oh my God, you ordered me a burger! Thank you. Although I almost didn't answer the door.*

Emmy: *Thank you. Truly. I can't think of anything more I needed right at this moment. Here's a pic. You may have noticed if you've been nosy in my photos that I like to take pictures of food.*

PICTURE OF A BURGER

Emmy: *I'm guessing my phone died. But that's not why you didn't call back, is it? I have something to say. I'll email it.*

I immediately open my laptop and go to my email.

To: Tmontgomery

From: Tmontgomery

Subject: Phone

I'm guessing you feel a bit like me right now; awkward about how weird it is that we were talking on the phone like that. I understand why you didn't call back. So just know, I consider the burger payment for the outstanding dinner recommendation I gave you. Nothing more. Now we're even. But it was a spectacular burger so here's a link to a breakfast place you'll love, and they make the best coffee and squeeze their own orange juice. Just turn left out of the hotel, walk three blocks, then left down the cobblestone alley. You'll see it on the right with the blue awning. Tell Armand I sent you, if you like. That earns me a free cappuccino every now and again. When you get a chance let me know the address of a place I can drop off your phone before I leave New York. Otherwise I'll drop it off at the front desk of the Planter's Inn when I get home to Charleston tomorrow evening. I hope you enjoy your stay in my spectacular city. It's a very special place. Maybe it's time to get to know your family. Thank you for agreeing to this phone swap rather than cancelling your phone. I apologize that it was so inconvenient, but know that the alternative would have been even more painful for me. So thank you. Again. It was nice to almost get to know a handsome stranger.

Regards,

Emmaline Angelique Dubois

I close the email without responding. I feel slightly ill.

Then I find myself staring blankly at the screen for a few moments. There's too much to process in the email. The biggest point I get is that I'm being politely brushed off. "You're hot, but not for me, before it gets weirder let's just . . . not."

Knowing I'm usually the one doing the brushing off, being on the receiving end pisses me off. I saw an Apple Store on my way to the hotel yesterday. I could easily walk in, and this could be over. But that would be callous to leave her without a phone. And I may not get close to people, but I'm never callous. Fuck, why am I still thinking about this? Shaking myself from her email, I scan through my inbox.

An email from Mr. Ravenel says the meeting at the law offices is confirmed for ten a.m. I don't like this pulling of the strings my grandfather is doing. It's dramatic and ridiculous. An email from Dorothy has an attachment. *Here's all the public information I could find about Montgomery Homes & Facilities and an estimated valuation.* I open the document and scan through until I reach the bottom line of the net profits and do a double take. Holy shit, the old man had been busy. I'm surprised Isabel hasn't tried to see me already. Then I see an email from her.

To: Tmontgomery
From: Imont@monthomesandfacdotcom
Subject: Your grandfather

Trystan

I apologize for my less than warm reception yesterday. It was an emotional day and a shock to see you. You have your mother's eyes, you know. I was wondering if there'd be a chance to pop by and see you, say for breakfast? Beau told me you are staying at the Planter's. I'll meet you in the salon at eight am.

Until then,

Isabel Montgomery

I check my watch. It's seven. No way in hell I'm seeing her. This isn't running away, I'm simply not ready. I take a shower, throw on my jeans, a button-down, and my brown boots, grab my phone and laptop, and I'm out the door in fifteen minutes and out the hotel a minute after that.

13

TRYSTAN

I leave the hotel and before I realize it, find myself following Emmy's instructions. Charleston has barely woken up, and the humidity has yet to rise. Before long I'm entering what I hope is the small cobblestone alleyway Emmy mentioned in her email. Instinct tells me these were the streets between the main fancy houses and where the horses were kept, similar to the mews houses in London.

Every ten meters or so there's a gate into a courtyard where a small carriage house or old stable can be found. Many of them have been clearly turned into residences, albeit tiny, some galleries and the like. I notice the blue awning not too far ahead, but my surroundings have me captivated. I don't miss London, I never have. It's not that it's so reminiscent of a place I don't miss. And it's eons away from even the most charming parts of the Village in New York, but something about this place feels . . . right.

I shrug off the feeling and head inside the breakfast shop, breathing in the scent of freshly baked bread. It's small, every square inch has been properly utilized. There are barn wood floors and corrugated tin. It's industrial in a rustic way. There are only seven tables inside, most can only fit two people. A man with slicked back dark hair with a white apron wrapped around his wiry frame is taking an order from a hipster couple in the corner. Other than them, I have my pick of tables. I choose a small table in the far right corner. The menu is a card presented on a small chopping board held in place by an elastic band, and there are only five breakfast items available.

"You must be Trystan," an accented voice says to me.

I look up, startled. "Armand, I presume?" He's of indeterminate age. His dark hair has some gray threading through it. His skin is olive, his descent of unknown origin. To me he could just as easily be Native-American as he could be Middle-Eastern or Greek. He's good-looking though, and something about that annoys me.

He grins and gives me a slow perusal from my messy post-shower hair, down to my beaten-in chukka boots that cost four hundred dollars to make them look old. "Well," he says.

"Well, what?" I counter.

He makes a *tsk* sound.

I lift an eyebrow in return.

"Hmm," he says. "*Bien*. Now, what can I get you?"

Weird.

After my rich dinner last night, I feel I should go little on the lighter side for breakfast. I order homemade gluten-free granola (nod to Emmy) with Greek yoghurt, local honey, bananas and blueberries, fresh orange juice, and an espresso. Armand hums with what I hope is approval then walks back behind the counter.

I wonder if there's a place like this near me in New York—simple, stylish, cozy—that I simply haven't ever bothered to notice, and I resolve to find one. The closest I can think of is perhaps something in Chelsea Market.

When my food comes I take out Emmy's phone and snap a picture. I'm not sure why I do it, and I definitely don't send it to her. Maybe just proof I took her advice.

I open my laptop and spend the next hour making sure I'm as knowledgeable as possible about Montgomery Homes & Facilities before Isabel Montgomery tries to argue I'm unable to run it.

* * *

WITH ABOUT FORTY-FIVE more minutes to kill before the meeting at Mr. Ravenel's office, I pay my check, wave at Armand, and decide to walk around the city. Some of the first horse-drawn carriage tours of the day have started up, and on almost every street corner I hear snippets of Charleston history. This famous person lived here, slaves were traded there, this used to be a church and now it's a restaurant, this pink house is four hundred years old, Blackbeard used to frequent that pub. If I ever come back to this place, I know I'd be fascinated by some of the stories. I almost studied history at university, but at the last minute chose economics. I'd loved these stories as a child the few years my mother tried to come home to the family. Right now, though, it does something to me inside, like opening up an emotional trash can lid that really should stay closed.

I grab the earbuds I keep in the outside pocket of my laptop bag, and I wonder what kind of music Emmy has on her phone. She has Spotify, but I'm disappointed to see it's the free version that needs Wi-Fi. I go over to her purchased music selection and scan it with a sinking stomach. It's a potpourri of girl power: Taylor Swift, P!nk, Katy Perry. I sigh and hit shuffle, making sure to turn it down more than usual so no one can overhear. By the time I take the last few steps to Mr. Ravenel's office, timed to be one minute late in order to avoid any small talk, I'm ready to take on the world and think most men suck. It makes me think of my reaction to the messages Emmy received from that dating app. No wonder the women are so pissed off in these songs. I resolve to make sure Dorothy knows she can wear trousers to work if she feels like it. In all the time she's worked for me she's come to work in a knee-length skirt, hose, and low sensible heels. She reminded me of one of my school teachers back in England, which was exactly why I'd hired her.

Everyone is already seated at the conference room table when I arrive. I greet Mr. Ravenel's receptionist, noting she's wearing a pantsuit today. Why am I so focused on women's apparel all of a sudden? "How long have they been in there?" I ask.

"They just sat down. Can I bring you coffee?"

"No, I'm good. Thanks." I smile tightly and head into the proverbial ring, avoiding the searing gaze of Isabel Montgomery.

"Let us begin." Mr. Ravenel stands and closes the door behind me and then pulls his chair in closer to the table and peers at each of us over the frames of his spectacles. "The reason for allowing an overnight reprieve was to allow any knee jerk reactions to the news yesterday to be processed before getting to the limitations and stipulations of the disbursements set out in the will. This was at the request of the late Mr. Montgomery."

He gives Isabel a meaningful glance. "At the time of the drawing up of the last will and testament of the late Mr. Montgomery, he was found to be of sound mind and had the blessing of his family physician. In addition, I personally asked that he see a mental health professional too, in order that there be absolutely no concern about his mental capacity." I feel sure the glance Ravenel gave Isabel was because she has already been calling the will into question. "Especially given that these stipulations are rather . . . unorthodox."

* * *

WHEN I LEAVE two hours later, shell-shocked and three times richer than when I walked in the door, I simply stand on the sidewalk. I'm not shell-shocked by the valuation of what I'm now worth, I'm shell-shocked by the stipulations that go along with it.

Someone walks into my back and I stumble forward, waking from my shock.

"Sorry. Oh hey, Trystan." It's Beau. The two of us face each other on the street outside the law office. He looks as stunned as I feel. Damn, but my grandfather was a twisted son of a bitch.

"You want to grab some lunch?" Beau asks.

"Sure." I shrug.

"I've been living out at the house on Awendaw. I don't know what's good around here anymore. Let's walk and see what we find."

"I know someone who will," I say and pull out the phone. The need to connect with Emmy at this moment is overwhelming. Someone completely removed from the weird shit in my life right now.

BREAKFAST WAS GREAT. *Lunch?*

THANKFULLY, she responds right away.

EMMY: *Are you close to Market Street?*

"ARE WE CLOSE TO MARKET STREET," I ask Beau.

He nods and points to the left and we cross the road.

YES.

EMMY: *Great. Head to 5Church. If you have any awkward silences you can just look up.*

I FROWN. That was a weird thing to say, but I go with it. It's like she knows I'm about to have lunch with my cousin for the first time in approximately eighteen years. Awkward, indeed.

"5 CHURCH," I tell Beau and give him the address she sends in her next text.

* * *

OPPOSITE the old slave trading market pavilions, which now sell sweetgrass baskets and bric-a-brac, and squeezed between two five-story buildings, is an old red brick church with a modern tempered-glass door. "Here we are, I guess." I lead the way up the stairs and inside.

We both stop and stare. Inside it's dim. There's a bar running the whole length of one side. The light fixtures are pendants covered with a curl of white feathers like a folded angel wing. But the most arresting sight is the massive, intact, stained-glass window soaring the entire height of the back wall and streaming fractured prisms of light into the room.

"Wow," says Beau. "I never even knew this was here." Then he points up to the ceiling, and I follow with my gaze. Lines and lines of text are painstakingly painted in row after row. There's not an inch of space without words. I read a few sentences here and there; it seems familiar. Every now and again a word is pulled out and written in supersize.

"What is that?" I ask squinting, though I recognize it the second the question leaves my lips.

"The entire text of *The Art of War* by Sun Tzu," the hostess at the stand responds. "Lunch for two?"

I nod and we follow her to a booth on the wall opposite the

bar. Of course it is. The only book I've read cover to cover several times over. One of my economics professors assigned it as part of his course in mergers and acquisitions; it has served me well.

My phone buzzes as we sit down, and I pull it back out of my pocket.

EMMY: I wish I could see your reaction right now.

I GRIN.

STUNNED. But with that introduction the food better be good.

EMMY: Ye of little faith. And you're in a church!

"YOUR GIRLFRIEND?" asks Beau, nodding to the phone.

I jerk my head up. "Oh, no. Just someone who knows the best places to eat in Charleston. I don't know her." I shake my head as if it's nothing, but Beau's still looking at me quizzically, and I decide if we're about to rebuild our relationship I may as well share. "Actually, it's kind of a funny story." I proceed to tell him the entire phone switching debacle. I leave out the fact we talked on the phone for over half an hour last night.

When I get done he slumps back against the high-backed bench seat. "And I thought *my* life just took a turn for the weird and wonderful. You have me beat."

I rub my hand over my jaw. "I wouldn't say that. So do *you* have a girlfriend? Are you even close to doing what he wants?"

"Getting married? Hell, no. I haven't ever gone past a tenth date to my knowledge."

"Ten. That's not bad. I draw a line at three. Four if we haven't . . . you know." I feel terrible saying that out loud. But it's the truth. I date women so I can have sex. I don't do relationships and commitments.

There's no judgement on Beau's face. "I should rein it back to four. Getting all the way to ten gets you in all sorts of trouble. Lots of women around here are looking to trap a Montgomery. Though," he looks up at the stained-glass window and crosses himself, "thankfully, I've been careful."

I give a mock shudder. "So how's your mom doing, by the way?" Beau's parents split up the same summer my mother managed to make herself persona non grata with the Montgomery family again.

Beau smiles. "Fine. Remarried. Lives out near Summerville."

"Good, that's good. Send her my regards, will you? She was always kind to me."

The waitress brings our drinks, and I order the soup and salad of the day. Something with goat cheese, but I'm too distracted by our recent meeting to pay much attention to the menu.

"Are you okay with not being involved with Montgomery Homes & Facilities?" I decide to cut to the chase with Beau. "I mean I thought I got a read that you were happy with the way it played out. Until today, obviously," I add.

"I never wanted to be involved, no. Of course, I would have done it for the family. But I think it's in the best hands now."

"What about your father? Uncle Robert? He looked ready to commit murder. Do I need to be worried?"

Beau looks at me seriously. "He's pretty upset. But to be honest, I think it's more about what people might think of him being passed over, that he might lose his social standing or at worst not be able to maintain his lifestyle." He lifts a shoulder and then drops it. "It's not about any sense of ambition. I doubt he could name half the operations we own. He'll still be a good source of information for you though."

I nod. "And Isabel? Was *she* more interested in the day to day?"

"I don't know, to tell you the truth. But I think it's more of the same feelings my father is having." He raises his hands to his mouth and widens his eyes. "What will the people at the club say?" he mimics.

"Ah."

"So what about you?" Beau asks. "I must admit, I didn't see that coming. It's like Grandfather is forcing us all back together in a way he was never able to when he was alive. So are you going to do it? Do you want to? Yesterday you weren't sure."

"I don't think I have a choice. My ego wouldn't let me walk even if my head tells me to run the other way. I have to hand it to the guy, he sure was a creative thinker."

"That's putting it mildly."

"So?" I grin and volley straight back to him. "Who are you going to marry in order to get your inheritance?"

The waitress comes back to top off our iced tea at that exact moment. She pauses mid pour and steps back looking Beau up and down. "Well honey, I'm available if you're stuck," she says with a wink.

Beau's skin color deepens about fifteen shades as he glares at me, and I crack up laughing. "Uh, thanks," he mumbles, not quite looking at her.

"He'll keep you in mind," I tell her.

"See that he does. Your food will be right out."

"Thanks."

We both watch her walk away.

"She's cute," I say. "You could do worse."

"Probably. What in the hell was Grandfather thinking putting that stipulation on me? Why not *you*?"

"Me? Never. Anyway, I hardly got off scot-free." I grimace. "It just so happens I'm about to sell my company in New York. I wasn't sure what I was going to work on next, but it sure as shit didn't involve anything to do with the Montgomerys. No offense.

I'm sure Grandfather knew if he added in a marriage stipulation to that bombshell, I'd walk."

"Well, I for one am glad. It'll be good to have you back here more." Beau brushes his hair off his forehead. "You can help me narrow down my prospect list."

Emmy pops into my head.

"Sure," I say. Emmy is single. Nice. Beautiful. Funny.

I open my mouth then immediately close it.

"You okay?" Beau asks, looking concerned by whatever he sees on my expression.

"Yeah." I sigh. "No. I don't know. Nothing. I'm fine."

There's an awkward pause. I look up at the ceiling.

"Today sure was a lot to take in," Beau says, relieving me of clarifying my comment.

Our food arrives, saving me from adding anything else. I pull out Emmy's phone, take a picture and start to text it to her. I stop myself and put my phone away. Beau is grinning at me.

"Shut up," I say.

He raises his eyebrows. "Didn't say a word."

14

EMMY

*T*he continuous rain made the already dilapidated neighbourhood seem that much more abandoned. Unlike the busy hustle of the city, where New Yorkers merely continued their day under an umbrella, the streets around David's nursing home were deserted. I'd planned on starting the day with a walk down to the water and a search for a coffee shop, but a peek between the buildings toward the shore showed only a misty view awaited me, so I pressed on. The coffee shop eluded me too, and by the time I arrived to see David I was soaked and irritable.

The email I'd sent last night to Trystan weighed on me. I felt vulnerable, like I'd exposed a part of myself to him and been left wanting. It was preposterous to even let it bother me. He was a stranger. And in a few days, after we had traded back phones, he would continue to be a stranger. After I'd sent the email, I'd gone through his photos. He wasn't a manic picture taker like me, but what I found fit with what I knew about him. He was a kind, beautiful man, with a tendency toward periodic assholery. There weren't any pictures of him with anyone who could possibly be categorized as family. None of him with any women. Nor men, though I thought I'd pretty much assured myself he was straight. And definitely not one of him with a dog. Every now and again, he'd capture a scene from the city—the leaves in Central Park, a bridge at sunset. He took pictures of art. Perhaps he was a collector and took pictures of things he liked on occasion to remember them. And the bulk of the pictures were of documents. If he was like me, I used an app where you could send faxes from picture files. I often sent our service agreements and contracts this way to clients. There were also several pictures of him with a younger dark-skinned boy, pictures of that boy playing basketball, hanging out, and receiving a diploma. I'd studied the picture of Trystan and the kid as I fell asleep, thinking I made out the sign for the Boys and Girls Club of America behind them. It made sense that my handsome stranger would do something as awesome as have a Little Brother. There weren't many people I knew who'd give their time to a cause like that. But then another notification from one of his dating apps or a text would come through, and it sobered me up. I turned on the Do Not Disturb around midnight.

* * *

I GREETED the nursing home staff in the downstairs office and headed to the cafeteria to see about getting coffee. David was still at his table eating breakfast. I went to the far wall and filled a Styrofoam cup with pale brown liquid and creamer then went to join him.

"Mind if I sit with you?" I asked David.

"Emmy!" he greeted me right away, and I leaned down to kiss his cheek. Inside, my tense stomach relaxed to know that at least I had my David back today.

D'Andre saw me drinking the coffee. "Baby girl, you can't drink that. Give it to me."

I raised an eyebrow and handed him my cup.

"You know we don't fully charge the coffee down here. Be right back."

It hadn't occurred to me that they didn't give their patients real caffeinated coffee, but it made sense. Caffeine was a drug, and with all the prescriptions going around in here, I should have thought about it. Sure enough, the coffee D'Andre brought me, in a real mug was heavenly. "Thank you," I said gratefully.

David and I chatted about everything and nothing, the old days and my new memories in Charleston. I explained his medical condition to him while he was lucid enough to understand as I'd done several times before. And as before, it made us both cry. But I'd been advised that it was important for him to understand as much as possible why he was in a home, so there was less chance of him trying to get out. We played cards, and then I walked him back to his room for a rest before lunch.

As always happened when I spent time with David, I was left feeling both full of love and emotionally drained.

I needed to go and clear my head in order to be back with him in the afternoon. Pulling Trystan's phone out of my purse, I ignored all the missed calls and messages and opened the web browser to find somewhere to eat lunch. I was under no impression that I'd be hearing from him today unless he needed some information off his phone, so I was taken by surprise when a text from Suit Monkey popped up at the top of the screen. Having absolutely no will power, I opened it immediately.

SUIT MONKEY: *Breakfast was great. Lunch?*

SO HE'D TAKEN my recommendation for breakfast, that gave me a small modicum of satisfaction. Actually, it made me insanely happy, which was clearly an indication of how depressed I was about the situation with David. I'd seen an email last night from someone called Isabel Montgomery and something about it rubbed me the wrong way. The fact she assumed he'd have breakfast with her, I guess. Or her tone. She made mention of Trystan's mother so carelessly in the email, that even without knowing him, I wanted to protect him. Was his mother even in his life? I had no idea. I was operating on pure gut-level instinct. So I'd offered up the breakfast suggestion, letting him in on one of my best kept secrets, my most favorite place. A place that happened to be almost next door to my little carriage house. It felt like inviting him into my world. Would he even appreciate it?

But then his text had come, and it all felt okay again. As if I'd done the right thing. So I gave him my next favorite place. 5Church. With his appreciation for art, I was sure its uniqueness would appeal to him. Especially at lunch. As beautiful as it was in the evening, the daylight coming through the window was a sight to behold.

When he admitted he was stunned, I couldn't help my smile. The fact that my stomach flipped over as I read his text was, however, a little concerning.

My madness was complete when I found myself looking up the number and calling Armand.

"Indigo Café," Armand's voice greeted me.

"Armand, it's Emmy."

"Emmy, *mi amor.* I saw your friend today." He whistled. "Aye, aye, he is *delicioso*."

"Stop it, Armand," I admonished. And then because I couldn't help it. "He is though, isn't he?"

"Darling girl, yes."

"So did he enjoy his breakfast?"

"Of course," he said, sounding affronted that I'd even suggest such a thing—especially since after the café closed at two in the afternoon, Armand spent the rest of his time hand-making menu items from scratch. "But he spent *mucho tiempo* on the computer, tap, tap, tapping."

"Right, well, he seems to be a busy man. So, how are you?"

"*Bien, bien.* Annie, she came for lunch with the baby. So cute!"

"She did? That's great. You didn't tell her about Trystan, did you?"

"But, of course. He is too handsome not to be news."

I cringed. She'd probably texted my phone, and if she hadn't she would as soon as she arrived home and got the baby down for a nap. "Shit. I have to go and do damage control. Love you, Armand. See you when I get back. Are we still going dancing?"

"*Claro, mi amor.* See you Friday."

I hung up and immediately opened the message app to text Annie and then froze. Oh my God. I didn't remember her number off the top of my head.

I bit my lip and sent a text to Trystan.

ANY CHANCE *you can forward me the contact information for my friend, Annie? Thx.*

I CAUGHT myself chewing on my thumbnail and decided I couldn't put off walking somewhere to have lunch, or I was going to eat my own hand with anxiety. Thankfully, the rain slowed but the forecast showed there was more coming.

OH AND IF SHE TEXTS, *just ignore it. She has a new baby and is a little woo-woo in the head. Says some crazy stuff. K, thx, bye.*

AFTER A FRUSTRATING MEETING with David's assigned social worker, the head nurse, and Penny, I was no clearer on what to do about him. They wanted hard and fast dates when they could count on David being gone. It came down to a liability issue where they simply weren't equipped or insured enough to deal with a dementia patient. Then I spent an equally frustrating few hours with David, who started slipping into confusion as he got tired. And I still hadn't had a text back from Trystan. It shouldn't have bothered me, but somehow it did.

Maybe my phone had died. The battery was for shit. Unfortunately, the lack of hearing from him was probably more along the lines of him having received a couple of texts from Annie that were meant for me, and was now, at this very moment, hiring personal security.

What a disaster. It was already weird between us. This had made it infinitely worse. And I didn't understand why I was so fixated on making a good impression.

When I looked at his phone, I almost expected to see no signal, showing me he'd given in and bought a new phone and cancelled this one. There was an Apple Store right there on King Street. It would take him approximately eight hundred dollars and twenty minutes to get rid of me. Clearly he had the means. He wouldn't even have to ditch my phone, he could just leave it with Armand.

Trying to untangle my feelings about whether I was more worried about not having a working phone for the next twenty-four hours or that I might never hear from Trystan Montgomery again was giving me a headache.

I came to a dead stop outside my rented Airbnb. I looked at the phone to make a decision about dinner, and some kind of instinct borne of always checking my work email when I looked at my phone to make sure I never missed anything had me opening Trystan's by mistake.

Shaking my head, I double tapped to close it just as I saw an email from Trystan. *From* Trystan. *To* Trystan. It took all my effort not to open it and assume it was for me. I'd just pretend I hadn't seen it. I had to kick this Trystan habit.

Except right at that moment a text appeared at the top of the screen, and my heart rate sped up. Shit.

SUIT MONKEY: *I replied to your email.*

15

EMMY

*T*o: tmontgomery
       From: tmontgomery
Subject: re: Phone

DEAR EMMALINE ANGELIQUE DUBOIS

THANK you for your restaurant recommendations today. Both came at very opportune times. And by the way, your town is lovely, but I wouldn't call it a city. New York is a city.

I decided to wing it tonight and find somewhere to eat without your help. I chose The Ordinary. Luckily the food was *extra*-ordinary. Ha. I sat at the bar. Did you know they have 412 different types of gin? At least it seemed so. I'm more of an aged single malt man myself, but when in Rome . . .

Leaving my phone at the front desk of The Planter's Inn tomorrow evening might be problematic. They are kicking me out in the morning. Apparently your *town* has some kind of festival starting this weekend and the entire hotel is booked. In fact it seems every hotel is over-booked. Perhaps they should move the festival to an actual city?

If you have a hotel hookup who can get me a room for the next few days I'd appreciate it. I can't leave at the moment as apparently my grandfather has decided he can dictate my life from beyond the grave.

Regards,

Trystan L. Montgomery

P.S. YOUR FRIEND Annie has some colorful language. She seemed to get annoyed when there was no return text from you, so of course I had to answer. It was about me, after all. Don't worry, she doesn't know it wasn't you.

Dear Trystan L. Montgomery

I think you'll find that if a town has a cathedral, it becomes, by definition, a city. We have a cathedral. Several in fact. The spires of the City of Charleston have graced many a postcard. I believe you might have been in one of them just two days ago. Perhaps you spontaneously burst into flames upon entering and that's why you are so ornery?

I'm sad for your lack of accommodations, I wish you good luck in that endeavor. It is indeed the largest festival of its kind in the United States, having exceeded the festival in Spoleto, Italy, from whence it was derived.

It is so popular, in fact, that I often stay with my *colorful* friend, Annie and rent my place out. But Annie has recently had a baby, my godson. She's quite sleep deprived, so I'm sure anything she says can be dismissed. Perhaps you could see your way to forwarding her contact information to me (this is my second request).

Perhaps you should stay with family.

The Ordinary was a satisfactory choice for dinner.

Regards,

Emmaline A. Dubois

P.S. I have greatly enjoyed corresponding with your matches on your various dating apps. It's been quite . . . educational to realize all the different expectations they have, depending on the app. So fun! And naughty! Don't worry, they don't know it's not you, *Jeff* .

. .

Dear Emmaline *Angelique* Dubois

Can I rent your house, condo, or whatever?

Regards,
   Trystan L. Montgomery

P.S. I can't believe the smut on your Kindle app. You've made me blush. I think you might be naughtier than I'll ever be. I found the one about the mafia boss to be particularly shocking.

Dear Mr. Montgomery

No, you may not.

Regards,
  Miss Dubois

P.S. In the interests of expediency, I went ahead and responded to the last six girlfriends who texted you and asked them all to head to your condo at nine p.m. next Thursday. I'm sure this will make your dating life more organized.

To: tmontgomery
  From: tmontgomery
  Subject: Best behavior

Emmy

Why not? Are you a hoarder?

Regards,
  Trystan

P.S. Is your hair color natural?

My stomach was teeming with slippery ribbons of laughter, outrage, lust, and excitement and I was utterly nauseated. I plugged in Trystan's phone to charge without replying to his email and set it down on the counter of the small apartment. I stared at the black rectangle like it was a live thing that might spontaneously fly up and smash me straight through the heart. Backing slowly away, I changed into my sweatpants and rolled out my yoga mat with shaking fingers. By the time I'd made it through fourteen Chaturangas, I'd finally managed to focus on nothing but my breathing and my muscles. I was centered. Focused.

And still obsessed.

I surrendered into Child's pose, my body folded and my forehead to the ground.

I had it so, so, bad.

16

TRYSTAN

J probably shouldn't have made friends with the bartender at The Ordinary because my gin tolerance is apparently quite low. I've been *flirtmalling* with Emmy, and it's gotten out of hand. When she doesn't write back, I'm left with a rock in my stomach that feels a lot like it could be rejection, if I was sure I knew what that felt like. Most of all, I'm asking myself how I can be behaving this way with someone I've laid eyes on for approximately ten seconds at the very most.

Checking my email one more time before I leave my laptop on the desk, I'm disappointed to see she still hasn't responded.

Instead I see an email from Isabel Montgomery.

SUBJECT: We really do need to talk.

OF COURSE ISABEL wants to talk. My grandfather basically stipulated that the only way she could continue to receive the same business disbursements into her spending account was to go through me.

I would have to sign off on them.

My grandfather, may God rest his manipulative soul, is basically forcing Isabel Montgomery to kiss my ass or go without. The whole situation is so messed up. Frankly, I'm sure it's destined to breed more hatred than mend anything.

Not one to run from conflict, I decide we may as well meet and get all the grievances aired and over with.

FROM: Tmontgomery
  To: Imont@monthomesandfacdotcom
  Subject: Re: We really do need to talk
  Isabel,
  That would be fine. I'll be available for coffee before our morning meeting with the firm accountants. Please be at the hotel by eight.
  Trystan

FEELING HAPPIER that I'm the one in control now, I close my laptop, strip out of my clothes, and climb into bed, letting inebriated and broken sleep claim me. Except it doesn't. And I get up to get Emmy's phone and bring it back to bed.

GOOD NIGHT, *Emmy.*

THE RESPONSE COMES IMMEDIATELY.

EMMY: *Good night, Trystan*

SIGHING HEAVILY and too mentally wired to sleep, I mindlessly surf her phone. Maybe I can find something, *anything*, that will turn me off.

Her Instagram profile, even though I scrolled through it before, becomes my focus. There are the pictures of food I've already seen, and halfway through scrolling and trying to find more than the couple of pictures of Emmy rather than her dinner, I realize there are repeating links to another Instagram account. The account I've been looking at is her work one. I tap her name at the top and a drop-down choice comes up with another name *AnAngelintheForest*. My frown clears as realize the reference to her last name, Dubois, loosely translates to The Woods or The Forest in French. And that's when I hit the motherlode. I grin and make myself comfortable. Pictures of her around town, sunsets over the water, the beach, her toes in the sand. I zoom in, even her feet are pretty. Pale skin, pink polished toes. And her ankles are slender.

I hate my stalker self right now, but I push on.

Pictures of her with a blonde woman tagged as her friend Annie. Emmy with a little baby boy—Annie's baby, I presume. Her with Armand. All three of them together. Clearly the three of them hang out a lot. Emmy with an older man with white-gray hair who has no family resemblance whatsoever. I read the caption: "The families you choose are the families that once chose you." Something about the way it's written sends a prickle of melancholy through me. It has a lot of likes. The man isn't tagged. But I wonder if it's David. I click out and go back to the main page of pictures and continue my search.

And oh, I really shouldn't have done it.

My thumb and my eyes zero in on a picture of people on the beach. I open the picture up to full screen. I see who I presume is Annie, her belly round and pregnant in a navy blue swimsuit. But I barely spare her a glance because there's Emmy, her red hair is wild and streaking sideways in the breeze and filtering the sun.

Her mouth is open and wide with laughter, and her sweet, curvy, little body is packed into a tiny yellow bikini.

Holy hell.

I sit straight up in bed as if I can see it better if I'm upright. My gaze slides down her body from her slender neck and collarbone, over the swell of her ample breasts, the barest hint of a tightly-budded nipple shadowing the fabric, and down the soft skin of her belly, pauses on the small yellow triangle, and on down her shapely legs to those pink toes.

Aaaand, I'm hard.

Fuck.

I have a headache starting to brew between my eyes, and I pinch the bridge of my nose. Surely, it's the gin and not the fact I was supposed to find something to exterminate my crush, not magnify it a thousandfold.

Now I know how she looks in a bikini, a visual I could have done without. Because, *Christ*, she is far from the skinny women I normally go for, but she is quite possibly, the sexiest woman I have ever seen. The image is seared onto my eyeballs. And even half an hour after I've put her phone safely on the other side of the damn room, I can still see it.

I turn on the TV in the dark and flick mindlessly through channels looking for ESPN, hoping for lots and lots of sports stats.

What have I been reduced to? Because even in my most hormonal teenage years, I never focused this hard on a girl.

* * *

THE INCESSANT BUZZING ring of Emmy's phone wakes me in the dark. The hands of my watch glow faintly, telling me it's just past six. Pushing myself from the bed, I stumble to the desk where I left her phone.

It's a Manhattan number. Naturally, I answer it.

"Oh," the voice responds to my raspy morning greeting. "Uh, is Miss Dubois available please? This is Penny Smith from Rockaway Nursing and Rehabilitation. It's an emergency."

I shake my head and scrub a hand down my face to wake myself up. "Um, she's not here right now."

"This is her phone, right?"

"Yes, sorry." I give her my cell phone number. "She's reachable on this other number until this evening." This is an absolute farce. How could two lives possibly get more complicated over a set of phones?

"Thank y—"

"Wait." I swallow. "Is everything all right? You said it was an emergency."

"Are you related to Miss Dubois?"

"No, but—"

"Then, I'm sorry. I'm not at liberty to tell you. But if you hear from her, can you please ask her to call us as soon as possible?"

"Is it . . ." I rack my brain for the name. "David. Is it about David, is he all right?"

"I can't tell you, I'm sorry. I need to hang up so I can call her."

"Sorry. Yes, if I speak to her, I'll let her know you called."

I press end on the phone and sit down heavily in the desk chair. Apparently I missed four calls before I'd answered. Grabbing my unfinished water bottle from last night, I chug down the rest of it. Realizing I never quite got to the bottom of who David is to Emmy, I pull out my computer and type in Rockaway Nursing & Rehabilitation, learning that it's a senior care facility. I remember a David calling several times the first day I had Emmy's phone, but as soon as I'd answered, he'd hung up. He probably thought he'd dialed the wrong number. I didn't answer the next few times he tried.

I open the text message app.

Rockaway Nursing trying to get hold of you urgently.

I start typing *Let me know if there's anything I can do* and then delete it. I only need to pass along the information.

God, I spent way too long stalking Emmy last night. I was using her as a distraction to what was going on in my life. She's obviously taken the place of my usual methods. And it has to stop. We are getting far too involved in each other's lives.

A quick workout and hot shower later, I check in with Dorothy then Mac to make sure everything is on for the closing of the deal next week. Dorothy still hasn't had any luck finding me a hotel. If Beau lived in town, I'd ask him if he had a spare room. Damn, I'd take a couch right now.

After I pack my roll-on, I head downstairs to meet with the Montgomery matriarch.

* * *

Isabel Montgomery stands, drawing my attention as soon as I enter the small but elegant lounge area.

She takes a step forward and holds out her hand. "Trystan."

"Isabel," I reply, accepting her handshake.

She clasps both cold, papery hands around mine and squeezes. It's a rare display of affection.

Clearing my throat, I look past her at the seating area. She's chosen two arm chairs in the corner that face each other and share a small table. A carafe of coffee and two cups are already there. "Shall we?" I ask.

"Let's." She purses her lips in what may or may not be an attempt at a polite smile, it's hard to tell, and holds her pearls as she lowers herself back to where she was sitting.

A server materializes silently.

"Are you eating?" Isabel asks me.

I don't have a menu, but I look up. "An omelet if you have it. Chef's choice."

"Very good, sir," the man inclines his head and melts away.

I pour some coffee in my empty cup and wait for Isabel to say whatever it is she needs to.

It's not until I've added cream, stirred, and taken a sip that she begins. I watch her over the rim of the delicate fine china cup I'm holding.

"It was . . . as I said, a shock to see you," she says and again her hand comes nervously to her throat. "I didn't know you'd heard of your grandfather's passing, let alone that you would come. And well, now with . . . the will, of course, it makes sense."

She looks at me expectantly, but I have no idea what I'm supposed to say. So I wait.

She breathes out, and her eyes flick away and back, becoming hard, "You're determined to make this unpleasant, aren't you?"

A stab of hurt, a memory from my childhood, hits low in my chest, but I do my best to use it to fuel annoyance instead. "I'm not *determined* to do anything, Isabel. You asked to see *me*." I take another sip of coffee. "And I do wish you'd get to the point."

She wrings her hands in her lap. They are bony with age, the knuckles a tiny bit out of proportion to the delicate line of her. Arthritic, perhaps.

"Look, Isabel." I soften slightly. "I'm sorry for your loss. I imagine it must be devastating to lose your life partner. And I'm sorry that seeing me was a shock. I am sure you were quite satisfied that you'd effectively cut my mother and me out of your life for good, and I—"

"I made a mistake." Her mouth pinches, and she looks away and blinks several times.

"Excuse me?"

"You heard me. I made a mistake. I . . . was hard on her. And perhaps I shouldn't have turned my back on her like I did if it meant we lost you too."

I stare at her, my breath stalled in my lungs.

"Don't . . . you . . . dare," I finally manage in a low tone. Then abruptly lean forward.

She glances around nervously and back to me.

I carefully set my delicate cup down before I throw it across the room or accidentally crush it.

"Now, Trystan, I . . . look, please." She reaches out a hand, but I stand and she's forced to pull it back. "Don't make a scene," she says quietly, nervously, eyes darting around the room.

Leaning down so to the passersby it might look as if I'm telling her a secret, I put my hands on the arm rests either side of her.

She leans back but has nowhere to go.

"I won't make a scene," I say quietly to the side of her head, "as long as you get something clear. All I wanted was a family. I was thirteen years old. I loved you. As cold as you were. I loved it here. I thought I'd come to paradise. Only, we were sent away again. And then I had to watch my own mother die a long slow death. Alone. For all her faults, she was your *daughter*, for Christ's sake," I hiss. "And you ignored her. Ignored me. It's a little too late for regrets, don't you think? The time to pretend you gave a shit about *me* would have been while I sat alone at seventeen in an NHS hospital as a stranger told me my mother had finally gone to God. If you think I'm hardened . . . difficult . . . heartless . . . ruthless, you haven't seen anything. You made me this way, Isabel Montgomery. And I'll do whatever I damned well please."

I pull back and stand.

Wet tracks mark Isabel's powdered cheeks. Her normally regal, statuesque features are crumpled and broken. I look away from her. The waiter takes that moment to arrive with my omelet. I grab a napkin from my place setting and hand it to her. My hands are shaking, belying my composed tone.

"I won't be eating after all," I tell the nonplussed server. I peel off some bills to cover the meal and then head to check out of the hotel.

I want to beat the shit out of something, but I have nowhere to go and nothing to hit. I don't care what Ravenel says about me sticking around, I need to go back to New York and get some distance from the clusterfuck my life turned into over the last three days.

I'm flying out of here tonight, no question.

TRYSTAN

I've set myself up in Ravenel's conference room with financials printed and spread out all around me. The company accountants are set to arrive and give me a proper rundown, and Uncle Robert is keeping to himself at the end of the table with his own files.

Ravenel's assistant pokes her head in the door for about the eleventh time. "Is there anything I can get you, Mr. Montgomery?"

"We're fine. But, thank you." I speak for both of us in the room.

She pouts. I should be hitting that while I'm in town, it would certainly go some way toward easing the tension brewing the last few days. I stare after her. Why am I not? I definitely noticed how cute she was when I came in a few days ago, and she would be more than willing, that much is obvious. What was her name again? Daisy, I think.

"I wouldn't if I were you."

I look up to where Robert is sitting at the end of the table with his own files.

He nods his chin toward the door. "She's Maybank's niece. As in Mr. Ravenel's law partner."

"Thanks for the heads-up," I tell him then cast my attention back to the papers in front of me. "Where is Maybank anyway?"

"Hunting in Africa."

"Gross," I mutter.

"Tell me about it," Robert concurs, and I give him a surprised look. "Please," he adds. "It's not like culling the deer population. Killing endangered animals with a gun from a safe few hundred yards away is pure greed."

"Fact," I say, begrudging we have common ground.

He looks at me over the top of his file. "My mother hasn't made it in. I'm assuming the meeting did not go her way this morning?"

I blow out a breath. I still feel like shit. It felt both good and horrible to get all that off my chest. "I wouldn't say it went well, no. I don't know what "her way" was, but let's just say we didn't get that far."

"I'm sorry, you know?"

"About what?" I ask stiffly.

"About Savannah. My sister. She was a screw-up, I know. But so was I. We'd have to be, with cold parents like ours. I tried to reason with them. Hell, I even tried to contact Savannah myself, but she wouldn't respond. I—I'm sorry, Trystan. I would have been there, if I'd known."

I swallow over my tongue that feels too large in my mouth.

"Thank you," I manage, but it comes out hoarse. My heart is pounding in my throat, my head heating up. Burning.

"Fuck," I mutter and stand abruptly. "I need some air."

Stalking out of the room, through reception and down to the street, I feel like I can't get outside fast enough. Like I might suffocate. I think I was about to fucking cry in there. Except I don't damn well cry. Haven't in fourteen years.

* * *

EMMY IS SOBBING SO HARD I can barely understand her.

"Shh, calm down," I tell her. "Sweetheart, I can't hear what you're saying."

I'd answered without thinking, desperate for the distraction she brought from my own family drama, only to be greeted by almost incoherent hysteria.

"D-David's missing. He wandered off. They can't find him, they don't even know when he left."

My stomach sinks as I stand on the sidewalk outside the law office. "Oh shit, honey. I'm sorry." I cross the sidewalk and lean against the building. Did I just call her honey?

"H-has he called you?" she asks.

I frown. "What?"

"That's why I called you. He calls me sometimes, repeatedly. I thought maybe he was trying to get hold of me and couldn't, and that's why he left, you know?"

She hiccups.

Shit. I look down at the phone and go to the missed calls in case somehow I didn't hear them. There's nothing but the calls from early this morning and then two I let roll to voicemail that was a Charleston number that said "Work."

I breathe out. "I'm sorry. Only your work called."

"W-Will you answer the phone though? If it rings? If it's a New York number? Or any number? He could be anywhere. Oh my God. What if something happens to him?" Her voice breaks to a whisper. "He's all I have left."

My bruised heart is taking a fucking beating today. Jesus. The sound of Emmy's desolation is killing me.

"He can't have gone far," I tell her. "I mean he has no money, right? And they've called the police?"

"Yes." Her soft sniffles are pathetic, and they make me feel helpless.

"Can you think of anywhere he might have wanted to go if he *had* money?"

"I—no. I don't think so. I mean he worked in the city, but I can't think where he'd go. And he doesn't have any money, so there's just . . . it's impossible."

"Where did he work?"

"He had a small investment firm near Wall Street. But I really don't think he'd go there."

"Look, I don't know much about how this stuff works, but my instinct tells me he might go somewhere that feels familiar."

There's quiet. "I'm scared, Trystan. God, why am I telling you this? I don't even know you. I'm sorry."

I squeeze my eyes closed. "It's going to be okay, Emmy. I'm sure he'll call, and if not, someone will find him and call the police, It's going to be okay."

"Okay." Her voice sounds tiny.

"Okay," I reply softly.

"Trystan?"

"Yeah?"

"You can rent my place. I can't come back tonight what with David missing. And I . . . if you still need to that is. But it would probably help me. Monetarily, I mean, if you did. Staying in New York is expensive—"

"Yes," I cut in. "I'll rent your place. Text me your bank details, and I'll deposit the money for two nights."

She's quiet again. "Th-Thank you," she says haltingly.

"Of course, Emmy. Let me know if I can do anything else, and I'll let you know if David calls."

"Wait! Are you allergic to cats?" she asks. "I have a cat. Armand's been feeding her. Is that okay? You don't hate cats, right?"

I frown. "Only if they sleep on my face," I say.

She giggles then.

I smile, but my brow furrows. "What's so funny?"

"No pussies on your face. Got it," she says, stunning me speechless.

Then she bursts out laughing which almost instantly devolves to crying again. "Oh shit, I'm a mess," she finally manages through her tears.

"Not gonna disagree," I counter, shaking my head but grinning at the same time.

"Thank you, Trystan," she says finally when she has herself under control.

"You're welcome, Emmy."

I press end, slip the phone into my pocket, and head back inside.

* * *

WE'RE an hour into the meeting with the accountants and going through all the profit centers. Every time the phone buzzes, I apologize and take it out of my pocket to check the number. Emmy sends her bank details, and I forward them to Dorothy asking her to make an instant transfer or go into a branch if she has to. I name a stupid amount, but I'd rather err on the side of too much than not enough.

The next time it buzzes it's Emmy, sending her address and telling me to call Armand for the key.

The next one after that she's asking if I've heard from David.

And the following one is a list of instructions including where to find clean sheets to change the bed and the Wi-Fi password.

"Are you with us?" Robert asks, frowning.

"I am," I say. "Apologies. I have a friend going through a crisis. Her elderly family member walked out of a nursing facility this morning. He may call me, so I'm trying to make sure I don't miss a message."

"Surely they had an anklet on him?"

I look at Robert blankly.

"Elderly residents, particularly those with a propensity to wander, have a digital bracelet or anklet that sounds an alarm if they near the exit. It's gross negligence on their part if he wasn't wearing it, or it wasn't working. Which facility is it?"

"Um, Rockaway Nursing in Far Rockaway outside of Manhattan."

"Oh. I don't know it. I thought it might be somewhere near here. We pretty much know of all the major competitors in the area."

I narrow my eyes on all the paperwork in front of me and the lists of assets. Most are student housing, apartments, a couple of emergency clinics, and a whole family of retirement and nursing home communities. Huh. I hadn't put two and two together, that Montgomery Homes & Facilities also owned nursing homes.

"What would it take to move someone into one of our facilities down here?" I ask.

Robert shrugs. "If they can pay, and there's a suite available, sure. It's not a problem. They'd need a medical evaluation to see what level of care they might require."

"Okay." I nod. I can at least let Emmy know she might consider moving David closer. I wonder why she hasn't already.

When she finds him.

I grimace.

"And also to check what kind of insurance they have," Robert goes on. "Now if it's someone dependent on Medicaid or something, it's harder. We have to assign a certain number of Medicaid beds to be compliant and equal opportunity, and there's a waiting list a mile long. And frankly, my father would try to fudge those numbers a bit to make a larger profit, if you know what I mean."

The man next to me coughs and shifts, looking uncomfortable.

Robert doesn't notice or doesn't care. "And it might depend on whether they are receiving social security and how much that is."

"Fine, fine," I say. "Let's get back to what we were looking at.

Profit centers." Then I look at the accountants. Two of them, the balding man with glasses who looks uncomfortable and his colleague with dark hair who's been running his finger down sheets, his lips moving silently all meeting, but who's now looking up at me.

"Please make sure that any report you show me has the actual number of beds available, and there is never *any* creative accounting. Am I clear? I'll fire anyone who tries to pull that shit past me."

Robert makes a sound I can't decipher, but I don't get a chance to dwell on it because we dive right into the weeds of numbers. Pages and pages and pages.

By three in the afternoon, after a lunch of delivered sandwiches and pages and pages of more numbers, my eyes are crossing and another headache is brewing.

Suddenly, the phone is buzzing again with an incoming call. From a New York area code.

"Excuse me," I say to the room. "Hello," I answer. There's silence. Ambient noise but no speaking. Then the line goes dead.

David.

Shit.

Of course he hung up, he was expecting Emmy.

I stand, willing him to call back. What if he doesn't call back?

"Anyone know how to reverse look up a phone number?" I ask the room.

18

TRYSTAN

"*D*avid, don't hang up," I say quickly when the phone rings again.

"H-Hello?" It's a man's voice, crackled with age.

"David is that you?"

"Where's Emmy?"

"She's not here right now. David, where are you?"

"What do you mean she's not there? She said this was her mobile phone. That she had this with her all the time."

"I know, David, I just spoke with her and—"

"Who are you?"

"My name is Trystan, and I'm a friend of Emmy's. I—I'm helping her."

"Helping her with what?"

"Well, right now I'm helping her get in touch with you. She's worried because she doesn't know where you are."

"I need to talk to Emmy."

"I know, sir. She wants to talk to you too. Can you tell me where you are so she can come and meet you?"

There's quiet then the sound of sighing. "I—I'm not sure. Oh, this is so embarrassing. I—I thought I . . ." He's beginning to sound panicked.

Thinking quickly, I try to keep him distracted. "It's okay, David. Happens to all of us. Are you in a restaurant?"

"Yes," he says. "I know this place. Well, I thought I did. Miguel was the maître d'. Excuse me, young man," I barely hear the last part as he's covering the phone. Then I hear talking and David saying indignantly. "No, I'm not lost!"

"David," I try and get his attention. "David! Can you listen to me?"

There's more muted sounds and then the line goes silent. I look at the phone to see he hung up.

"Shit. Anyone find out where he called from?" I ask, even as I dial the number back.

"I think it's called the Paris Cafe?" the dark haired accountant stammers.

It rings. I know the place. It's in the Seaport near the financial district. That makes sense.

"Paris Cafe, can I help you?"

"Yes, that elderly man that was there, please don't let him leave."

"Sir?"

"The man. David. Can you keep him there? I'll cover his tab. Just feed him and keep him there."

"Sir, we're not open for dinner yet. And he was belligerent and rude to—"

"This is Trystan Montgomery, I will literally read you off my credit card number and you can charge me whatever you see fit for your trouble. But he is confused, and he's a missing person. His—" Damn it. What was Emmy to him? Niece? "His family are looking for him."

"He's left, sir."

"Christ! Well, get him back and offer the poor man a safe place to wait while we get him back to his family. I don't think you want the bad press if something happens to him, do you? This is the equivalent of a lost child right now. So get off the fucking phone and go and find him."

"Yes, sir!"

I hit end, my chest heaving. "Fucking incompetents."

I blow out a breath. I dare not tie up the line by calling, so I text Emmy.

DAVID CALLED, he's near the financial district. Paris Cafe. I don't add that he might not still be there. But then I realize they might not get him back. Shit. I go back and delete the text before sending and try again.

David is okay. He's in the financial district. Tracking him down now.

EMMY: *OMG. Did you talk to him? Is he okay? Where is he? How did he get there?*

HE'S FINE. More when I know. Oh, and what's his last name?

EMMY: *Same as me. Dubois.*

SOON AS I talk to him again, I can have a car there in under thirty minutes to pick him up and bring him back out to Far Rockaway. I'll let you know as soon as he's safely picked up.

IT's a promise I hope I can keep.

I BORROW Ravenel's phone to call Dorothy and get the number for my driver and explain the situation to him.

Then I dial back the bar. "This is Trystan Montgomery, did you manage to get David back?"

* * *

I LOOK up Armand's number in Emmy's phone as I massage the tension in the back of my neck. What a day.

Hi, it's Trystan. Not sure if you heard from Emmy, but I'm renting her place tonight and apparently I can get the key from you?

I PULL up the address Emmy sent me and when I map it, I realize I can walk there pretty easily. Charleston is still bustling in the early evening. Bars and restaurants are starting to fill. I find myself in the same cobblestone alley she sent me to the first morning to have breakfast at Armand's place. Makes sense then that he's taking care of her cat and has a key since he works such a short distance away. The café is closed up, I hope he knows I'm coming. I find the address pretty easily and stop by a gate in a wall. It's locked.

Looking through the bars down the narrow plant-lined pathway, I look ahead to the periwinkle blue front door. It's so Emmy, I think, even though I have no idea why I should assume that. As I look at it, it opens and Armand steps out.

"Ahh, Trystan! Emmy told me you are renting her little casa." He reaches back inside the house and the gate buzzes open.

"Armand." I greet him.

He nods, looking at me speculatively as I approach. "Interesting new development, no?"

I shrug. "I needed a place to stay."

He nods slowly. "Of course, of course." He stands aside and gestures me inside.

I have to duck slightly through the doorway as it's basically built for a hobbit. Inside, the space is rectangular with a small kitchen against the closest wall to me, an eating area in its mirrored spot to my left. The rest of the room is a cozy living area facing a fireplace. One side of the fireplace has shelves stuffed with books, the other is the beginning of a narrow staircase that disappears behind the chimney.

Luckily, I can actually stand up straight, though I probably shouldn't do any jumping jacks. It doesn't feel claustrophobic though. The wide windows on three sides showcase the lovely gardens surrounding the tiny house. I look outside the window. "Emmy do this?"

"Si. Fireplace has gas," Armand informs me and shows me how to turn it on. Though I can't imagine using it in this town. Does it ever get cold? I can't remember.

"Hot water takes a few minutes and bedroom is upstairs. Beer is in the fridge, Emmy told me to buy some. I must go. But I'll see you for breakfast?"

I'm looking around taking in my surroundings. It feels both familiar and strange to be in Emmy's home. It's tiny. But somehow it fits her. There are small, framed pictures on the walls, covering any white space that isn't filled with large colorful paintings. The dining table, if you can call it that, has a sewing machine on it, and rolls of fabric are leaning, stacked in the corner. Books are piled here and there, but it doesn't seem cluttered.

In fact, it's everything I imagine Emmy to be. It's the Emmy in my mind personified. It smells enticing, clean, but unfamiliar. There's a sense of a life well-lived and opportunities seized. It's vibrant, a bit edgy in parts, fun, yet comfortable. Unexpected but still . . . traditional.

"Where's the cat?" I ask

Armand makes a disgusted sound. "Who knows? But she eats her food and makes her shit, so I know she's here." He shrugs. "I'll be back to check on the cat tomorrow. Unless you want to?"

"No, not really."

"Okay. Well."

"Wait. You want to stay for a beer?" It's weird to ask. I mean he's a friend of Emmy's. But then, I don't really know Emmy.

"I wish I could, but I'm meeting someone, and he seems like a punctual type of guy. Maybe tomorrow?"

I nod, his revelation answering a question about his relationship with Emmy I wasn't sure I wanted to ask. "Maybe tomorrow. Thanks, Armand."

"Night, Trystan."

He closes the door behind him, and I breathe out a long sigh of relief.

I head up the stairs, stooping to get up there without hitting my head. The stairs open up into a large room built into the eaves of the roof line. Despite its use of space, it doesn't feel like an attic. It's light and bright. The floor is covered in sisal, and the bedding on the queen bed is white and fluffy. The main event, though, is an old antique claw-footed tub set under a long shed dormer window on one side of the room. I stare at it. Visions of that yellow bikini-clad Emmy with soapy, glistening skin and pink from heat and steam assault me, except now there are just bubbles where the bikini used to be.

Jesus. It was a really bad idea to think staying at Emmy's place wouldn't be fodder for many a spank bank fantasy in my future.

I drag my eyes away from the tub to a door into what I presume is the actual bathroom on the other side of the room. I drop my laptop bag off my shoulder down to my hand and lay it on the bench that's at the foot of the bed. I inhale the smell of sunlight, natural fibers, and a light floral scent that's all Emmy. I suddenly remember noticing the scent of Emmy at the airport when she sat next to me briefly.

The bathroom is small but clean. A sink, toilet, and shower decorated in white and off white.

The phone in my pocket buzzes.

EMMY: *You settled in? Armand says you found it okay. I'm sorry if it's messy, I normally declutter before I rent it out. And don't forget to put clean sheets on the bed.*

I TURN AROUND and stare at her bed again. My pulse is doing weird erratic things, and . . . I blink and shake my head. I should go back downstairs.

SETTLED IN FINE. Thanks. How's David?

EMMY: *Can I call you?*

19

EMMY

$\mathcal{W}$hen a long and sleek black town car pulled up outside Rockaway Nursing and Rehab, I wanted to cry with relief. D'Andre was waiting with me as well as an officer from the local 101 Precinct. The driver hopped out of the car as I jogged toward it.

"Are you Emmaline Dubois?" he asked as he headed around to open the back door.

"I am."

"Mr. Montgomery wanted me to make sure you were here before I let Mr. Dubois out of the vehicle."

D'Andre was by my side as the door opened and David blinked up at us.

"David," I greeted him, my voice wobbling with emotion.

"Had a little outing, did we?" D'Andre said and took David's other arm as he used us to leverage himself out of the car.

"I'll be right back," I told the driver. "We'll just get him inside."

David blustered. "I can walk by myself."

"That's for dayam sho," D'Andre muttered. "You walked your-self right outta this joint."

We accompanied him through the front doors. The alarm

started blaring from his anklet, so we coaxed him farther in and away from the sensors. The officer went and conferred with Penny, presumably to be assured they could cancel the Silver Alert they were about to issue.

I stepped in front of David. "D'Andre's going to take you up to your room, okay? Then I'll be right up to see you."

"Okay." David smiled, all relaxed, like we all just came back from a fun afternoon at the freaking zoo.

I smiled tightly, hugged him, and headed out to the driver, scratching around in my purse for some cash. How much were you supposed to tip a guy who transported the most precious person in your life to safety?

"If you're looking to tip me," the driver said, "Mr. Montgomery already took care of it."

"Oh." I stopped. "Are you sure?"

"Yes ma'am. I'm instructed not to take it anyway. Your grandfather, is he? He's an interesting guy. I enjoyed the ride. I'm Bobby, by the way."

"Thank you, Bobby," I told him, not bothering to correct him about my relationship with David. I put out my hand, and he shook it.

"No problem," he responded with a grin. Then he gave me a card. "In case you ever need wheels. I'll be in the area for the next hour, then I'm headed into the city anyway. If you needed a ride." He headed back to the driver's side, opened the door, got in, and pulled the car away from the curb.

I was left standing there wondering how immense my owed favor was to Trystan Montgomery. I didn't like feeling indebted, but I was so grateful that if the guy was in front of me at that moment I'd hug him for an eternity and have a hard time letting go. Mostly due to aforementioned gratefulness, but also because I remembered him smelling really, really, good.

And now to add it, he was a freaking hero in my eyes.

* * *

As soon as I'd seen David settled, I'd gone back outside to sit on the steps outside and breathe calmly or the first time in what felt like forever. It had been less than ten hours since I'd first learned David was missing, but it felt longer. I logged in to my bank on Trystan's web browser to make sure I had funds for a hotel.

The closest option would be to stay in one of the hotels near JFK. But damn if I didn't want to stay in the city tonight. It had been years since I'd spent any time in Manhattan. After the day I'd had, I would walk toward Times Square, buy a single scalped ticket to Springsteen on Broadway, and lose myself for three hours before collapsing into a hotel bed.

"Son-of-a-bitch," I hissed out loud, straightening up as I saw my bank balance. Never mind a hotel and a show, I could take a week-long Caribbean vacation for the amount of money deposited in my account.

As soon as the shock passed, I felt the rise of immense irritation. God. I already felt in debt to him, and now it was worse. He was throwing his money around. Either he didn't value money, or I was his charity case. Both scenarios made my stomach turn.

A text popped across the top of the screen. Armand letting me know Trystan had arrived to rent my place, and I had to remind myself that while he may be overpaying, he was in fact *renting* my place. That part wasn't charity. Rescuing David, maybe, but I could explain away the rest of it.

"You okay out here?" D'Andre's voice made me jump. "Oops sorry, didn't mean to freak you out."

I smiled up at him, and he joined me on the top step. "Sorry. In my own world. What a day."

"What a day, indeed. So how'd you get the limo hookup?"

"Well." I blew out a breath and held up the cell phone. "That was cell phone dude's doing. Life works in mysterious ways. The most annoyingly inconvenient thing that's ever happened to me led me to "not meeting" this . . . guy, who ended up being the one to pretty much save David."

D'Andre's eyes were wide, his eyebrow cocked is disbelief.

"Believe it," I said. "David called Trystan Montgomery on my number, and Trystan somehow convinced David to stay where he was, have something to eat, and then get in a limousine to come here." I shook my head. "I honestly don't know how I'll ever repay that debt."

"Maybe it's not meant to be paid," D'Andre said thoughtfully. "I mean sometimes things have a value beyond, you know? Maybe you just pay it forward."

"I guess."

"Sounds like a good guy though. Maybe you two should actually plan to meet for real."

"Ha." I let out a nervous cackle. "One minute he's soooo . . . everything. And the next he acts like a prick. I don't know who I'm going to get. And I can already tell from all these many, many dating apps," I brandish the phone out in front of me, "that this one runs a mile from intimacy and commitment. Two things I value above everything else."

"Everything else?" D'Andre teased.

"You laugh," I said seriously, "but I'd settle for bad sex as long as I had intimacy and commitment."

"Girl, you must have dated some assholes."

"Probably," I agreed. "But mostly no one whose character's been worth settling everything else for."

"Now, I don't call myself a dating expert," D'Andre said, his voice taking on a higher pitched preaching tone. "But I'd say what that dude did for you today showed his character."

I squinted. "Don't," I complained. "I'm already crushing hard on the dude. Please don't give me more reasons to. I need less reasons."

"Well, he keeps doing shit like today? Girl, you in trouble."

The setting sun chose that moment to streak rays ▪etween the buildings. I raised my hand to shield my eyes.

"Are you clocking out?" I asked, noticing he was out of his scrubs and wearing designer-looking jeans and a lightweight jacket.

"Sure am. I'm headed into the city to see Logic." He shook his head side to side, his bright smile contagious.

"Your idol."

"You know it. I got a friend with a hookup at the club he's playing. I may get to meet him after, you know?"

My eyes widened. "That's awesome."

"You wanna go? I could get you in. I'm going with a crew. It's real. You'll love it."

I laughed. "I was thinking earlier I'd love to go to a show, but I was thinking more along the lines of Bruce Springsteen. You probably don't even know who that is."

D'Andre reeled away from me, his hand on his heart. "Baby girl. Stop it. You hurtin' me. I grew up in Jersey, yo. And that guy? Those are some lyrics right there. He may not be street, but he's talking the same shit."

"Never thought of it that way. David was a fan. *Is* a fan. I don't know. Anyway, I grew up knowing all his music."

"Well it's not Springsteen, but you'll have a good time. You in?"

"D'Andre, be serious." I laugh and look down at myself, straightening my jean clad legs out in front of me. "I'm not dressed for a club."

"Look. I ain't hittin' on you. But you hot. Just, like, put some makeup on or some shit."

"Stop it. Tell me about your YouTube thing."

He leaned back on his elbows. "Been rappin' and posting my lyrics. On Instagram too. I have followers, not many, but it's been cool. I just like need a big break, you know? Like if I get mentioned or picked up by another YouTuber it'd go big you know?"

I thought about my little phone hacker friend and his YouTube channel, though I didn't know much about what he actually did. While I thought about it, I dug out his card. "This guy." I showed it to D'Andre. "Know of this guy?"

"Xanderr? Shit, yeah. He's a gamer but, like, he's pretty famous."

"Is he?" He had seemed pretty cocky, but then I wasn't around a lot of the current crop of teenagers. And not famous enough not to be stuffed into economy class next to me. Then again, that was probably his parents doing.

"Wait, you know him?" D'Andre asked.

"Not really. Well. A bit, I suppose."

"Whoa." D'Andre leaned back and looked at me with increasing respect. "Would you send him a link to my channel?" he asked. "Or . . . man, he lives in New York, right? Does he want to come out tonight and see Logic? I can hook him up too. Then I could meet him."

"He's young. Like sixteen or something. He probably can't get into a club."

"For real? Damn."

"I can ask."

"Call him. Call him, right now." D'Andre elbowed me. "Pleeeease?"

"Fine." I rolled my eyes with a smile and dialed the number on the card.

It rang twice.

"Al?" I asked. "Alex?"

"Who is this?"

"It's, uh, Emmy." Silence. "From the plane. With the phone . . . situation." I winced.

There was a muffled sound, then an expletive, then a deep breath.

"Emmy, girl. Sweet Emmy. How are you?" His voice came out calm and deep like he was pretending to be super relaxed.

I laughed silently. "Great, actually. How are you?"

"Can't complain. Back with the old man in the Big Apple. You get your phone sitch sorted?"

"Nope. Still have that guy's phone."

"Dude. You must have sweet talked him."

"Ha. Well, anyway, the reason I called is I have this friend, D'Andre. He's a musician. A rapper."

D'Andre nodded approvingly.

"A poet," I added, and D'Andre put a hand to his chest in thanks.

"Yeah?"

"He has a YouTube channel. The only other person I know who has one is you, and I don't know how these things work, but I thought maybe you all should connect. You might like his stuff or . . . something."

"Give it to me, I'll look it up right now."

"Oh, uh sure." I gestured wildly at D'Andre. *What's the link?* I mouthed to him. He pulled it up on his phone, his face hopeful, and I read it out to Alex.

"Cool. Cool," Alex said. "Just gonna give it a look and listen, back in a mo."

There was silence on the phone, and I imagined him slipping on those massive earphones of his.

"He's listening right now," I told D'Andre, who jumped to his feet and paced back and forth in front of me.

"Calm down," I told him.

"I need a paper bag," he said.

After a few minutes, Alex was back. "I need to get hold of this guy."

"Oh, uh." I looked at D'Andre who had both hands covering his mouth. "He's standing right next to me. I'll give you his number."

"Extra. Put him on, will you?"

I held out the phone to D'Andre who looked at it aghast.

"He wants to talk to me?" he whispered.

I nodded.

He took the phone and cleared his throat. "This is D'Andre. Yeah, sure." He got his own phone out of his pocket and typed something into it. Then walked back and handed me Trystan's phone.

"Is this happening?" D'Andre asked me, looking nervous.

I smiled and shrugged.

The phone in his hand buzzed, and he answered, walking a few feet away along the sidewalk. It must have been good news based on the size of the grin he was wearing.

Remembering Armand's text, I decided to get hold of Trystan. Dude had some explaining to do about the price of a two-night rental in Charleston. I wanted to call him but didn't want to risk getting barked at if he was in the middle of something. Instead, I texted him to make sure he'd settled in and found clean sheets.

A response came back almost immediately.

SUIT MONKEY: *Settled in fine. Thanks. How's David?*

CAN I CALL YOU? I typed. I refused to thank him via text, it was too big.

THE PHONE RANG immediately with an incoming call. *Suit Monkey.* My heart jumped to my throat as I hit "Accept."

20

EMMY

"*T*rystan," I greeted him as soon as it connected.

"Yeah."

There was a beat of silence and I rushed to fill it. "I wanted to thank you. I never got a chance to do that after you found David. So, thank you. Officially. Thank you."

"How is he?"

"Fine. Thanks to you. I—I don't know how to thank you," I rambled.

"It was nothing. He called me, it was easy at that point."

I let out a breath. "Thank you. I mean it."

"You've now thanked me four times. Stop it." But suddenly I heard him smiling through his words, and inside I relaxed.

"How was he?" he asked.

"He was fine. Better than fine. Apparently you bought him dinner, discussed business and told him there was a car and driver waiting on him?"

"All that was true." He laughed. "He's a smart man. I enjoyed chatting with him. Anyway, did you ever find out what happened?"

"Not really," I confessed. "I mean he had money for a cab, and honestly, I think he took it from my purse because I realized this afternoon I was missing sixty dollars in twenties. I just don't know when he might have done it. And I can't imagine him stealing from me."

"And his anklet? He didn't set off the alarm?"

"We don't know what happened there. He was wearing the anklet, and Penny Smith, the administrator, swears the alarm sensor is working. But maybe the power was out or something. It's a mystery."

"You could sue, you know?"

It wasn't like in my worry-crazed hours earlier today those thoughts hadn't crossed my mind, but now . . . "You know, apart from this incident, they've been pretty great. And his one main caretaker, D'Andre, well he's pretty awesome. I fear he could lose his job if they had to scapegoat someone. I don't think it was negligence. I wouldn't be able to live with myself if they got the blame for something they couldn't control. Besides, I'm not sure it would be worth it anyway since he's okay. Accidents happen."

"Well, he's safe. That's what counts."

"Yes."

"Have you thought about moving him somewhere closer to you?"

I pursed my lips. "Yep. Of course. Unfortunately, it's a little complicated, but somehow I'll have to figure that out."

There was a long pause, and then I thought of him in my house while I sat on a dirty set of steps on a dirty sidewalk. "Are you at my house?" I asked.

"I'm actually in your bedroom," he answered, and my stomach experienced a weird dropping sensation.

"I'm sorry you have to get the bed ready." I talked over my reaction, trying to ignore it. "I should make it a rule to never go away without changing the sheets and tidying my stuff away first. Just in case."

"In case you have a stranger to stay," Trystan said. His voice had an odd timbre to it.

"You don't . . . you don't feel like a stranger anymore," I said honestly, and my stomach hollowed out as I made myself vulnerable. "You feel like a friend. After today, you feel like a friend."

"Yeah. A friend." Trystan cleared his throat. "So, now you have David back, do I need to sleep on the couch? Are you coming home?"

Be in the same house with him? My insides flipped over. I'd be far too nervous to even breathe with him in my space. Trystan Montgomery was . . . a presence.

"No," I answered him. "I cancelled my flight. I guess I'll stay. Besides I want to see David tomorrow and see if he has any recollection of what he did today. It was too hard to talk to him when we got him back this evening because he was tired. He gets more confused when he's tired."

"So, is he, like, your uncle? Grandfather? I've been trying to figure out the family relationship."

"It's a head-scratcher for sure." I smiled. "He's my adoptive uncle. Random, right? I was in foster care until I was legally adopted by my foster parents. Unfortunately, he's the only family I now have left. I guess that's why he's so important to me. I just . . . don't want to be without family again . . . alone again. What a selfish way to put it." I laughed deprecatingly at myself. "That's not the only reason, obviously. It's also because I adore him. He's a pretty cool guy. I miss the man he used to be."

There was a long silence.

"Trystan?" I asked. "You there?"

"I'm here," he said, his voice thick. "And to think I spent the last fourteen years avoiding the family I have."

My throat closed as I tried to swallow. I wanted to ask why. How could anyone not want a family? Or rather, what could a family have done to make someone not want to be with them? And I thought of the funeral and wondered if Trystan had regrets, causing something uncomfortable to twist in my chest. "I'm sorry, Trystan," I managed, finally. Because what else could I say?

"Don't be." I heard him take a breath and let it out long and slow. "Before I forget, your work number called several times. Did you tell them you're not coming back?"

"Ugh, I'll call Steven, my boss. He's just throwing his weight around. There's big pitch tomorrow I was supposed to be at."

"If you're as good as you say you are, he's probably panicked you won't be there to win the business for him."

"Ha. You're probably right. Well, maybe he'll learn to appreciate me more."

"So where are you going to stay tonight?" He changed the subject. "Can you go back to your rental?"

"I think I'll have to find a hotel. But on that note, you paid me way too freaking much to rent my place."

"I asked around what I'd be paying during Spoleto to rent a one bedroom apartment in downtown, and sorry Emmy, but that's the going rate. Apparently you should have been charging more."

"Trystan, something tells me you hear what you want to."

He laughed, a low rumble of thunder. "Yeah. That's probably true. I usually get what I want too."

"I don't doubt it."

"What I want right now is for you to call me back from a nice, safe, cushy hotel in a nice neighborhood so I can relax."

"You worried about me?"

"Emmy. You have no idea. And frankly given that I didn't even know you three days ago, I apparently have no idea either. It just is. So take my advice, okay?"

"I was going to stay near the airp—"

"No."

"Hey!"

"Bloody hell. Seriously, Emmy. Take my driver, he'll take you to a hotel I'm part-owner of in the city. You can get a room there, relax, order room service, and give us both a freaking break, yeah?"

I was stunned silent.

"And tomorrow," he went on, "after you're well-rested, he can take you back out to see David. Then you can decide if you're coming home or not."

"You're quite . . . overbearing, did you know that?"

"I'm going to pretend you just said, 'okay, Trystan.' My driver will be back there in ten minutes to pick you up."

"What? No. Don't be ridiculous."

"Emmy, I'm not bloody fucking around."

"I'm not either," I said sternly.

"If you don't take me up on my suggestion I'm going to sleep on your sheets and look through your bedside table drawers."

My breath left me in a sharp exhalation, my stomach bottoming out and my face growing hot and prickly.

"What will I find, Emmy?"

"Okay, I'll do it. I'll go," I squeaked.

"Interesting."

"No. Not interesting. Goodbye, Trystan." I pressed end. Oh my God, I thought I might throw up. He'd find my vibrator and I'd die.

Fully die.

At the very least, I'd never look at another human in the eye again.

Maybe not even my cat.

Never ever.

And after my reaction, there was no way he wouldn't go through my drawers now. I was such an idiot.

"Woohoo!" D'Andre came jogging up the sidewalk and fist pumped the air.

Thankful for the distraction, I stood and dusted my butt off, wobbling slightly with lightheadedness. "I take it that went well?" I greeted him, hoping he didn't notice my flushed state.

"You just paid it forward, girl!" D'Andre was practically giving off sparks of joy.

"I did?"

"You did."

The black, shiny, town car chose that moment to purr silently back up to the curb, reminding me I wasn't done paying anything forward just yet. "You need a ride into the city?" I asked D'Andre, pointing at the car and pursing my lips.

"For real?"

"For real," I confirmed and went back inside to get my suitcase. I just had to send a quick text.

SERIOUSLY. Don't you dare.

SUIT MONKEY: *Challenge accepted.*

I GUESS *I'll head to the airport hotel then.*

SUIT MONKEY: *Fine. Your secrets are safe. For now.*

"UGH," I said out loud in exasperation and headed toward the black car.

* * *

THE CAR RIDE into the city was full of chatter from an excited D'Andre. It was infectious, and it was a good thing because if he hadn't been there I would have been grilling the driver all about Trystan.

Apparently, Xanderr was able to come out and meet D'Andre at the club he was going to.

"Are you sure you can't come?" D'Andre asked, his palms together in entreaty.

I leveled a serious look at him. "I'm exhausted."

"Just for a couple drinks. You don't even have to go to the concert. Let me buy you a couple of drinks to say thank you."

I smiled. "Maybe. Let me get settled first, okay? Then you can text me and let me know where you are."

"Where are you staying anyway?" D'Andre asked me.

Bobby looked in the rearview mirror. "Mr. Montgomery asked me to take Miss Dubois to the Chelsea Grand."

"Oooo, *Mr. Montgomery*," D'Andre sang, echoing Bobby. "*The Chelsea Grand*. Hey, that's a pretty swank hotel."

"Stop it."

D'Andre's eyes narrowed. "Is he paying for you to stay there?"

"No!" God. No.

He nodded his chin once. "Good. 'Coz there only be one reason to do all this for a lady, and that's coz you buyin' something. Know what I mean?"

I narrowed my eyes right back at him. "Buying what, exactly?"

His hands came up. "I'm jus' sayin'. And before you get all offended, I ain't saying you sellin'."

"You better not be." I pointed my finger in his face.

As if summoned, my phone buzzed.

SUIT MONKEY: *Who's your friend?*

I SAT upright and glanced around.

"What?" asked D'Andre.

SUIT MONKEY: *Bobby told me we're giving someone a ride*

SINKING BACK in relief I typed back. *This is creepy behavior, Trystan. Don't make me regret going along with your suggestion.*

"NOTHING," I informed D'Andre.

"If I may?" Bobby piped up from the front seat. "Mr. Montgomery's a good man. He looks out for people."

"That's good to know," I answered, giving D'Andre the stink eye.

* * *

WE PULLED up outside a hotel with a carpeted sidewalk.

"There's a red carpet on the sidewalk," I said stupidly as a doorman opened my door, and Bobby jumped out of the driver's seat.

"That's so them rich people don't dirty up their kicks, yo."

"Welcome to the Chelsea Grand," the doorman said. "Checking in?"

"Um, yes."

Bobby joined us with my bag, and the doorman took it.

"Guest of Mr. Montgomery's," Bobby said to the doorman, whom he clearly knew.

"Thanks, Bobby." I put out my hand to shake his. "What do I owe you?"

"You're welcome, Miss Dubois." He tipped his hat. "I'm on call for Mr. Montgomery. You have my card, and my number is also in his phone. Just text or call, no matter the hour. Especially if you decide to go out for cocktails. Mr. Montgomery asked me to be sure you were safe."

"Thank you," I said, taking my wallet out. "But—"

"Like I said. I'm on call for Mr. M." He smiled, tipped his hat toward D'Andre too, and trotted back around to the driver's side of the car.

"Baby girl done got her a sugar daddy," D'Andre said with a chuckle.

"Shut it," I said with an eye roll. "All right. I'm going in. You say hi to Xanderr. Don't get him in trouble, he's underage."

"Yes, Mom."

I grinned.

D'Andre put out his fist. I tapped it with mine.

"Thank you, Emmy. I mean it."

"You take care of yourself D'Andre. Good luck tonight. Don't forget about us little people when you see your name up in lights."

"Never." He grinned then swung away, loping off down the sidewalk.

I took a deep breath and went inside the hotel and farther and farther into Trystan Montgomery's life.

21

EMMY

*T*he staff at the hotel were solicitous and practically falling over themselves to make me feel comfortable. All it did was make me feel a bit like a specimen. They were clearly curious.

I was shown to a room that was really more of a suite. It had a sitting area and desk as well as a large king-sized bed. The building wasn't as tall as some others in the area, so there was no skyline view. But at least it was overlooking the street below and not the back of another building that so many of them did in New York. The room was modern but sumptuous—clean lines and comfortable furnishings. The bathroom had a large glassed-in shower that was a rare size for this city, and hanging behind the door was a large white fluffy robe.

I sighed with happiness. I'd order room service just as Trystan had suggested, take a long hot shower, wrap myself up in the robe, and maybe watch a chick flick. For one night, I wouldn't let myself worry about anything. What had Trystan said? Give us both a break? It was true I needed a mental break from worrying about money and David.

On that note, I thought I better get the call to my boss over with. I got his voicemail of course.

"Steven, sorry to call the office number so late. I don't have my phone, so I don't have your cell phone number with me. My uncle went missing today. It was awful. He's safe now, thank goodness. But of course I had to cancel my flight, and I have to make sure I deal with any fallout from that tomorrow. I won't be back for the pitch, but everything is ready for it, the deck is finished and saved on the server. Sorry, again. Thanks, Bye."

Grimacing, I hoped that would do. Steven was a stickler for people sticking to time off organized months in advance. I couldn't prove it, but I was convinced Trina the receptionist lost her job last year because her son had an emergency dental appointment after an accident at school and had to take time off without notice. Steven was an asshole, and for once he would just have to cope without me.

Hunting around the desk area, I found a simple grill-style menu from the hotel, but apparently one could order from any restaurants in the area too. I settled on a piece of fresh fish and vegetables from downstairs because it didn't look like it involved any gluten. Picking up the phone, I was about to dial zero when a voice spoke. "Good evening, Miss Dubois, may I get something for you?"

"Uh, hi." I looked at the phone, then put it back to my ear. "Um, may I order some dinner?"

"What can I get you this evening?"

"I was thinking of the fish."

"This evening we have two choices; an Adirondack Mountain Trout or an Alaskan Halibut. Both outstanding choices."

"The trout please. And is it prepared gluten-free?"

"It can be. I'll let chef know. Any other allergies?"

"Er, no."

"Very good. And Mr. Montgomery instructed that you would

be having wine with dinner. Since you've ordered the fish, may I suggest our Sancerre?"

He did, did he?

"Um," I paused, quite taken aback by the whole affair. Trystan was certainly making sure I blew through all the money he'd sent me.

"If you don't like Sancerre, I can sugg—"

"No, no. Sancerre is fine."

"Very good, and what time would you like to eat?"

I looked at my watch, knowing I wanted to shower and wash my hair. But I was also starving. "Maybe in about forty minutes?" I could dry my hair later.

"Very well. Good evening, Miss Dubois."

"Thank you, bye." I set the phone back on its cradle and stared at it for a few minutes. Interesting set up Trystan had here.

* * *

I TOOK my time in the shower, letting the delicious stream of hot water beat down my neck and back, pummeling away the stress of the day. The steam swirled with the scent of lavender and bergamot. At least, that's what the labels on the full-sized bottles of shampoo and conditioner said. I was pink with heat by the time I emerged. I dried off, put on a tank and sleep shorts, and slipped into the large fluffy robe. I combed the tangles out of my hair and then wrapped it in an extra towel to squeeze some excess water out and keep it from dripping down my back while I ate my dinner.

Just in time. There was a knock at the door, a waiter brought in and set up my dinner on the desk. "May I get you anything else?" he asked as he backed toward the door.

"I'm fine. Thank you."

"Very well. Good evening." The door clicked closed behind him.

Picking up Trystan's phone as I sat down to eat, I saw he'd texted me.

SUIT MONKEY: *Why does someone who doesn't eat gluten have a pizza menu on her refrigerator?*

WHILE I CONTEMPLATED how to respond, I took a bite of trout and moaned. Wow, it was delicious. So was the sautéed spinach with artichoke hearts. Picking up the glass of wine the waiter had poured, I took a small sip.

Within minutes I had cleaned my plate and poured myself another glass of wine. I picked up the tray and plate and set it outside in the hall, then I picked up my glass of wine and fairly crawled into the bed. I felt decadent and relaxed.

SOMEONE WHO HAS friends who aren't gluten-free?

SUIT MONKEY: *Fair point. It's good pizza.*

OF COURSE. I'm guessing you didn't go out.

SUIT MONKEY: *Too tired to contemplate going out and eating alone.*

EATING ALONE. I took a sip of wine, feeling its warmth spread through me. Relaxing me. Trystan's family situation intrigued me. It must have been some few days for him if he hadn't seen his family in fourteen years and then showed up to the funeral and apparently the reading of the will. It was like a novel.

THERE MUST BE *someone in your family who would put up with you for one dinner? I typed and then deleted and started again. Why alone? Aren't you mending fences after fourteen years? Ugh. No. Not that either.*

SUIT MONKEY: *What are you too nervous to ask me? I keep seeing dots appear then go away.*

Suit Monkey: *And no I didn't look in your bedside table, in case that's what you were wondering.*

I LAUGHED. *No, that wasn't it.*

SUIT MONKEY: *Well?*

YOU SAID *you were eating alone, and that you haven't seen your family in fourteen years. I have questions. I'm curious. I don't know what or how to ask, and I know you probably don't want to talk about them.*

I STARED at the phone wondering if I'd stepped over a line.

I BET you're sorry you pushed it, huh?

STILL NO ANSWER.

GRRR. Texting sucked because you never knew if you'd said the wrong thing or it'd been taken the wrong way. But calling him now felt weird. We'd already spoken a few times today. For two people who didn't really know each other, that seemed excessive. So was asking him about his family, actually. It felt normal at the time, but if I had to describe what was going on to someone, I wasn't sure I'd be able to.

Just then he texted back.

SUIT MONKEY: *I'm back. Bathroom break. Been drinking all that local craft beer Armand left in the fridge if you know what I mean. And your damned phone needed charging. Again.*

SUIT MONKEY: *To answer your question: It's complicated. So did you eat dinner?*

I DID. And I'm currently drinking your prescribed wine. Didn't I mention earlier how overbearing you could be?

SUIT MONKEY: *But you like it. The wine, I mean ;)*

IF I DON'T SLOW down I may drink the whole bottle. The Sancerre. It's good.

SUIT MONKEY: *Look at us, we're having a drink together. Cheers.*

CHEERS! This hotel is lovely.

SUIT MONKEY: *It is. Glad you're enjoying. By the way, I think you were lying about having a cat.*

I CHUCKLE OUT LOUD. *Nope. He just doesn't like most people. Especially men.*

HOPPING OUT OF BED, I poured another glass of wine and grabbed the TV remote, and then climbed under the comforter. I really should have dried my hair, but it was so cozy, and I was so relaxed. The phone was quiet for a while then, and while I tried to concentrate on a Lifetime movie I came across that looked interesting, I couldn't seem to stop glancing at the phone. Eventually I gave in and texted him again.

I HOPE you don't mind that I had to turn off all the notifications for your dating apps. They were getting a bit much.

AND I GUESS it was the wine that made me do it, but I kept going to see if I could get a response from him.

ALSO BECAUSE I actually started to find myself really liking this one girl. She wanted to get together tonight. It would have been a bit awkward when I showed up instead of you.

THE RESPONSE CAME IMMEDIATELY.

SUIT MONKEY: *I would have paid good money to witness that meet up.*

UGH. Men, I typed, but I was grinning madly. It felt like I had a bubble in my chest that could explode at any moment. *Why do men get off on thinking about girls hooking up?*

SUIT MONKEY: *We're simple creatures. Visual creatures. And I'm sure women know how to make other women feel good. Since they have the same parts to practice on :)*

SO IT'S women's pleasure that turns you on? I bite my lip as I hit send.

SUIT MONKEY: *Never thought of it quite that way, but . . . yes. I guess so. Among other things.*

MY OWN GIRLY parts were buzzing with pleasure. What was I doing? I didn't know but thought maybe I should stop.

SUIT MONKEY: *Where do you keep your meds, I need an aspirin or something. I have a tension headache brewing.*

MY BUBBLE of I-don't-know-what-this-is deflated somewhat as I was brought to reality.

IN MY BATHROOM CABINET?

SUIT MONKEY: *I looked.*

OH, so he'd seen all my personal items, including my birth control pills. Why that bothered me but flirting with him and asking what turned him on didn't, was anyone's guess. I was a mess of confusing feelings.

TRY THE PANTRY CUPBOARDS?

THE PHONE RANG in my hand. I took a deep breath and swallowed. "Hello?"

"Sorry, it's easier than typing. Which pantry cupboards? I looked, but I'm not sure I know which you mean?"

"There's a pullout pantry, and there's a basket in one of the shelf drawers that has painkillers and stuff in there."

"Shelf drawers?" he repeated. "Not sure what you mean by that." I heard shuffling around and the opening and closing of doors.

"No, it's a pullout one. Regular cupboard door to the left."

"Hang on," he said.

The phone in my hand started doing a high-pitched ring. A video call.

Oh my shit.

I put my wine down and sat straight up. God, I was make-upless, and my hair was up in a towel. Argh! I had to answer otherwise it would seem like I was avoiding it. With a wince, I accepted.

There was a beep and then Trystan's face and bare shoulders appeared.

"Emmy? Hey."

Holy mother of all Godlike creatures.

The screen focused, and he was brought into sharp relief and high-definition glory.

I stared at him wide-eyed and speechless. Damn, but he was gorgeous. Even with that crinkled, furrowed brow and brown hair shiny and disheveled like he'd stepped out of the shower and had just towel-dried it. He'd been naked in my shower. In my bedroom. Thoughts and visions torpedoed through my brain a mile a minute.

"Emmy? You're frozen. Can you hear me? Shit." He moved, his arm dropping down and . . . I got a drive-by view of his torso.

Suit Monkey wasn't wearing a suit.

A squeak left me—a gasp that had exploded from the pressure, and I realized I hadn't been breathing. I spurred into action, slamming the phone against my robe to muffle the sounds of me letting the air out of my lungs and trying to normalize my breathing. I pulled the towel off my head, and my damp hair flopped down. I raked fingers through it, over it, smoothing, and tucked it behind an ear.

I counted to three then brought the phone up. "Hi," I managed, my voice sounding stupidly breathless to my own ears.

Trystan was staring straight at the phone, one eyebrow quirked waiting for me. As we locked eyes though, something shifted in his expression. His eyebrow dropped, and we really looked at each other for a beat. His eyes looked dark gray, his jaw strong and shadowed. And his lips . . . I didn't think I ever noticed how perfectly formed they were.

"Hi back," he said softly after a moment, and I saw his Adam's apple move heavily. Could he tell on a small screen I was staring at his mouth? Holy shit, but he was absolutely stunning. My memory and his scarce phone photos did not do him justice.

At.

All.

"You're shirtless," I said stupidly.

His perfect lips quirked. "And you're in a robe."

"Did you just shower?" I asked.

"Did you?" he countered.

Fuck. What was going on? This was some crazy foreplay right here. I was so turned on. I squeezed my legs together.

He stared at me.

"So, painkillers?" I asked when I could no longer bear the tension.

"Ahem. Yeah." His gorgeous face disappeared and was replaced by the cabinets in my kitchen.

"Walk forward to the cabinets on the left," I started, then took a break to bite my own knuckle. "The end one has pullout drawers." I watched him open the door. "Okay see the third drawer?"

"Yeah." He slid it out.

"At the back is a basket."

He pulled the drawer out farther until the basket was in view. Sitting right next to the bottle of generic brand painkillers was a box of condoms I'd forgotten about.

Nausea swirled through me. How many times could I feel mortified in only a few days? Something about Trystan made me feel like I was operating on some flayed open level of vulnerability that made everything feel embarrassing.

Of course I had to watch as his hand went for the condoms instead of the painkillers.

"Well, well. Good to always be prepared. But why are they in your kitchen, Emmy?"

The camera angle swung around so I could see Trystan's amused face and cheeky eyebrow.

I covered my eyes.

"Don't you think they should be in your bedside drawer? With your *other* secrets?"

I took a deep breath, refusing to cower under his teasing. "Do people only have sex in bedrooms, Trystan?" I asked haughtily.

His eyes flickered and he pursed his lips. His gorgeous lips. He held up the box to inspect it. "Well, well, well. You haven't been having sex in here that's for sure. These are unopened, and . . ." He narrowed his eyes as if really examining the box. "Oh, Emmy, these raincoats are expired."

I slapped my hand over my eyes again. "Just get your painkillers and stop embarrassing me," I whined.

He laughed, slow and smooth, making my skin prickle. "Okay. Back in the cupboard they go. Just don't forget you need to replace them."

"If you don't need anything else," I started.

"Wait. Don't hang up."

I slowly took my hand away from my eyes.

"Can we?" His eyes flicked away and then back to mine. "Can we just talk?" He put the pills in his mouth then held up his beer before taking a swig. I got a nice long look at his beautiful neck and watched it move as he swallowed down the pills.

My mouth felt dry. I took a long gulp of wine.

22

TRYSTAN

I let out a refreshed *ahhh* sound and hold up my beer to the small screen that shows Emmy's face staring back at me. She takes a large sip of wine.

"We'll have that drink," I tell her, hoping she'll stay online with me.

I can tell she's nervous. I shouldn't have teased her about the condoms. I almost feel like if I push her too hard she'll scurry away. I prefer it when she's feisty and teasing me back, turning me on.

She bites her lips together, then lets them pop free. "I guess so." She shrugs, affecting a nonchalance that I'm not sure I buy. "And you really shouldn't do that," she says.

My mind grasps around. "Do what?"

"Wash down painkillers with alcohol. Your liver doesn't like it."

"Probably not," I concede.

"There's one condition though," she says and smooths her fingers through her damp hair, "to us chatting on video." Where her hair was dark from water before, it's now starting to lighten and curl. I wonder what it feels like. Her skin is pale and flawless. Stunning. She should have this as her dating profile.

"What's the condition?" I ask warily.

"You tell me about your family."

Oh.

I'm halfway to bringing the beer bottle to my mouth, and I stop. Having an evening of flirting and conversation is one thing. Discussing my family? Not so much.

"I told you about David. About my family. It's only fair," she says.

"I've already told you about how they kicked my mom out. I'd say we're even."

"The math doesn't add up," she says. "You said you've been avoiding them for fourteen years. Correct me if I'm wrong but you're a little older than fourteen. Thirty-one if I'm not mistaken."

I walk across the room, prop the phone up on the coffee table against a stack of books, and sit down across from it. I pulled on jeans after my shower; I may not have fully buttoned them up. I let my legs splay slightly and lean against her sofa back, relaxed as can be.

She's frozen with her wine glass in front of her mouth as her eyes drink me in.

They roam down my bare chest as I'd wanted them to. I spend a lot of time on my abs, it's only fair they should be appreciated. She puts her wine glass down, but her expression is inscrutable. I'm trying to distract her, but I'm not sure it's working.

"And you're twenty-eight," I answer her, confirming what we already know—that we've both checked out each other's dating profiles.

"Correct," she says. "And you don't have a dog, do you?"

"My friends have dogs." I laugh.

"So what did your grandfather leave you in his will that has your grandmother all in a tizzy?"

I narrow my eyes at her. "If I tell you a bit more, can we drop it then?"

She lifts a shoulder, and I wonder what she has on under that robe.

"You don't have to tell me a thing," she says. "We can end our call and both get a much needed early night."

I drop my head back on the couch back and lift both forearms across my closed eyes. Hearing her soft intake of breath I know she's not as unaffected by her view as she's pretending to be. For that, I'll give her something.

"My mother died when I was seventeen." I can see she immediately regrets asking me, but she did and here it comes. "We were living in England."

"Hence the accent." She nibbles her bottom lip nervously. "I'm sorry about your mother, Trystan."

I nod once and sit forward resting my forearms across my splayed knees. And I look Emmy in the eyes. "Okay, here's everything. I'm going to go through it once, and then I don't want to talk about it again. They kicked my mom out when she was pregnant with me. After I was born, she went to England. Maybe to try and get back together with my father, I guess. He obviously didn't want anything to do with her. But he made allowances for me, his bastard child. She was set up with a sort of common-law alimony, though I never saw him."

I take a deep breath. "When I was eleven we came back to Charleston. Got to know the family again. My uncle also had kids. I have two cousins. Beau was . . . I guess he was my best friend. But then my mother started having an affair with another married man—this one a prominent member of their country club. Let's just say, they weren't going to go through that again. When I was thirteen they kicked us out once more. I woke up one morning, and my grandmother said, "You and your mother are leaving." She didn't hug or kiss me that I remember. We just . . . . left. Flew back to England. I was confused. Betrayed. Angry at

Grandmother. Angry at my mother." I frowned. "But she was my mum, you know? I loved her. Then she got sick. I wanted to come back here, but my mother told me they wouldn't care. They didn't come when she was sick, and they didn't come when she died. I vowed right then that they may as well be dead to me. I'd just finished high school, so I stayed in England where higher education is subsidized and got my degree. Then I moved to New York."

I sat forward. "Right away I put a few warehouse buildings under contract, then I filed city paperwork to adjoin the lots. I officially bought and resold them in a simultaneous closing to an import company looking for a distribution center. I built myself up quickly after that. I had a knack for a deal I guess. Maybe it runs in the family, or maybe failing wasn't an option.

"The first time I heard a Montgomery was buying a building in New York City, I figured out it was my grandfather, and I quietly snuffed out the deal. I did it twice more." I rake my hands through my hair and let my head hang for a second before I look back at Emmy. "I thought maybe he'd ask to see me. Arrange a meeting. Ask me why. Something. It's not like I was hiding. I was baiting him. But after that, he never tried a deal again in New York, and he never tried to see me. And then the real estate crash happened. I lucked out. I was between projects, I lost less than most. But I *knew* he knew I was there. And I knew he was watching me. But he never, not once, reached out."

I took a few deep breaths and the last sip of now almost warm beer. The label was starting to slip off, so I worked my thumb under it, trying to get it loose. "My grandmother had made it clear to my mother when we left that she would never allow anyone in the family to communicate with her. With us. I figured my grandfather knew that, and that's why he kept quiet. His weakness in standing up to Isabel Montgomery filled me with . . . rage. But also hurt. I missed him. I missed *them*. I never stopped wanting him to reach out. I even toyed with maybe making the first move. But I feared I might be rejected. Again. Then last week I get a letter from his attorney telling me he died."

I exhale. Telling this story, even though it's short and brutal is untying something in me. But fuck, it hurts. I rub my chest.

Emmy waits, not saying a word, knowing I'm not done. Her eyes are large, glistening, filled with emotion.

I pinch the bridge of my nose, thankful I've taken painkillers. The label on the beer bottle still needs help, so I pick at it again.

"So the will. He basically gave me control of his company. He cut his other two grandchildren out of it, although it seems like they're fine with that. Except he wants them both to get married in order to get their inheritance. Not to each other," I amend quickly. "What a twisted request." I shake my head.

A faint smile crosses Emmy's lips.

"And I'm supposed to pay my grandmother a stipend at my discretion. Can you imagine more of a way to piss her off than not giving her the company that should rightfully be hers or my uncle's, and then make her beholden for spending money to a grandchild she despises? What the fuck was he thinking?" I almost yell it.

I sit back. "There. Now you have it all. I'm not sure this was a fair trade, but now you know everything."

"Wow," Emmy says after a moment.

"Wow, is right," I agree.

Just then the smell of dead fish and the funk of forty thousand years breezes across my nose. "Christ!" I grimace and turn my head, only to see a pink puckered butthole surrounded with white fur pointing right at me.

"Jesus! Fuck!"

Something screeches in surprise and flies right at me in a hissing streak of black and white fur, though I think it was trying to jump down and lost its balance due it its ungodly size. Swinging my arms out in self-defense, I accidentally hit the creature in midair, and it clatters across the coffee table, sending the phone, the empty beer bottle, and books flying all over the place.

With one more outraged yowl it disappears.

It's all over in seconds, and I stand there alone, in shock and utter silence, clutching my chest.

No, not silence, there's the muffled sound of Emmy laughing uncontrollably from the phone face down on the carpet. I think she's trying to ask if he's okay, but she can't breathe.

"If *he's* okay? What about if *I'm* fucking okay?"

I guess that was her cat.

* * *

WE'RE STILL LAUGHING about it a few minutes later when I turn off the downstairs lights and head up to the bedroom.

"I'm crying, Trystan. Actual, real tears I'm laughing so hard." She's had to put the phone down.

"I haven't heard you apologize yet," I tell her as I trot up her stairs.

"Me? Apologize? Why?" Emmy can finally breathe.

"It's *your* cat."

"Okay, I'm so sorry, Trystan. Especially as you told me you don't like pussies on your face."

Oh, she went there, and I'm not letting her out of it. "It would depend on the pussy, Emmy."

There's a sharp inhale.

An instant visual of Emmy over me, me looking up her sweet body with all its secrets on display, to all that glorious red hair surrounding her flushed face. Her sinking down to meet my mouth. God, I'd love to know how she tastes.

A punch of lust rips through my gut, and it almost brings me to my knees.

I look at the phone screen, but all I see is the hotel ceiling.

"Emmy," I say. My voice is rough to my own ears. She must know what's in my head.

"Don't go there, Trystan."

"Why not?" I ask.

"Because."

"Because why? Look at me, Emmy."

"No."

"Because why?"

"Fine."

The camera angle moves and her face, cheeks flushed and eyes bright, comes into view. I sink onto her bed. "Christ, you're beautiful," I say, cutting off anything she's about to say.

She swallows heavily. "You're not so bad yourself."

"Why can't I go there, Emmy?"

"We don't ... know each other. Not really."

I stare at her. I've never bared myself to anyone the way I have to her. Probably *because* I thought we didn't really know each other. But maybe we do. Today, I heard her at her most vulnerable. Her most scared. And instead of running away, I ran toward danger. I've shared. She's shared. I'm in her home surrounded by her scent.

"I do know you, Emmy."

"You don't." She shakes her head.

"And you know me."

"No."

"Better than anyone alive." It's the God's honest truth.

"But I've only seen you once in my life. And it wasn't the greatest first impression if I'm honest."

I wince and blow out a breath. This is the pushing too hard too fast thing I've been doing. It makes her bolt. I have to reel it back in. Go slower.

"Okay. Maybe you're right. What don't I know about you that matters?"

"That's not how this works."

"Isn't it?"

"No."

"So tell me."

"You don't know what makes me cry—"

"David," I interject. "Families. Injustice. People who are alone. Christmas movies, I bet."

"You're guessing."

"Well. Am I right?"

"Partially. What makes me laugh?"

"Apart from me being attacked by your cat?"

She smiles. "Apart from that."

"The absurdity of life," I tell her. "You find the ironic and the absurd in every situation. Particularly the tough ones. It's what helps you through life."

Her smile falters, and she blinks. "How can you—?"

"But also people. Their quirks. Their gifts. Your friends. Your godson. You seek out the joy. You find it even when no one else can."

She blows out a long slow breath.

"Trystan," she says, and she props the phone up, presumably on the side table, and lies back on the hotel bed, rolling to face me. Her head is resting on her hand, and her hair is a tumble of red waves, her cheeks tinged pink. The robe gapes slightly showing me a curve of breast and the beginning of whatever she's wearing underneath it.

"Emmy." I breathe her name. And when I do, I breathe her in. Her scent is all around me in her room.

Knowing she's watching me on the screen, I lie back and turn my face into her sheets and inhale deeply. Her light floral scent intoxicates me, not sweet exactly, mixed with clean detergent, but also with a hint of something like vanilla that makes my mouth water. "You smell amazing."

She lets out a small moan, and I can almost hear her swallow before her lips drop open.

"What else don't I know about you, Emmy?"

"That this scares me, whatever this is happening here."

"I know that," I say.

I know because I'm scared too. But I feel like I'm base jumping. I just voluntarily threw myself off a cliff, and I'm living in the free-fall terror for as long as it will have me because it feels fucking amazing.

The screen goes gray. *Video connection lost*

Shit. "Emmy?"

23

TRYSTAN

The phone tries to reconnect the video signal to no avail. "I have poor internet connection in the bedroom, sorry." I hear Emmy walking around.

"What are you doing?" I ask.

"Going to brush my teeth. Don't worry, I'm taking you with me." Her voice becomes echoey as she goes into the bathroom.

I grin and get up to go brush my teeth too. "Wait, do you have any mouthwash?" I ask when I'm done. "I didn't pack mine."

"Right below the sink."

I squat and open the cabinet. All I see are—

"Behind the new toilet paper rolls and next to the tampons," she says. "Sorry."

I reach forward, blindly feeling my way, and my hand grabs the top of a plastic bottle. "We're rapidly discovering all of each other's secrets, finding out you use tampons is not a shock, Emmy. Why are you hiding the mouthwash though?"

"I hate the look of the bottle."

I look down with an amused frown. "It looks pretty normal to me. Lots of big writing, but nothing offensive."

"I don't know what to say. I find it ugly. Okay, I'm putting you outside for a second. Actually can I call you back?"

I look at the phone as if I can see her. "Sure," I say, hoping she won't second-guess herself or feel weird and not call back. I realize out of the two of us, I've already done that to her. "Talk to you in a minute." I take the opportunity to grab the charger and plug the phone in by the bed since her battery is low again. Then I take my jeans off and slide into her bed. Onto her sheets. Normally I sleep naked, but I keep my boxers on.

The phone rings. "Hey," I greet her. We're just talking, no video call this time.

"Hey," she says and I hear the smile in her voice. "Are you in bed?"

"I am."

"Me too."

"What side do you sleep on?" I ask, looking at the bedside tables on either side of the bed. The table nearest me has books piled up versus the other. I'm assuming I'm on her side.

"The left," she says. "Closest to the bathroom. I mean who wants to walk farther than they have to, right?"

"True."

"You? What side?"

"At this moment, the left." I imagine the bed in my own room at my apartment. "But at home, the right side for the same reason."

"Where's home?" she asks. "Now you know so much about where I sleep, and I know nothing about where you usually sleep."

Thinking about my apartment in New York makes me feel lonely, cold. "I have a condo on Fifty-first."

"Central Park?"

"Nearby." Actually overlooking it. I picked it up from a day trader who'd lost his entire life savings in the crash.

"Wow. David lived in Manhattan. Not too far from this hotel actually. I loved to come and visit him here."

"It's a great area." I don't say that I actually spend more time there than at home because that would beg the question as to why. "Do you miss visiting New York City?"

"I miss David. But I love Charleston. I've . . . been happy there."

There's so much she's not saying between the gaps in her words. Earlier she mentioned David was all she had left, which begs the question of what happened to her parents. I know I could ask and based on the fact I poured my soul out to her, she'd probably answer.

But I don't want her sad. Not now while she's alone and after the day she had. I want her happy, sleepy, relaxed. I want her falling asleep with me with a smile on her face.

We talk for hours.

We talk about everything and nothing.

"Like Japanese haiku poetry," I say at one point after we've both agreed to turn off our bedside lights. We're on speaker phone, and her voice emanates from the phone that I've laid face-up on the bedside table.

"What about it?"

"What's the point? I mean, I don't get it."

"There's nothing to get." She laughs. "They're little vignettes of everyday things meant to be observed for just what they are."

"It's a big joke propagated on the literary community, is what it is."

She giggles. "Go downstairs and get my book of Japanese haiku, it's sitting on the small desk in the corner by the book shelves. There's an art to it. I'll prove you wrong."

"You want me to go downstairs in the dark, with a beast on the loose who could leap out at me any moment?"

"He's not a beast."

"You were there, you saw the whole thing!" I fire off indignantly.

"Fine. Well, he likes you or you wouldn't have seen him at all."

"Likes me? He farted in my face."

"Exactly. He feels comfortable around you. He'll probably come visit you in the night."

I sit bolt upright in the dark. "Emmy, you better be fucking kidding." I look toward the shadowy opening of the stairwell.

"Oh, and I also have a ghost. But I don't hear from it much."

My skin goes cold and clammy. I can do pretty much anything. But I don't do ghosts. "You what?" It comes out as a whisper. "Are you serious?"

"Wait," Emmy murmurs. "Do you believe in ghosts?"

I cringe. "Yes?"

She chuckles. "Oh my God, you're serious."

"Fuck, yes, I'm serious. Please tell me you're fucking joking, Emmy."

She's still laughing.

"Do you or do you not have a ghost?" I very slowly and very quietly lie down and draw her duvet all the way up to my chin so I don't draw attention to myself.

"I—I don't know," she manages, and I know she's trying hard to stop laughing.

I'm rigid, my eyes squeezed shut. "You don't know?"

"I mean, I hear things sometimes. It's an old house."

I moan. I can't breathe.

"You're really freaked out, aren't you?" she asks.

"Mmm hhmmmm. You better not get off the phone with me. Like, ever."

The phone buzzes with a text, and I open one eye.

Snaking one arm out from under the covers, I unplug it from the charger and bring it in bed with me. She's sent me a text.

"We can stay on the phone as long as you need to," she says. "I'm sorry I freaked you out."

EMMY: *Did you really read the books on my Kindle app?*

"I DON'T WANT to know what you've heard that makes you think you have a ghost," I tell her, "but I think you should probably get the place saged or cleansed or whatever when you get back. In fact, I'll get it done tomorrow morning. Maybe I'll have Father Pete come over and bless the place."

I DID. I'd love to know which ones, and which PARTS are your favorite.
I hit send.

"TRYSTAN," she's saying. Then I hear her pause and know from her quick inhale of breath she read my text. She clears her throat and continues. "I'm surprised you know what saging is. Along with your fear of ghosts it doesn't seem very manly."

"My decorator insisted I sage my apartment when I bought it from the previous owner to get rid of his karma or whatever."

Her text response comes through.

EMMY: *It depends on my mood, but all of them usually open to my favorite parts. Try one.*
Emmy: *Read me a story. A sexy story.*

I GROAN. Out loud. A vision of her reading erotica and touching herself in the bed I'm in right now is almost too much to bear. "Emmy, if you were here you'd see, and feel, just how manly I am right now." I don't bother texting her back. She was trying to distract me from my fear and it worked.

Her breathing changes.

I'm hard as granite and desperate to slide my hand down to get some relief. "Emmy?"

"Yes?" she whispers it.

"I have a confession. I went through all of your photos, and I found the one of you in the yellow bikini. I can't get it out of my head. I thought about it when I was in the shower this evening. In your shower."

"You did?"

"I did. I was washing with your soap, lathering up my whole body, and bam there you were in my head, in that tiny, indecent bikini, and God, you turned me on so much. I was so hard."

I give in and slide my free hand down my stomach until it reaches under my boxers. I fist my cock and squeeze hard once, letting out a groan I can't keep in.

"D-did you touch yourself?" she asks.

"Yes, Emmy."

She makes a sound that almost make me want to come in my hand right then. It gives me confidence to say more. "I imagined you in the shower with me, the bikini wet and see-through. Your nipples showing through the fabric, your skin shiny and slick."

I swallow, my mouth dry, my breathing erratic. She doesn't respond, but she doesn't tell me to shut up either.

"I sucked your nipples through the fabric, Emmy."

She gasps, and I give my cock one long stroke to get the edge off. But it makes it worse.

"More," she whispers and my stomach hollows out. "Tell me more."

"But it wasn't enough," I go on. "I slipped those little bikini top triangles aside to see your tightly budded nipples begging for my mouth. Pink or beige, Emmy?"

"Pink," she gasps out.

"Fuck. Are you touching yourself, Emmy?" Jesus, please let her be touching herself.

"Y-Yes."

Thank, Christ.

"Am I on speaker?" I ask.

"Yes."

"Good, you have two hands. Use them, Emmy. I want you to touch yourself like I want to touch you. Tell me, Emmy. Are your fingers between your legs?"

Her breathing is coming in light, sharp bursts.

"Emmy, if your hands aren't between your legs, they need to be right now. I want you stroking your clit. Are you doing it Emmy?"

"Yes." Her answer is just breath, no sound.

"What does it feel like? Are you wet?" I ask, my voice sounding strangled to my own ears.

"Yes. Oh God, yes."

"Spread your legs, Emmy. Wider."

If I was there, I'd have them so damn wide.

"Tell me what it feels like," I coax.

"Slippery. Warm."

"God, Emmy." I can't stop my hand, it's stroking up and down, squeezing, desperate. I imagine it's her warm wet body sliding up and down my cock. That I'm already inside her. I squeeze harder. "Slip a finger inside, Emmy." I can barely form the words.

"I am."

"Two. Make it two, three if you can, I want you to really feel me."

"Trystan," she moans. "Oh . . . my . . . Oh my God." Her whispers are frantic. She sounds shocked.

Jesus, what I wouldn't give to see her face right now. To feel her body spasm. See her lose it. I want to know if her skin turns pink, if she squeezes her eyes closed, if she arches her back.

She's gasping, panting, and I know she's almost there. I can almost feel it. My fist pumps harder, tighter, faster.

"That's it, Emmy. Are you fucking yourself, Emmy?"

"Y-Yes."

"Feel my cock sliding in and out of your sweet wet pussy while you rub your clit. Hard. God, you're beautiful. I want to feel you come, Emmy."

I'm on the edge, it's building, taking over. My heart is pounding so hard it feels like it's outside my body. "I'm going to come, Emmy." My words are grunts. I don't know how I'm coherent. If I'm coherent. "I'm so close. I'm going to imagine pumping into your sweet body, and I'm going to come so deep inside you, Emmy."

"Oh, God. Oh my God." Her breathing is erratic, desperate, picking up speed. "I'm coming, Trystan. Oh my God. Oh, oh, oh . . ." her voice fails and a long low moan takes over. It's endless. And oh my shit, if it's not the sexiest fucking thing I have ever heard.

I lose it then. My body goes rigid, I kick the comforter off my belly, and throw my head back into her pillow, the smell of her surrounds me as everything builds and rushes south and I come so damn hard, erupting into my own hand and across my stomach.

24

TRYSTAN

*T*he silent darkness finally creeps back as my breathing slows.

"Emmy? You still there?"

"Yes." Her voice is tiny.

"Don't hang up." I say it out of instinct. I don't know how I know she's probably lying there, her hand covering her eyes, mortified.

"Okay," she squeaks.

"Just breathe," I tell her. I sit up and by feel, grab a dirty T-shirt from my suitcase at the end of the bed and clean myself off. "That was amazing. *You're* amazing."

"I cannot believe we just did that. I've never—"

"Me neither." I climb back in bed.

She exhales. "You've never had phone sex?"

"Never."

"I'm embarrassed, Trystan."

"Why? Didn't it feel good?"

"God, yes. It felt good. Too good. I just feel . . ." she trails off not finishing her thought, and I worry she's going to say dirty or something.

"There's no such thing as 'too good.' Emmy, it was beautiful. You're incredible. I will replay the sounds you made in my head probably for the rest of my life."

"Oh, God," she moans and lets out an embarrassed laugh. "And you, Mr. Montgomery, are a really dirty, dirty talker."

I chuckle. "I can hardly remember the things that came out of my mouth, Emmy. I was in flow state. But I think, though I can't be sure," I say in a dry tone, "I think you liked my dirty, dirty talking."

"Oh, God, I'm mortified." Her voice is muffled like she's covering her face, but I still hear laughter. Thank God.

"Be honest, Emmy," I warn.

"Yes, I did."

"Did what?"

"I liked your dirty, dirty talking."

"That's my girl. Now, do you need to go to the bathroom or anything, coz I'd really love to fall asleep talking to you."

I roll over and lay her phone on the bedside table. And we do just that.

The last thing I remember is Emmy asking, "What makes *you* cry, Trystan?"

"All your unread emails," I mumble as my eyes close.

* * *

I TEXT Emmy as soon as I wake up. It's Friday. I'm supposed to do tours of an apartment building and a student housing project at some point today, but I'm waiting on the details from Robert. After my initial frosty reception from him, he seems to at least be going through the motions of helping me get my bearings about everything to do with Montgomery Homes & Facilities. I change into shorts and a T-shirt and check my email on my laptop, then I pull up a map of Charleston on Emmy's phone, pop my earbuds in, and pick a playlist entitled, "If I ever decide to start jogging." I smirk because it's so her.

I head out and follow the map of downtown, jogging to East Bay Street. Turning left would take me out toward the docks and warehouses, turning right will take me toward the Battery and the water. I turn right as I listen to Sia telling me she's the greatest and how much stamina she has. I push on, dodging a few early tourists, passing carriages, hopping over horse shit, and checking out the architecture. By the time I'm on East Battery, I catch sight of the morning sun sparkling silver across the water in the big soup bowl where the wide Ashley and Cooper Rivers merge before they join the Atlantic Ocean. I'm in stride, working hard. Sweat is a second skin and I'm humming along with U + Ur Hand by P!nk. I head along the waterfront sidewalk then cut right to pass under the majestic live oaks to a bench I spot. This town—I can't quite call it a city yet—has a great energy. I like it.

I feel . . . happy. I haven't felt this much lust for life in some time. For months now, I've had a feeling—odd dissatisfaction creeping in my life. Like there was nothing left to accomplish with my business, hence my decision to sell it. But I love New York.

Or do I?

I contemplate this as I breathe in the sea air.

I'd heard a couple of buzzes cutting over the music as I ran, so I pull the phone out of my bicep wrap, but there are no texts from Emmy. There are two missed calls from her work number I'd seen and ignored and then two texts from someone named Steven. I frown. I hope she was able to tell her boss she couldn't be in today. I slide the text open.

STEVEN: *Emmaline. I haven't heard back on the email I sent you. I expect you to be in this morning as previously arranged. We have an important pitch at noon, and they specifically requested you attend.*

STEVEN: *I don't think I need to tell you that not being able to keep to your approved time-off schedule speaks of unprofessionalism.*

I TEXT Emmy again even though I haven't heard from her yet. *Your boss is texting. Apparently he sent you an email. I'll forward it to you now. You should probably call him.* My watch says it's nine o'clock. She could still be sleeping, but something feels off.

In the email icon on her phone, which shows thousands of unread messages and makes my neck itch, I spot two emails from her boss that came in. One last night and one this morning. I forward them to my own email without reading them. I wish she'd text me or call me.

Continuing my run, I turn right to pass the Montgomery house on South Battery. I don't have clear memories of it from the outside from when I was a kid, but I check it out as I pass the grand entrance, the facade in original brick with wide porches to take advantage of the breezes off the water. From the looks of it, many of the neighboring homes have been turned into inns.

Armand is outside Indigo Café, clearing cups and saucers off the two bistro tables he's set up outside.

"Morning," I call, out of breath.

He straightens and smiles as he sees me. "Come have breakfast."

"I will. I'm starving. Just let me get showered. Ten minutes."

After my shower I realize Emmy still hasn't texted me back, and I feel another twinge of concern.

Armand is slammed with customers when I return, but he's reserved me a spot in the corner. He points to it, and I nod gratefully. "Same as before," I mouth, hoping he remembers what I had so it saves him the time of coming over to take my order.

I scroll through my emails on my laptop, seeing the two I sent Emmy and hoping she answered them. Then I call Mac.

"Hey old man," I greet him.

"Trystan. How did it go? You disappeared on me. Are you back?"

"Nope. But I'll probably fly back tomorrow." Then I fill him in on the will. It feels good to talk about it again, and I realize I should be talking more with Mac generally. He's been a good business-mentor-turned-friend since I did my first deal with him.

"So you're going to run the operation from New York?" he asks.

"I'm going to try. At least for now."

"I heard Charleston's a neat city. It's not New York of course, but there could be worse places."

"Ha. Nah, I'm used to New York," I say. But even as the words come out of my mouth I think of Emmy. Although, since we've never actually spent any time together, there's no reason why we can't continue to be "phone friends" when I get back up north. I experience an uncomfortable sensation as I think it, but mentally I move on. We chat about the logistics for closing next week and then say goodbye as Armand brings my breakfast.

"Do you have a break soon?" I ask him. "It's busy."

"Busy, but I love it." He grins. "Maybe come by later."

"I'll see. I have a few meetings."

"Everything okay at Emmy's casa?"

"Perfect," I tell him, though my smile feels tight. Emmy still hasn't texted me.

Beau calls me then, and Armand nods and goes back to work.

"Hey, Trystan?"

"Beau. Hi, how you?"

"Good. So I'm going to tag along today. And I've been tasked with asking you if you'll attend a family dinner at the town house."

I swallow. "Seriously?"

"Yep."

"I'd have thought Isabel had heard enough from me. I don't want you and Suzy trying to patch things up between Grandmother and me."

"Actually, the invite came from her. She called and asked me if I'd please invite you."

I run a finger under the collar of my shirt. I want to say no, but suddenly, I think of Emmy and her hanging onto David with everything she has. She'd go, if it was her. It can't hurt to humor Isabel before I go back to New York. "So you and Suzy will be there? Your dad too?"

"Yeah."

"Okay, I'll come. What should I bring?"

"Just yourself. But wear a jacket. She's formal. A bottle of wine wouldn't hurt either."

"I'll need it." I laugh and we say our goodbyes.

I'm consumed by the need to tell Emmy I took her advice. Not that she's been explicit about it. But I got the sense she thought I should at least give my family a chance.

As I dial my number again, I experience a wave of awkwardness. If she hasn't texted, she's either asleep or doesn't want to talk to me because she's having an attack of the morning-afters. I feel certain it's the latter. The phone rings and then goes to voicemail. I hang up and dial the hotel.

"Hi, it's Trystan Montgomery. Can you put me through to my room, please, I have a guest staying there."

The call is patched through, but there's no answer. She said she used to visit David in the Village, she's probably gone for a walk in the neighborhood. But even as I think it, I doubt that's the case.

I open another text message, but I'm clueless what to say. Everything is starting to feel weird and cold in the daylight. I think over all the things that came out of my mouth last night and realize they are starting to feel lascivious and disgusting. My breakfast doesn't feel too settled either. Everything feels wrong.

EMMY, can we talk, please? Call me.

25

EMMY

J forgot to close the black-out blinds, I realized as I blinked bleary-eyed against the shaft of light coming in the room. My mouth was dry like I had a cotton ball for a tongue, and my head was pounding—a long slow thudding. I might have drunk that whole bottle of Sancerre last night. Though my body was hurting, it also felt lethargic, relaxed, satisfied. I stretched on a long moan and then froze.

Everything came rushing back to me. Trystan's voice. Oh, God. His sexy commands. I could hear them blasting through my brain right now. Instant, aching arousal swirled through me at the same time I was slammed by acute embarrassment. Oh God. What had I done?

Maybe it was just a dream.

A very, very, sexy, incredible dream with no consequences. At least no physical consequences.

I shifted in the bed and realized I was very, very naked below the waist, my sleep shorts balled up against my thigh. Dragging them out from under the covers, I stared at the pineapple design like it somehow was to blame. Not a dream then. I chucked them away from me.

Just as I slid my gaze over to the phone, it buzzed. As if it might bite, I slowly and carefully picked it up.

SUIT MONKEY: *Morning, beautiful. P.S. Stop overthinking it.*

"AAARGH!" I said aloud to the room. What the hell was I supposed to say to him today?

What did last night mean? We lived in different cities for God's sake. What was this?

I kept hearing myself in my head along with his words. I let him hear everything, and in the cold light of day it made me feel vulnerable and so embarrassed. Mortified.

Should I quickly nip this in the bud with my pride intact? Maybe say: sorry, I had a bit too much wine, I don't know what came over me?

The phone buzzed again.

SUIT MONKEY: *Call me when you wake up.*

I LAID the phone on the side table. The worst part was I remembered I was the one who started it. He was getting freaked out about my resident ghost, and I figured I'd tease and distract him. Little had I realized how successful that tactic would be.

I didn't think I had the courage to talk to him right now. God, I hardly knew him. How did I manage to have phone sex with someone I'd never met? What should I text back?

Spread your legs, Emmy. Wider. His voice was in my head, and I was aching again. I don't think, in my whole life, anything had ever turned me on as much as Trystan had last night.

I let out a shaky breath and got up on weak legs, took

another shower, and blow-dried my hair. After I checked in at work, I would call the airline. In my panic over David's disappearance I hadn't tried to change my ticket, I'd had to cancel it, not knowing when David might be found. And the chances of getting on a last minute flight on a Friday were slim to say the least. I looked around. There'd be worse places to stay another night, but I'd rather not blow all the money Trystan had sent me for my place. I could put it toward David's move.

Feeling braver, I finally picked up Trystan's phone. There was a missed call from him and two more text messages. I shifted uncomfortably from one foot to another. I should text him back and stop being a coward. But then I saw the words. Something about my boss. Shit.

I opened his email and found the email he'd forwarded from my email to his. It was a curt email from my boss about time off and our pitch today. My stomach sank. Honestly, I'd already prepared everything for it before I left, he was being dramatic. Not that I was saying I was expendable, but surely this one time they could manage without me?

I sat at the desk and picked up the room phone.

"Miss Dubois," a voice intoned from the handset. I jumped. I'd forgotten about the beck and call thing they had going here. "Good morning," the voice went on. "May I order you some breakfast?"

"Oh, uh." I hesitated. I'd thought about walking to find some coffee. "Actually I just wanted to make a phone call."

"Yes, ma'am. Connecting you to an outside line now. Go ahead."

A dial tone came over the line, and I punched in the office number for my boss. At least that was a number I knew by heart. Which said a lot about my work-life imbalance.

"This is Steven," my boss answered.

"Steven, it's Emmy."

"Emmaline, you better be on the way in to work, but I'm guessing by the two one two area code you are still in New York."

"I am. Sorry. I hope you got my message yesterday about what happened."

"I did. But Emmaline, this pitch is important. I assumed you would be on the next flight back here."

"I'm sorry. No. But the pitch deck is ready, it's saved—"

"Not good enough, Emmaline. I'm not sure you really value your job here. We were counting on you to bring this in. *I* was counting on you. I didn't want to have to make this public," he dropped his voice, "but if we don't hit our quarterly revenue projections, I'm afraid there'll have to be some downsizing. I'm sure you don't want to be responsible for people losing their jobs."

My stomach fell further. The reality was I wouldn't put him past laying people off just to make his point. And I was especially curious about how much he took out of the company to pay for his lifestyle and his flashy deep-sea fishing boat, *The Lucky Hooker*.

"Of course not, Steven. This was unavoidable. And there's no way I can meet the noon deadline even if I got on the next flight."

"You'll call in then."

"I can't." I strengthened my resolve and swallowed. "I'll be with David. I need to make sure he's okay today after yesterday."

"Emmaline, I expect you to participate in this pitch."

I blew out a frustrated breath, not wanting to say a hard *No* again. "I'll try."

"Good. It will have to do. Just know I'm extremely disappointed in your work ethic. I'll text you the call in number."

"O—"

The line went dead. "'Kay," I finished lamely.

"Ugh," I complained to the empty hotel room. "Steven is *so* annoying!"

God, I really needed coffee. I'd started my morning embarrassed, now I was pissed off too. This was definitely not a situa-tion to be in without several shots of espresso.

I threw yesterday's clothes in my bag. Retracing my steps around the room to make sure I didn't forget anything, I opened the wardrobe even though I hadn't used it and froze.

A couple of men's suits and three shirts hung there. My gaze tracked to the narrow set of shelves where I saw underwear, socks, and a blue tie laid out neatly. Next to the tie was a toiletries bag with the initials T.M monogrammed on the side.

What the hell?

Wait. I knew Trystan was a part-owner. He said he could get a room, but this must be *his* room.

I frowned.

But why did he have a permanent room at a hotel in the city where he lived? His apartment wasn't that far away.

Unless . . .

Oh my God.

Acid from my empty stomach threatened to crawl up my throat.

This . . . this was where he had all his hookups so he never had to take anyone home for the night.

I stepped backward, my calves colliding with the bed, and sank onto the edge. Did we basically hook up? Was I one of his hookups?

Shame and humiliation tore up and down inside me, free-wheeling with all my insecurities until my stomach was aching and in shreds.

I'd been touching myself while he listened, from this very same bed where he'd heard countless other women screaming his name. God, he must have been laughing at how easily I came apart for him. For a stranger.

So ironic that it would be in his hookup hotel.

I suddenly felt dirty and . . . stupid.

I was so, so stupid.

My nose burned as I fought tears. God, what a morning.

I took a deep breath, trying to think clearly. It wasn't like he'd forced me. I was angry at myself more than I was at him.

But he wasn't getting any more from me, certainly not tears. And I was *not* staying another night here in this high-end bordello like a concubine. Ugh.

I stood and took five deep, long breaths. Then I walked calmly to where I'd laid my purse. I picked it up, grabbed the handle of my wheelie bag, and headed toward the door.

Trystan's phone was buzzing again on the desk, but I left it there and opened the door of the room.

Two seconds later I returned to the desk and picked up the damned phone.

Because of David.

Obviously.

*　*　*

"WHAT DO YOU MEAN, there's no bill?" I whisper shouted at the poor frightened girl at the front desk.

I was trying not to make a scene, but failing miserably.

"Th-there just isn't. It's Mr. Montgomery's room, and it's already paid for." She lifted her shoulders helplessly. "It's just his. There's no billing attached."

"But—but what about the food? My dinner? And the wine?"

"Same?" She winced.

"Asshole!" I exploded and immediately regretted it. "Sorry. It's not your fault. I just, I never would have stayed if I'd known."

"Why not?" she asked in confusion. A phone rang incessantly in the back office.

"Ugh, never mind. Can you call me a cab?"

"Mr. Montgomery has a car—"

"No, just no. Please. For the love and dignity of all pussies everywhere, please just call me a cab."

The girl sucked her lips between her teeth, her shoulders shaking as she tried to hold in a laugh.

"I was talking about cats."

"Sure," she said and picked up the phone receiver in front of her. "Let me ask the doorman outside to hail you a cab."

A man's head popped out of the office behind the front desk, eyes scanning the reception area. His gaze landed on me. "You Emmy?"

Oh, hell no.

"Mr. Montgomery would like a word."

"I just bet he would. Tell him . . ." I sighed. Defeated. I had no fight left. "Just tell him . . . no."

"No? That's it?"

"Yes. Just tell him *no.*"

The man shrugged and slunk back inside the office. The girl at the front desk was smirking. "Your cab is waiting."

"Thank you. Sorry about my outburst." I gathered up my stuff.

"It's fine," she said. "And I'm not sure if this helps or makes matters worse, but he, uh, Mr. Montgomery, only uses his room himself. He, uh, gets another one if he has, um, company . . ." she trailed off in obvious discomfort and scratched her nose.

"So that he doesn't have to actually spend the whole night with someone," I finished her sentence. "You're right, I don't know if that makes it better or worse." I walked away then stopped. "But thank you," I told her and headed out to my waiting cab.

26

EMMY

*S*itting in the back of the cab, my lack of caffeine and late night with Trystan knocked me out.

"Lady," the cab driver yelled.

I snorted as I came to and wiped my mouth.

"We're here."

I blinked, feeling like I'd woken from an eighty-year slumber. "Thanks. Sorry." After paying, I stumbled from the cab, making sure I had everything. Phone!

"Hey," I yelled as the cab driver pulled away. I abandoned my bag and went yelling out into the street after him. Luckily, there were no other cars coming that direction. The cab squealed to a stop.

"Lady!" the driver yelled out the window, his hand gesticulating a series of symbols I was sure were an A-Z of curse words in Urdu sign language.

"Sorry." I pulled open the back door, and of course there sat Trystan's phone. I breathed out a sigh of relief. "Thank you," I said as the driver tutted and shook his head. I picked the phone up and closed the door, having to leap back as the car sped away. I almost lost my toes.

Suit Monkey: *Are you actually alive? Can you at least tell me that?*

Barely, I answered mentally. I exhaled hard. I had to talk to him. I knew it. And now my boss had made it necessary.

Yes.

What a cop-out. He'd know something was wrong, and I didn't want to act like a weirdo.

I'm good. Sorry just had a busy morning.

Suit Monkey: *Sure.*

He wasn't buying it one bit. And it sounded like my avoidance might've started pissing him off.

I cringed that the only reason I was communicating was because I needed something from him.

Any chance I got another text or email from my boss with a call-in number?

There was no immediate response. I negotiated my bag into the building and signed in. "Is D'Andre working today?" I asked the new lady at the sign-in desk.

"Nah. He's off Fridays," she responded.

I thanked her and trekked to Penny's office to let her know I was here. She was on the phone, but she waved at me, and I went to find David.

SUIT MONKEY: *Email forwarded.*

THANK YOU. TTYL

SUIT MONKEY: *Sorry. I'm in my 30s. TTYL?*

TALK TO YOU LATER.

DAVID HAD no recollection of his outing the day before and seemed in good spirits. It made me feel as if I had no reason to hang around. I should go home today, at the very least to get some balance. Some equilibrium. Then I'd also be able to use my laptop to follow up with the Medicaid consultant I'd told Penny I'd found. We'd spoken on and off for months but suddenly this week, I wasn't talking hypotheticals with David. I *had* to move him.

Flying back today was impossible though, and I couldn't stay at home. Trystan had rented my place for another night. This was so messed up.

I had about twenty minutes until I had to call in for the pitch. Raiding a vending machine downstairs, I made my way to the staff break room D'Andre had shown me and had a healthy lunch of a nut bar and a Snapple.

Then I went to Trystan's emails to find the one he'd forwarded for me. Underneath the one from my email were all his work emails. And lots about Montgomery Homes & Facilities in Charleston. And lo and behold one from a real estate company in Charleston. I couldn't help the bubble of stupid hope that fizzed up inside me. He'd said he'd been left some of his grandfather's business. Did this mean he might also be moving to Charleston? It took a colossal effort of will not to open the email and read it. I knew I was semi mad at him and annoyed at falling for his charms. But also the idea of not being remotely near each other's lives was equally . . . unpleasant. Him moving to Charleston could either be amazing or an absolute disaster in the making.

Trystan's phone buzzed and a text notification blocked my view while I was checking the time.

NATALIE: *Haven't heard from you, but we have plans tonight, right? So looking forward to "dinner." What should I wear? Or what shouldn't I wear? ;-) Xoxo*

I REARED BACK from the screen as if the text was a literal slap in the face. Nothing like a booty text to remind you to keep your wits about you. I couldn't resist the snarky text I sent to Trystan.

NATALIE WANTS *to know if you guys are still on for tonight, and what she should or shouldn't wear. Wink, wink. Should I postpone her until you're back in New York next week?*

DOTS IMMEDIATELY DANCED across the bottom of the screen then disappeared. Agonizing seconds passed.

The phone rang as I stared at it. *Suit Monkey.*

"Hi," I managed.

"What in the hell was that?"

"What?" I asked and shrugged my shoulders even though he couldn't see me.

"Just . . ." Trystan exhaled roughly. "God, Emmy."

The sound of his voice brought my insides to a simmer. I squeezed my eyes closed. "What Trystan?"

"Do you want me to go? To postpone it?"

I winced. He had me there. Why did he have to turn it around on me? "Do you want to?"

There was silence. And I found myself pulling on a thread of my sweater. And pulling and pulling.

This was ridiculous.

Trystan broke first. "You've been avoiding me."

"I haven't."

"Emmy, I'm not an idiot. You are talking to the prime-minis-ter-in-chief of all avoidance. Trust me. I know it when I see it. Are you okay after last night?"

"The prime-minister-in-chief? I don't think that's a thing."

"It's a thing." I could hear the laugh in his tone. "Because that's my title. I even had cards made."

"Huh," I acknowledged.

"So?"

I bit my lip. "So, what?"

"You're exasperating," he said. "And I don't think I've ever used that word."

"Er no. You can add the prime-minister-in-chief of *that* to your list of titles too."

"What's going on, Emmy?"

"Nothing. So what's the latest?" I sang, leaning back and putting my feet up on the chair in front of me. "I missed the episode of the *Young and The Restless* that just ended in the staff break room, so I could use some of your family drama to tide me over."

"Emmaline."

"Oh God, don't. That's what my boss calls me. And to think I used to love my name."

"Apologies. That won't do. Speaking of. Did you get that situation with your boss sorted out?"

"I did. He wants me to call-in to the pitch he's doing at noon."

"That's—"

"In a couple of minutes. I know."

"How's David today?"

I smiled. "He has zero recollection of what happened yesterday."

"Impossible!" Trystan huffed. "He and I had a connection. How does he not remember me?"

"He didn't mention you, sorry," I said, grinning.

"I'm so hurt."

"You do seem sensitive to stuff like that," I deadpanned.

"Hey."

"Hey, what?"

"Nothing," he said. "You better go. I need to as well. I'm going to visit some student housing."

I swallowed. I did have to go, but I didn't want to. How did he make it sound so easy and act so cool after last night? How could I be mad at him, yet still be addicted to talking to him? I was a head-case. I sighed. "Bye, Trystan."

"Bye, Emmy."

I noticed neither one of us mentioned making a plan to return phones.

* * *

I SAT up straight and dialed in the conference number Trystan had forwarded from my boss.

The line beeped to tell me I was connected. "This is Emmy joining the call."

There was silence.

"Hello?"

"Emmaline, it's Steven."

"Hi, so are we ready to go."

"No, Emmaline. The client cancelled."

"What? When?"

"This morning. Apparently the company is going through some changes, and all budgets are on hold for now."

"Oh, okay. That's a shame. Wait," I said, frowning. "Then why did you make me call-in?"

"To make sure you'd actually do it, of course."

My blood heated like a scolded toddler. "Are you serious?"

"Excuse me? I don't think you're in a position to question me."

"In a position to—" I stared at the phone. The urge to quit right at this moment was so overwhelming I had to suck my lips between my teeth to stop myself saying the words. Tears of frustration sprung to my eyes. I worked my butt off for Steven—often going to all of my clients' restaurants over and above the call of duty or reimbursement to keep them happy and feeling like I was always keeping them in high priority.

I inhaled deeply, taking note of where I was. I couldn't afford to be out of work right now if I was going to help David. Swallowing all my frustration like a lump of clay, I told him, "Steven, you can count on me. I won't overstay my leave again."

"See that you don't. See you on Monday bright and early."

"See you Monday," I replied dejectedly.

The call ended.

I HATE MY BOSS.

SUIT MONKEY: *What happened?*

PITCH WAS CANCELLED. He knew that but still made me call in. I'm feeling . . . stabby.

SUIT MONKEY: *Stabby?*

MURDEROUS!

SUIT MONKEY: *So you texted ME? Great.*

SORRY.

I FOUND MYSELF GRINNING.

SUIT MONKEY: *No it's fine really. It's nice to know I spring to mind when you're stirred to great heights of passion. Was just hoping they'd be less murderous and more amorous.*

IN THE MIDDLE of the day?

SUIT MONKEY: *A noon delight? Why not?*

I GASPED DRAMATICALLY in the empty break room and typed double exclamation points of shock and hit send.

SUIT MONKEY: *I'm kidding. Kind of. Not really. But I bet you're smiling now. Or at least rolling your eyes.*

I AM :)

TRYSTAN: *I'm in a car with my uncle and my cousin going to visit some of the properties I now own. But if I weren't . . .*

STOP.

SUIT MONKEY: *Okay.*

Is this what we are now?

SUIT MONKEY: *What?*

PHONE SEX BUDDIES.

SUIT MONKEY: *Do we have to label it?*

YOU CAN'T EVEN COMMIT to phone sex? You're worse off than I thought.

SUIT MONKEY: *Ha. You think you're pretty funny.*

I WAS SMILING, but I was only half joking. The truth was I was still feeling pretty raw about the hotel room situation and imagining all the countless women he'd brought there. A physical shudder jolted through me. Somehow when we texted, it was just easier to pretend everything was okay though. I mean, who created relationship drama with someone they'd never even met?

"Knock, knock," said a voice from the door.

I looked up to see the administrator, Penny.

She entered the room, and I slipped my feet off the chair in front of me, so she could sit down.

"Hey, Penny. I'm so sorry about David yesterday."

"Honey, don't apologize," she said, wafting down with a thud onto the empty seat. "These things happen. I found out we had a short power outage at about five in the morning yesterday." She shook her head. "It must have been some crazy confluence of events that David managed to get up unseen, get downstairs before the morning shift, and then pass through the doors at the exact time the power was out."

"Wow," I said because what else could I say? That was some crazy synchronicity right there. "That was bad luck."

"And good luck that he was found safe and sound. I'm glad you were able to get someone to help you. We panicked when we couldn't get you on your phone." She tutted. "So," she said and settled into the chair. "I took the liberty of calling around some places near you in South Carolina."

"You did?"

"Yes, I spoke with the Medicaid consultant you'd found. I thought perhaps a call from me might spur on the situation and have her move a little faster identifying places. We went ahead and put David's name down for four facilities that have dementia care in South Carolina."

"You did? Wow, that was fast. Thank you."

She inclined her head. "Sometimes it's easier to get through to the right people when you know the system. I believe the best one is in a place called Summerville."

"Oh, that's super close to Charleston." Hope ballooned in my chest. "It's a drive, but doable. With urban sprawl it's practically become part of greater Charleston."

"Well, there's no guarantee. They have a limited number of Medicaid beds. None of these places do more than they are required to by law. They have to be financially sustainable after all. But I'm going to suggest that when you get home you go and visit them. Have them put a face to a name. See if there's any way to speed up the process." She handed me a manila folder. "All four are in here with phone numbers and contact information. Then you'll have to rely on the administration staff to file all their paperwork in a timely manner so you can get coverage as soon as possible. They always have a backlog though, so you need to be prepared for out-of-pocket medical expenses in the interim."

"Thank you, Penny."

"Don't thank me. I'm relying on you to do everything you can to get him a spot before the end of next month."

"I will. But thank you for giving me a place to start."

She reached out and put a hand on mine. "You were on the way. But I was glad I was able to help speed up the process. I know this isn't easy."

"He is a good man, Penny. David was there for me like a parent. Anyway. Thank you. I know he seems crazy and belligerent, but he was kind."

She smiled. "That's good to know. He talks sometimes like he did something very bad."

I lift a shoulder. "He managed other people's money. It was a big responsibility. And like so many others invested heavily in mortgage-backed securities, he lost everything. Everything for his clients, himself, and his family."

"I had a feeling it was something like that. When are you flying back?"

"I don't know. Tomorrow, maybe. I had to cancel my flight yesterday."

"A lot of these facilities are geared for visiting and tours on the weekends. So maybe if you can get back today you could go this weekend?"

It made more sense to fly out tonight than pay for a hotel room, but it was Friday and flights into Charleston due to the Spoleto Festival were probably full. Maybe I could try standby and stay with Armand.

"I'll see if I can get on a flight."

Penny nodded and stood.

Going back today meant seeing Trystan today. I felt sick with nerves.

EMMY

*a*s I suspected the flights were full. I called the airline to see about standby and after a lady explained I should probably get to the airport as soon as possible because the flights would get busier and busier, I went upstairs to say goodbye to David.

"David," I greeted him from the door to his room.

He waved me in absently. "I had a dream, Emmy. You had a fella. Then I spoke to him!"

"You did, huh?"

"Well, I spoke to him in my dream. But then again just now. On the phone."

I perched on the end of his bed. "That's lovely, David. What do you guys talk about?"

He grinned. "You, of course."

"Me?"

"And business, of course."

"Of course."

"You should tell him, Emmy. He thinks I'm a nice person. You should tell him what I did."

"You are a nice person, David—"

"No. I was stupid. You should tell him all those things."

"*I* know those things, David. And I still think you're a nice person."

David huffed. "Well, he loves you. That makes me happy."

"That's lovely," I said. "Maybe one day I'll meet this dream fella. I'd sure love for him to be real."

"What are you talking about? He's the one with your phone staying with you in Charleston."

"What? Oh no. That's Trystan. He's not my fella."

"Could've fooled me."

"David—" I started, then sighed. "It's complicated."

"Nothing's complicated when you love someone. And he loves you."

"David." I took his hand and squeezed. I really should let this go, let him have his fantasy, but the idea he had was preposterous, and God forbid it took on any kind of permanence in his mind. I'd be hearing about it and fielding questions about where Trystan was for years. "David, I don't really know Trystan. I've only known him for three days, and even then—"

"Psshh," David cut in, waving his hand. "Three days. Let me tell you about three days. I met Dolly on a Greyhound bus on my way to California in 1972. If you don't think you can fall in love with someone in three days, missy, then ask me why I never met anyone again for the rest of my life."

David had been a bachelor as long as I'd ever known him. At one time, I'd thought maybe he was gay, and then perhaps simply asexual. I'd heard about Dolly once, but he never spoke about her. This was a new development.

"Tell me about her," I pressed.

"Nothing to tell. We spent three days together on a bus just talking, sleeping, laughing, learning about each other's lives. When we arrived, I kissed her, and well . . . then we went and spent the night together at a motel. It was the most beautiful night of my life. In the morning she told me she was married." He looked away and blinked.

"Oh, David. I'm so sorry."

"In all our three days together she'd never shared the biggest thing about her."

"Maybe she didn't think it was the biggest thing about her."

David looked at me sharply, and I shrugged. "I mean, maybe that's not how she identified herself. And maybe there was a reason she was on a Greyhound bus traveling to California rather than home with her husband."

"What did that singer fella say? Too young to reason and too grown up to dream. That was me."

"That's beautiful. And sad."

"I couldn't think of it in those terms back then. I was hurt. She left. I never saw her again. But I never forgot her. Sometimes there's just someone like that. Maybe most people never meet that someone, or maybe they don't recognize when they do. Maybe they pass them on the street and share a look, but they don't realize the size of the opportunity they are passing. Or they do but their hands are tied."

"Maybe they accidentally switch phones," I said and cringed. It was bad enough I'd been crushing so hard on Trystan, but ascribing anything more to it than happenstance and chemistry was a dangerously slippery slope.

We sat quietly for a while, and then I got up and began straightening the clothes in his closet. David dressed himself every morning, and he wasn't the most agile person anymore, so if he dropped something or it slipped off the hanger it usually stayed where it fell.

"I'm sorry, Emmy."

"What for?" I straightened and hung up a hooded waterproof jacket. When would he ever need one of those again? Why was it even here?

"Where do I start? For the predicament I'm in that you have to deal with. For losing all our family's fortunes. For sending my sister to an early grave. All of it."

My breath caught. "David—"

He held up a hand. "No, let me say it. I feel awake. Everything seems very clear today. I know why I'm here. I'm not right in the head. It's a terrible burden I've placed on you. After everything I did—"

"David, you didn't do it on purpose. Shit happens." I swiped tears from my eyes. I hated how broken and lost he sounded. "The whole world went through a financial crisis. It wasn't your fault."

"Greed, Emmy. That's a choice. That's on me. I deserved what happened to me. But none of you deserved for me to take you down with me."

I crouched down in front of his chair and put my hands on his knees.

He laid his hand on my hair. "You're a good girl, Emmy. You were a gift to my family."

"And you were a gift to me. You *are* a gift."

"Listen." His tone took on a new urgency like he knew his mind might slip away at any moment. "Take a chance. Put yourself out there. Fall in love. Start a family of your own. Do it soon. Throw yourself into love, Emmy. It's scary, I know. But don't be like me and shy away from it."

Tears rolled down my face, and I gave up wiping them away. I hadn't had such a lucid moment with David for years. There was so much I wanted to ask him, but I felt stuck in his words and overwhelmed with emotion I couldn't identify.

A strange look came over his face. "Now get up," he said. "I'm about to pass gas."

I scrambled to my feet.

"And tell that lovely Asian lady I wouldn't mind a walk down to the beach this afternoon. Maybe after the concert?"

"Okay, David."

I had no choice but to get David closer to me, no matter what it cost. I'd take on more side hustles in the interior design business with my sewing, do whatever I had to to meet the shortfall from my PR paycheck until I could get his Medicaid sorted out again. I didn't know how much time I had left with him, and I didn't want to waste it.

* * *

I STARED at myself in the mirror of the downstairs bathroom off the lobby of David's nursing home. David's thoughts he'd shared today hit me hard. It hurt that he carried so much guilt. My eyes stung again as I thought about him feeling so afraid and alone and worried about me in his moments of lucidity.

At least my hair was clean and nicely blown with waves because the rest of me was a fright. I was pale, and my eyes were red-rimmed, wide and frightened.

SUIT MONKEY: *Let me know what time you are arriving tomorrow so we can exchange phones before I leave.*

AND THERE IT WAS. It was only me who was dreading trading phones back with Trystan.

If I headed home, I'd have to see him and return his phone. It was frightening to realize I didn't want to. I didn't want this to be over. Being stuck in New York gave me a reason to stay in touch with him. Going home would mean having to see him, knowing it would burst the bubble. We were living in a fantasy. At least *I* was.

In this fantasy, I was in a relationship with someone who was there to talk to and laugh with and have sexy times with.

In real life, Trystan was a commitment-phobic serial dater.

In real life, he'd never be there for me the way he was now.

David had stuck this idea in my head that Trystan could be something more, and as soon as he had, cold fear had gripped me deep to my core. The signs all pointed to him not being relationship material. I'd be absolutely stupid based on evidence I had, including being another numbered woman in his hotel regardless of whether he was there with me or not, to think otherwise. But the stupid kernel of hope burst forth like popcorn.

The only thing I could think of was to go home tonight and not tell Trystan I was home until tomorrow. He'd rented my place for another night anyway. If he thought I was coming home, he might offer to move out or something, even though he'd already paid me. And where would he stay?

It would be weird and awkward. It would suddenly establish real life rules and distance because I'd be deliberately choosing not to spend the night with him when everything since last night seemed to say otherwise. I'd be coming home and . . . *coming* at home. Ha.

I guessed that was where the frightened look in my eyes was coming from—I felt caught on the cusp of something. Stuck between going home and lying about it, which didn't sit comfortably, or going home and bursting the bubble of whatever this was between us.

A knock at the door startled me. "Miss Dubois?"

I splashed water on my face and dried my hands and face with a paper towel. Unlocking the door, I saw the lady from the security desk. "Your cab's here," she said.

"Sorry. It's always emotional saying goodbye to David." Giving her a smile, I thanked her and grabbed my wheelie bag, heading out to the cab. Climbing in, I hunted around in my purse for my charging cord. Shit. Where was it? I glanced at Trystan's phone. Ten percent. Then I had a vision of the cord I'd plugged in in the hotel room. Dammit. Looking up Armand's number at the cafe, I dialed. It rang and rang. Annoyed again that I hadn't memorized any of my friend's cell phone numbers, I let out a long annoyed sigh and leaned back against the seat.

* * *

"YOU AGAIN," Phillip said at the information desk on the airport concourse. "Still no phone, I see."

I held Trystan's phone up. "It's dead."

"Buy a new charger."

"I have. Can you please do me a favor?"

"It depends."

"I need information. You provide that, don't you?"

Phillip released a long-suffering sigh. "I do."

"I'd like you to look up the number for Indigo Café in Charleston, and then I'd like to use your phone to dial that number."

Phillip stared at me, un-reacting. "That's got nothing to do with your flight or airport information," he said.

Without breaking his stare, I reached into my purse and grabbed one of my last remaining five-dollar bills and held it out between two fingers. "It's all I have," I whispered, staring him down. "And that information has everything to do with me flying home today."

I assumed he wasn't supposed to take money for information, so my action broke him, and he quickly glanced both ways before his hand darted out and nabbed the money so fast I barely felt it leave my fingers. I was aghast. "Train on the streets, did you?"

"You have no idea," he muttered and typed quickly into his computer. He read off the address to confirm it was the right place and then dialed the number and handed me the phone.

"Armand?" I said as soon as he answered.

"Emmy?"

"Yes. Listen, I'm coming home today. I wasn't going to because something happened with David. And then, well, anyway with Trystan renting my place tonight, I just . . . can I stay with you? Or can you call Annie since I don't have her number with me and ask her?" It all came out in a big long rush.

"*Si, Si.* Are you okay?"

"I'm okay. Yes. No. It's . . . complicated. And please don't tell Trystan I'm coming home if you see him. Just . . . can I stay with you?"

"Of course, Emmy. The couch isn't great but—"

"I'll take it. Thank you, Armand. You're a good friend."

"A good friend who you better give all the Trystan details to later. Because that man is fine!"

"Armand," I whined.

"Deal or no deal."

"Fine, deal. I'll grab a cab to your place. I'll get in around seven, I hope. I'm on standby. And we can still go dancing."

"*Perfecto*, Emmy. See you then."

"See you." I hung up and slumped against the information desk in relief.

"You know?" Phillip's voice cut in. "I see and hear a lot of weird shit every day with all these people passing through. But Emmy, I have to say, your situation intrigues me."

I looked up at him.

"Don't get me wrong"—he put both his palms up—"not enough to ask you about it. And please, don't share. But nonetheless."

I laughed and shook my head. "You're a character, Phillip."

"So I've been told. Bye, Emmy."

"Bye, Phillip."

The gate attendant said I was first in line on standby so she was pretty sure I'd get on the next flight. I didn't dare move from the gate while I waited. And even though I'd bought a new charger, I perversely didn't plug in the phone. This way I couldn't communicate with Trystan while I decided if I was going to tell him I was coming back or not. I needed more time to think it through.

TRYSTAN

*B*eau, Robert, and I walk through the student housing cafeteria. We've been given a tour of the halls we built that are currently leased by The College of Charleston, and they seem in good shape. Well-lit, freshly painted, clean. Students sit around in groups or dart here and there, late for afternoon class.

I wonder if Emmy went to college here. I never asked specifically, but in our long talk as we fell asleep last night, I thought I remembered her mentioning it. Checking my phone I see she hasn't contacted me in the last several hours. Not that she needs to. It's ridiculous how much I've grown to react to the vibration of a message that might be from her. To need it.

"Okay, well," Robert finally says. "I think that should do it for today. Are we seeing you for dinner?"

"You are. Beau already mentioned it." I nod at my cousin as he hands me a water.

"Great, then I'll leave you two here if you don't mind. Beau, you'll take Trystan by the office and introduce him around?"

"Will do."

We shake hands and my uncle heads out the exit.

I look at my watch.

"You late for something?" Beau asks, his eyebrows raised.

I shake my head. "Nah. I think Emmy might be coming back today, and I need to make a plan to switch phones with her." Something shifts unpleasantly inside me. It feels like disappointment. And I'm not sure, but it feels like I'm disappointed in myself. I have this feeling like I'm on the brink of something that's about to disappear unless I'm careful, and part of me feels like it's already too late.

"Do you think you'll ask her out?"

I exhale. "I don't know," I answer honestly. The thought of not asking her out is ludicrous, after everything we've shared. But on the other hand it also feels like the very reason I shouldn't. I'm so conflicted. "Anyway, I'm headed back up to New York."

"How long for?"

"At least until the sale of my business goes through. But I'm not sure I'm ready to leave New York. I'll have to be here often, of course. But moving here?" I shake my head.

"From what little you've shared, it seems like she's not the one-and-done type of girl."

"You've got that right. She's in a different category, but I'm not sure I know what that is."

"Maybe just friends?"

I think of what that could be like. We could still talk to each other. I'd tell her about my life and my dates, she could tell me if she was having any luck finding normal guys on the dating apps. My stomach turns. No. I can't hear about Emmy dating other men. Imagining those little sounds and gasps she makes when she comes . . . happening with someone else? Fuck no. I close my eyes. "Definitely not just friends." Shit. I think I really complicated things. But I don't know her in real life. That's probably what's making it feel different. So confusing.

"Question," Beau starts. "Do you think it would be better for me to marry a friend or a stranger?"

"Wow, hit me with a big one, why don't you?" I laugh, and we walk outside onto Liberty Street.

"Ha. Well, it's pretty big. I want to build boats. It's all I've ever wanted to do. Now I get a chance to do it, but only if I get married. I have a good friend. Not sure if you remember Gwen from when we were growing up?"

I wrack my brain, searching into the memory banks of the two summers I'd spent here, but come up empty. "No, sorry."

"Okay, well. We're friends. Good friends."

"Ever anything more?"

"Never. I mean, don't get me wrong, when we were teenagers I thought maybe we could have a thing, but she never really gave me that vibe, and I was too shy to push it. So it kind of morphed into a friendship. I'd even say she's one of my best friends. So it makes me think . . . should I just ask her to marry me, knowing we get along great but it means she misses out on her chance to find someone? Or do I find a stranger and have a neatly drawn up business arrangement?"

I discard my empty water bottle in a nearby recycling can and stuff my hands into my dark jeans pockets. "I'm about as far from the best person to advise you on this, having never been, nor ever planning, to be married."

"I know. But I thought maybe if you were me for a second . . . what would you do?"

"If it were me, I'd keep it as clean as possible. No room for misunderstandings. I'd still be able to date without worrying about confusing anyone."

"So . . . marry a stranger?"

"You asked what I would do." I shrug. "I also know I've been pretty relentless about keeping my distance from women's feelings." Even as the words come out of my mouth, I think of Emmy. But knowing someone over a phone, and hearing them cry and cheering them up, is different. "But you're you," I tell Beau.

He frowns. "I'd have to pick someone Gwen got along with

though. I don't plan on losing her or any of my friends because they don't like my business wife."

"Yeah, definitely be careful. You'd have to find someone for whom the arrangement was equally beneficial. How long do you have to stay married?"

"I have no idea. The stipulation is I have to get married. It doesn't say stay married."

I shake my head again at my grandfather's perverse sense of humor. "He was a real piece of work."

"Grandfather? Yeah, he was. But Suzy and I were talking about it. Look at us. Here you are in Charleston. Grandmother is trying to make nice, which she never did before. And planning a wedding? Two weddings? That's going to require everyone to talk to each other. He might have been a sadistic son of a bitch, but he sure knew how to get us all in a room together to sort all our shit out."

"True."

We hit Broad Street and Beau points left. "Let's swing into the office."

* * *

AT THE MONTGOMERY offices I see the two accountants I've already met and also meet some other support staff. Then after an hour I say my goodbyes to Beau and walk back to Emmy's. If I ever move to Charleston, I'll definitely look at living in the French Quarter. I love this part of the city. Ha, city, not town. I catch myself. With a smile, I pull the silent phone out of my back pocket even though I know it hasn't buzzed just as it vibrates.

My pulse spikes.

But it's a text from Annie.

ANNIE: *Have fun tonight at Django. I'm so jealous, can't wait to dance the baby weight off with you and Armand. Have a shot for me!*

I GUESS Annie still doesn't know Emmy doesn't have her phone and is stuck in New York. I realize I never forwarded Annie's contact info when Emmy asked me. I do it now while I'm thinking about it.

The hotel told me Emmy left this morning. I haven't told her I know this, but it made me think she might be coming back today. Surely if she is she'd have let me know. I'm staying in her place after all.

I give in to curiosity and pull up the *Find My iPhone* screen on my laptop. I log in and wait as it zeros in on a map of the New York area. I zoom in all the way and I'm super aware of my heart beating heavier in my chest. I'm not nervous. Maybe I'm—my stomach swoops.

The airport.

Last seen a few hours ago.

Emmy's coming home.

And for some reason she hasn't told me.

* * *

AFTER A QUICK SHOWER, where I'm completely incapable of shutting out thoughts about all the reasons Emmy hasn't told me she's coming home, I brush my teeth then wrap a towel around my waist and jog down the stairs to the stackable washer and dryer in a cabinet by the kitchen area. I open the dryer and pull my clothes out, hastily taking them back upstairs and dumping them on the bed. Then I pull on a clean pair of boxers and jeans. I'll have to re-wear a white button-down shirt to go with the jacket I need to wear to dinner. I roll up all my other clean clothes into my suitcase, in case I have to vacate her cottage, but God knows where I'll stay.

I slip on my jacket and check my watch. There's just enough time to knock on Armand's door before I have to leave for dinner.

Why does it bother me so much? I'm completely off-balance. I should be happy I'll get my phone back.

Last night has crept into my mind so often today that just the sound of her voice on the phone earlier gave me a semi.

Emmy hasn't read anything more into our call last night than what it was. I don't think. But what was it exactly? I'm not sure I know. It felt exhilarating and terrifying all at once. As soon as it was over, my main fear was that Emmy would retreat. And I hung on to make sure she didn't. If that had been two people hooking up in real life last night, my main fear would have been how to leave. I would have been out the door so fast, I'd have left a scorch mark on the carpet.

The fact I'm still thinking about it should bother me, except I'm relieved it's taken my mind off the fact I have to face Isabel Montgomery this evening.

I leave the cottage and head to Armand's. He'd mentioned he lives above the café, so I head to the fire escape stairs on the side of his building and knock on his door.

"Trystan," he greets me, surprised. "Everything okay at the cottage?"

"Yeah, I think so. Can I come in for a second? I can't stay long."

We shake hands and he steps back. "*Si, si,*" he says and offers me a seat.

"How was business today?"

"Good. It's always good. I'm lucky. Can I offer you a *cerveza?*"

I put my palm up. "I'm good. I—" This is stupid—sitting here ferreting out info about a girl like I have a crush or something.

Shit.

Of course I have a crush. That much is pretty clear. I stand up.

I'll be late if I don't leave now. "Is Emmy coming back to Charleston tonight? She hasn't told me, and I feel like she should have her cottage back if she is."

Armand looks conflicted. "*Si*," he says. "She is coming back. But she said you must stay at her cottage, she made another plan."

My stomach clenches. She didn't tell *me* that. I look around. It doesn't seem like a big enough apartment to have guests. Maybe she's staying with Annie or something. "Okay, well. Thanks." I stand. "Oh, I need to buy a bottle of wine. Can you direct me?"

Armand gives me instructions as he sees me to the door. "See you, Trystan."

"Bye." Lifting a hand, I give him a short wave and leave.

29

TRYSTAN

"Grandmother has had a few too many G and T's." Beau greets me at the front door of the Montgomery home on East Battery.

I shake his hand in greeting and raise my eyebrows. I'm sure it's a stressful prospect to have me over for dinner, but I kind of wish if it was such a hardship the invitation hadn't been offered. I greet Magda, who offers to take my jacket. Beau looks me up and down.

"Jeans and no tie? Leave the jacket on."

I apologize to Magda and follow Beau through a wide wallpapered entryway and to the right into a paneled sitting room. Isabel rises from an armchair facing the doorway as I enter. Suzy and Robert get up from a sofa. I stop and take in my surroundings. Everything is dark and heavily decorated. It feels familiar as if I should remember it but distant because it didn't feel this oppressive when I was thirteen. Or perhaps I wasn't tuned in to the heaviness of family dynamics back then.

"Isabel," I say. "Thank you for having me to dinner." I step forward and take her hand, and then because I'm in her home, I move farther forward and kiss her cheek and hand her the wine.

She pats my arm and swallows heavily. "Thank you for accepting the invitation," she says.

I greet Suzy, who hugs me with a smile, and shake hands with my uncle.

"So have you given any thought to moving down here from Yankeeville?" Robert asks as we move to the dining room.

* * *

THE DINNER SOUNDTRACK consists of small talk and discussion about the food, the weather, real estate development in the city, and of course new restaurants. Immediately, this makes me think of Emmy.

No one asks me about my life in New York. It's almost as if I'm a blank slate in this room, and I can't figure out if that's a good thing or a dismissal of everything I built and accomplished outside of their control.

By the main course, my collar, despite no tie, feels tight. I reach for my wine and take a large sip. It doesn't matter what Emmy said about family, I'm not used to this. I wish I could pretend they were simply business associates at a business dinner, but my compartmentalizing skill has deserted me.

"So what did you think of the properties we've seen so far?" Robert asks me, and everyone turns to look at me.

"Honestly," I say, "it's been great to see they are all stable and solid investments. But I'm in the middle of selling my own company, so I have a lot on my mind. As soon as I return to New York and concluded that sale, I'll be better able to focus on the project down here." I don't mean to sound dismissive, but I'm feeling out of sorts. I feel raw.

I stand abruptly. "Please excuse me," I say and head to the hall where I saw a bathroom and absently scroll through the messages on Emmy's phone again. *Django*. A nightclub? She still hasn't told me she's back. I decide to be direct. Let her lie or outright ignore me. I need to know.

ARE YOU BACK IN CHARLESTON?

WHEN I SEE the dots that she's responding, I lean my forearm against the wallpapered bathroom wall and rest my head.

EMMY: *Yes. But your phone was dead and I couldn't tell you. Sorry.*

I'M NOT sure I believe that's the reason she's been distant today, but I decide to play it cool. I feel uncomfortable enough as it is being here. I don't need Emmy brushing me off too.

SO TOMORROW WE'LL *meet up and trade phones. Oh by the way, you should know I'm following your advice tonight.*

EMMY: *What about?*

GETTING TO KNOW MY FAMILY.

EMMY: *Good luck. No matter how much they've upset you, family is precious.*

I SNORT. But then grin as I see her next text.

EMMY: *But also, take no shit. Gotta go.*

FEELING BETTER that we've at least communicated, I take a leak, then wash my hands and splash water on my face. Taking a deep breath I pull myself together and open the door.

"Trystan," Isabel says as I exit the bathroom. I start in surprise at her presence. "Let's you and I go and have a chat." She turns.

I follow her stiff back down the hall.

She enters a small office off a large kitchen. It's a lighter room, all the furnishings done in pale greens and pinks and pale wood. Seeing me look around, she rolls her eyes. "Suzy insisted on decorating this."

"I like it," I say.

"Me too." She gestures to two small club chairs.

We both sit down—me playing at relaxed with an ankle propped over a knee and Isabel perched on the edge of her seat with her hands clasped.

"Trystan," she begins, her voice cracking. Then her face creases.

Oh shit. My eyes search wildly around the room, thankfully finding a box of tissues. The box is upholstered in fabric matching the throw pillows. Suzy may have gone a little far.

"Thank you." Isabel sniffs as she takes a tissue. "Apologies. It's still so raw. And seeing you . . ."

I sit quietly, waiting.

Then she stands abruptly and goes to a small writing desk. Opening a drawer, she pulls out a stack of letters.

"I wrote to her." She looks at me and answers my unspoken question. "Savannah."

Hearing my mother's name from her lips is a shock, just like it was from Robert.

"They were all returned." She slaps the letters down on a small table. "I may have made mistakes, but she didn't want me in your lives."

My throat is closed, and I sit utterly still.

"I asked your grandfather to contact you in New York." She looks at me. "He was reticent. I thought he could speak to you on a . . . business level."

Isabel returns to her seat next to me and lowers her thin, bony frame while holding on to the chair arm. "But of course, you reacted as he would have. He was so proud of you."

I can't prevent the sharp jerk of my head.

"Yes," she says. "He was aware of what you were doing. But then . . ."

I lean forward, my forearms on my knees.

"Well, then he got sick. His heart was weak. We planned—he planned—well . . . it doesn't matter now, does it?" Her voice is brittle.

I inhale and lean back against the seat. I probably would have enjoyed getting to know my grandfather as an adult.

"All that said," Isabel continues, her voice wobbling, "I made mistakes, dreadful, heart-shattering mistakes . . . but I tried to fix them. Maybe not hard enough. I guess we were both too stubborn to make things right before it was too late. But please"—she looks at me, her watery blue eyes fixing on mine—"never think you don't have a family. That you don't belong. We're honored to have you be a Montgomery."

I sit forward. Then unsatisfied with that, I stand. I walk to the table and rest a finger on the stack of letters then turn. The door. God, I want to leave so badly. I look back at Isabel. She looks so hopeful. Sad too.

"It'll take some getting used to." I finger a paperweight next to the letters, picking it up and hefting the weight. "I've never had a family."

Isabel's eyes flicker at my statement.

"But rest assured," I go on, "I have no intention of being unreasonable regarding your income."

"That's not—Oh, Trystan. That's not why I wanted to talk to you."

I manage a humorless puff of laughter and replace the paperweight.

"Of course. I just wanted to make sure you knew that."

She purses her lips.

"I'm going to go," I tell her then look at the letters. There are only a few. I'm not sure how hard she tried, or if I believe her, but I guess I'll have to see for myself. "Can I take these?"

Isabel stands, hiding any offense well. "Of course. Though, Trystan"—she wrings her hands—"I hope you know you always have a home here. I hope you do come here. Back to Charleston. The company could use your presence. I can't help thinking Wilson had a greater plan in death than he did in life."

"Thank you for dinner." I smile stiffly. "Please give my excuses, but I need some air."

"Of course."

Twenty steps later and I'm on the sidewalk of East Battery. I follow the salt breeze to the left and make my way across the park I was in that very morning and finally reach the water's edge. Standing at the metal railing on the seawall, I breathe in deeply, trying to fill my lungs. I think I do believe my grandmother. And none of us can say we've lived our lives without regrets. But how big are they? And how long until you realize and start trying to make better choices?

MY PHONE BUZZES.

IT'S A MESSAGE FROM EMMY, but it begins:

THIS IS ARMAND . . .

30

EMMY

*T*he cab from the airport pulled up at the corner of my pedestrian-only street. I'd had the driver stop at the other end so I didn't have to walk past my own place to Armand's, but still I peered warily ahead. To think I'd left here at the beginning of the week totally clueless at how sideways life could go so fast. Four days and three nights later and everything looked the same, but I was a completely different person.

I hadn't even gotten laid, but I felt vulnerable and a bit screwed over. How weird was that? Had we had sex? Did phone sex count? It felt like it did. If I was honest with myself, it felt categorically like the most intimate sex I'd ever had.

My wheelie bag made an absolute racket as I walked up the road, bouncing along the stones, but it drowned out the fact my heart was pounding in my ears. I started jogging as the gate to Armand's place around the side of his little café came into view, and I didn't stop until I'd made it through his gate, past his little courtyard, up the iron stairs that hugged the building and was banging on the door to his studio apartment.

I'd barely gotten in three knocks before the door swung inward.

"Something chasing you?" Armand asked, his eyes wide and amused.

"Just my self-esteem," I grumbled as I breezed inside. I let go of my bag and went straight to his French doors with the Juliette balcony that looked over the street. Sweeping my gaze left and right and not seeing anyone but a group of tourists outside the art gallery four doors down, I breathed out a huge sigh of relief.

"Is it out there?" Armand asked, settling himself onto the corner of his futon he'd probably gotten up from to answer the door. He was in jeans and a black button down and looked great —already dressed for our night out.

"No," I answered and turned back to the room.

He was drinking a cup of something with one leg propped up, ankle over knee. "Trystan came by. You just missed him."

I turned sharply. "He did? Did you tell him I was coming home?"

"He asked as if he already knew."

I swallowed. "What did you tell him?"

"When I realized he'd figured out you might be coming home, I told him he could stay at your place, that you made other arrangements."

"Oh. Good."

"I told Annie we were going out dancing tonight. Maybe she texted you and he saw it. I don't know. I forgot to tell her about the phone situation."

So all my deciding what to tell him was for nothing. And now I felt horrible as if I'd lied.

"Emmy, he seemed like a guy who just got brushed off by a girl he really liked. He seemed . . . disappointed."

I refused to pay attention to the brick forming in my stomach that felt a lot like guilt. As if I'd done something wrong. "What else did he say? He must have said something else for you to think that."

"He didn't. But I also know *you, mi amor.*"

"What's that supposed to mean?"

"I think something happened between you two. And I think *you* got scared. Things maybe happening too fast?"

"That's not fair. And not true! I'm not the one with the intimacy problem."

Armand took a calm sip from his cup. "If you say so."

"Ugh!" I threw my hands up. "That's not fair. You don't know what happened."

"You could tell me."

I flounced across the room and landed on the other end of the futon. "I'd rather not. And I'm not even sure if I can explain it."

"Okay. So we don't talk about it. Fine."

"Good," I said. But I went and plugged in Trystan's phone. I'd have to face him sooner or later and return his phone. "So what's the plan tonight? Oh no!"

"What?"

"I have nothing to wear. As it is I'm a day past my three-day travel wardrobe." Getting anything from my house was out of the question. "Do we have time for me to throw everything in your washer and dryer? I'll wear jeans and my black cami."

"We'll coordinate." Armand gestured down his body.

I had a quick flashback to one night a year ago when we'd all gone clubbing and crashed here because my place was rented. "Did Annie ever pick up her dress?" It wasn't like she'd have been able to wear it while pregnant.

Armand got up and opened the laundry cupboard doors. Hanging on the inside of the right hand door was a little black dress. "I can't tell you how many questions I get about this thing when people stay over. I'm almost sad to let you wear it."

I laughed. "I can give it back when I'm done."

"See that you do. And don't tell Annie I still have it."

"Weirdo."

"That's me. Now go shower and get ready, then I'll tell you all about my mother coming from Colombia to visit this Christmas.

If you're still single by then"—he nodded to the charging phone —"you may need to pretend to be my girlfriend."

"Yikes. And don't look at Trystan's cell phone like that."

"Like what?"

"Like it has something to do with my single status."

"Doesn't it?"

"Ha. No." I pursed my lips. "Maybe?"

Armand's eyebrows popped up.

"Kidding," I grumbled. "Kind of." I slunk over to the coffee table and picked up the device. Was it weird that when I looked at it, I was aware of a low-grade fever bubbling away inside me? As the phone came to life, there were texts on the home screen and my insides swooped like a rollercoaster. "Shit."

They were from earlier today.

Armand cackled. "Your hand is shaking."

"It's not," I argued.

"*Mi amor*. What happened between you two?"

"Honestly, Armand. I'm really not sure what the hell happened this week. Let's just go out. I'm going to dance my ass off and have a good time."

I laid the phone gingerly on the table.

"Okay, *mi amor*. Go get ready." He pressed a kiss to my forehead.

I showered quickly in Armand's tiny bathroom, careful to keep my hair dry, then put makeup on and slipped on Annie's short black dress. I'd have to wear my flats though, which sucked.

A knock came at the door.

"Yes?"

The door opened and a pair of strappy black high-heeled sandals came through the gap, hanging off Armand's fingers. "She left these too after the Cinco De Mayo party."

"God, I'll kill myself in those. No way."

"Come on!"

"No, they're too big anyway."

"Try them."

"You're a bully."

"I'm a good friend is what I am."

"Argh. Fine. Give them to me." I took them and opened the door to pass him.

"Ooh la la! You look good."

"Whatever I look, it will have to do."

Armand smiled.

"You're being weird, you know that?"

"I'm always weird. It's why you love me."

"Meh," I tossed out over my shoulder as I went to the couch so I could sit and tie on the female torture devices. The phone still sat charging on the side table.

* * *

THE FIRST TEXT from Trystan came in as we were leaving to head to *Django*.

SUIT MONKEY: *Are you back in Charleston?*

MY PULSE SPED UP.

"What is it?"

"It's him," I told Armand. "My instinct wants to respond but . . ."

"Instinct? Your heart? Your gut?"

"You're saying I should?" I asked.

"Emmy, I have no idea what the guy did wrong—"

"He didn't do anything wrong. But he might *be* wrong."

"Okay, but I can't help because you won't talk about it. So I don't know what you should do. But he's got you tied up, and you're no fun right now because you are not here. You are wherever he is."

"Which is ironic because he's likely less than three hundred yards away from us."

"*Exactamente.* This is crazy."

I let out a sigh and texted him back.

YES. *But your phone was dead and I couldn't tell you. Sorry.*

ANOTHER TEXT CAME through as I negotiated the cobblestones in Annie's shoes.

SUIT MONKEY: *Tomorrow we'll meet up and trade phones. You should know I'm following your advice tonight.*

WHAT ABOUT?

SUIT MONKEY: *Getting to know my family.*

GOOD LUCK. *No matter how much they've upset you, family is precious.*

THEN I FELT a little on my high horse.

BUT ALSO, *take no shit. Gotta go.*

ARMAND GREW EXASPERATED. "We should go home," he moaned. "Actually, better idea, let's walk back two minutes and you can have this conversation with him in person."

"No way," I said, and at that moment our Uber arrived. I shrugged at Armand then got in the back seat. "Anyway, he's with his family. I promise as soon as we get there, I'll put it away and not think about it."

He climbed in behind me, and the car began moving. "Do you want to hear from him again?"

"I—" I looked out the window as the sidewalks flashed by. "Yes. No. I don't know."

"Let me help you. The answer is yes. So stop brushing him off."

I glared at him. "He's a man-whore," I hissed.

Armand shrugged. "Why do you say that?"

Pulling up all the dating apps, I started reading them out loud. "Why does this not bother you?" I asked when I got to the end.

"Because I don't think it's a big deal. So he dates? So what? That's what normal hot-blooded single people in their thirties do. It's what *I* do."

"So you're okay if I show up sobbing into my granola in your restaurant with a broken heart," I snapped.

"Oh, *mi amor*. Listen to yourself."

"What? Okay, maybe not a broken heart, but you know what I mean. A very bruised ego. I'd like him way more than he'd like me, and then he'd be gone, and I'd be here."

"So you should stay in your safe castle with your kitty cat. No chance of getting hurt. Or having *fun*." Armand shook his head at me.

"Stop looking at me like that!" I turned my head away in irritation. "I have fun."

He shrugged. "Sure. How long has it been again?"

"Ugh. I haven't found anyone I could be bothered to get naked for." Until Trystan, I added in my head.

"Well, let's hope he's as taken with you as you seem to be with him. Because one of you needs to take the first step, and I guess it needs to be him."

* * *

THE BEAT of the Latin music spilled out onto the night air outside the club. Annie, Armand, and I had been coming to Django since we were friends in college. Being from Colombia in South America, he'd sought out any flavor that reminded him of home. But the lines on Friday and Saturday nights had become annoying. Not enough to stop coming, obviously, but still.

"Remember when this place was uncool?" Armand grumbled.

"Was just thinking the same thing. It's like when your best-kept-secret breakfast place three doors down is suddenly seven deep at the counter when you're late for work and only want a coffee." I looked at Armand pointedly and slipped my arm through his. Heads of all genders swiveled as we passed because Armand was basically a dead ringer for Enrique Iglesias with slightly longer hair.

"I told you I can have a cappuccino ready to go at the same time every morning. You just need to get into a routine."

"I know, I know." I was chronically disorganized in the mornings.

Greeting the guy who'd worked the door as long as we'd been going, we then slipped through the rope and into the darkness and the swirling sultry beat.

Keeping my promise to Armand, I handed him my phone since I had no evening purse. It lit up as he took it.

"What?" I shouted.

"Nothing," he mouthed and slipped the phone into his back pocket. Then he made a let's get drinks motion, and I followed him to the bar.

EMMY

*a*nnie, Armand, and I had decided long ago that there was no point standing around drinking fancy drinks here because you couldn't talk over the music. So we either took a shot of Patron or drank water, and then we danced. It made things easier. Armand mimed short or long with his fingers to distinguish the two drinks. I held my thumb and forefinger out in an approximation of a shot glass. Smiling and nodding at regulars we knew, I scanned the bar area. There were lots of new faces and several men looked boldly at me, trying to catch my eye. Their gazes dropped away as Armand came back to my side.

We both took a shot and made it onto the dance floor as the DJ began spinning a classic Colombian cumbia beat in with the dance music. Armand's mother had insisted he learn to dance as a child, and I for one was thankful. The man's hips did not lie. He was a sensual and beautiful creature when he danced, and he made me look freaking awesome. We swirled, sidestepped, ground together, swayed, and danced ourselves into a sweaty stupor for the next hour. We moved together so well we often drew a small crowd. It was a high like nothing else when we were absolutely nailing it like this, it was like having pure sexual heroine running through my veins. It made me feel powerful and strong.

The DJ dropped the beat and slunk into a bachata rhythm and some people we knew whooped and cheered, knowing this was our favorite. Especially because Armand was so freaking gorgeous and his hips were a continuous writhing, fluid, pulsing attraction all on their own. The bachata, to me was the sexiest Latin dance of all, maybe even over the tango. Armand and I goofed it up and over-performed for the bystanders, convincing pretty much everyone who didn't know us we'd be doing this naked later that night.

Balanced astride Armand's thigh, I let him arch me backward. I hung loose with his arm under my back even as our hips moved, my hair almost grazing the ground. He ran his hand from my throat down my front, making people hoot and whistle. My view of the club was upside down and there was a brief millisecond gap in the crowd. I swear I thought . . . my insides went into free-fall, and I lurched upward even as Armand pulled me back. He looked at me in concern, then brought his face to my ear. "What happened?" He had to almost shout in my ear.

"Trystan?" I yelled. "Behind me?"

Armand looked over my shoulder, his eyes scanning. Then he shook his head.

Weird. But our flow was compromised. I mimed I needed water, telling him he should stay. He wouldn't have a problem finding a new partner. He nodded and handed me my phone so we could find each other easily.

I wove through the people, dodging a few handsy ones who thought I might be free for a dance, and headed for the end of the bar. Out of the crowd, I appreciated the movement of air against my hot damp skin.

I managed to squeeze between two couples and nodded to the

nearest bartender to let him know I was waiting as he mixed some drinks, then I looked past him and my heart stopped.

Trystan was at the opposite end of the bar, his sharp gray gaze skewering me from twenty feet away.

I took a surprised breath, but it caught in my chest.

He was leaning forward, resting his forearms on the bar, a tumbler of amber liquid in one hand. His white shirt, poking out of the collar of his black jacket, was stark against his skin.

Oh my God, he was so damn gorgeous. Memories of his voice and the sound of his breathing as he brought me to orgasm last night streaked through my head, and my sweaty body suddenly felt too sensitive in my dress. My skin prickled. Why didn't I want to see him again? For the life of me I couldn't remember why I was avoiding him.

Then the bartender was in front of me. I shook my head to catch up with my new view and ordered water. When Trystan was in eyesight again, I saw him take a sip of his drink and then pick his phone up from the bar in front of him and type something. Then he laid it down just as my water appeared. He'd made no move to come over to where I stood, and I knew I wasn't going to go to him.

The phone in my hand vibrated. And like a perfectly trained pet, my stomach swooped. I wondered if my body was now permanently conditioned to react to phone notifications. My embarrassed feeling from waking up this morning after what we'd done had apparently evaporated.

I drank thirstily, delaying the gratification of looking to see if it was him texting me.

Trystan narrowed his eyes.

I grinned, because I couldn't help it, then looked at my phone.

Suit Monkey: *You are absolutely stunning.*

I sucked my bottom lip into my mouth, trying to play it cool, even though I felt like grinning like an idiot. I was a sweaty mess, my hair sticking to the back of my neck, probably curling at my temples, my breathing still exerted, my skin hot. He had a funny idea of stunning.

You stalking me?

Suit Monkey: *Yes.*

He lifted a shoulder in a gesture of helplessness. He typed something else into his phone.

Suit Monkey: *It's a good thing I know Armand is gay.*

I looked up at Trystan with an eyebrow cocked and wondered how long he'd been watching us and if he'd liked what he saw. I'd seen others dancing like us. I knew it was hot. I texted back as Trystan picked up his drink and took a sip.

Armand is gay?

Trystan froze mid swallow, or maybe his throat suddenly closed, because from where I was standing, he choked. A big swarthy man next to him, wearing a tank and a bandana saw what happened and gave Trystan a massive thump between the shoulder blades, causing him to lurch forward.

I slapped a hand across my mouth in alarm, even as I lost control of the giggle that burst out of me.

OMG. Are you okay? Lol

Trystan thanked the guy next to him and then looked at me, smiling and shaking his head, his eyes watering. I was still laughing, but I laid a hand to my chest indicating I was relieved he was all right. Even while he laughed, semi-embarrassed at himself, his eyes became serious.

Suit Monkey: *You and Armand?*

Never. We're friends.

Suit Monkey: *Ever?*

No.

Suit Monkey: *Almost?*

I rolled my eyes. *No!*

Suit Monkey: *Impossible. Watching you dance was the hottest thing I've ever seen. That's why I had to find a spot against the bar.*

Apart from the fact I can barely stand, I thought my hard-on might get me arrested.

It was hard not to imagine Trystan's erection, and my mind flew back to last night and knowing he was bringing himself to relief as he listened to me. God, just thinking about it for a second had me so turned on I was aching.

I licked my lips.

Suit Monkey: *Don't lick your lips. I won't be able to walk.*

I laughed.

Sorry. I was imagining your erection.

Trystan dropped his head down on the bar, earning a concerned look from his previous savior, who shook his head in despair.

God, Trystan had beautiful thick hair. I wanted to grip it in my fists. I wondered if it was soft or coarse.

The bartender popped up in front of me. "Anything else?"

"Uh," I managed, reorienting myself to time and place. "A shot of Patron for me and one for that suit monkey at the end of the bar. Thanks."

The bartender swiveled his gaze down the bar. "Lucky guy," he said and grabbed two shot glasses.

Suit Monkey: *Where'd you learn to dance like that?*

Here. Every Friday night.

A shot appeared in front of me. Then the bartender delivered one down the bar, letting Trystan know it was from me. I held mine up in a toast.

He looked at me, bemused. Then he lifted his shot glass and we saluted each other. I slammed the drink back and grimaced against the fiery burn.

Suit Monkey: *That would have tasted better if I could have licked the sweat off your skin first.*

My mouth dropped open. The lines of text sank through my stomach and lassoed my libido. It wasn't possible to be this aroused by someone surely?

Why are you here, Trystan?

Suit Monkey: *You really asking me that?*

You want your phone back.

Suit Monkey: *That's not why I'm here.*

I blew out a breath and summoned the common sense that had made me walk out of his hotel room this morning. I willed it to stamp all over my flaming libido and snuff it out.

I can't be one of your hookups.

A crease crossed his brow. His mouth flattened to a serious line. He closed his eyes. When he opened them his gaze locked with mine. The lights at the bar accentuated the piercing gray-blue. I wondered what they really looked like close up. Would I see all the shades of blue and silver?

Suit Monkey: *I've thought of nothing but you all day.*

I took a deep breath. *Same. But . . .*

Suit Monkey: *Are you scared what we have won't translate to real life?*

He was frowning—legitimately trying to understand my hesitation. I guess he was used to these situations being certain. Uncomplicated. Easy.

I wasn't. So far from it. I couldn't do one-night stands. I'd tried a couple of times at college between boyfriends, and I simply wasn't wired to lay myself bare with someone, no pun intended, and find I'd left them with a part of myself they had no care for. I felt like I'd lost something valuable, something I could never get back. I realized it was a little how I'd felt this morning. No matter how much I liked this man, I simply didn't think I was designed for the likes of him. It wasn't that I had to be in a long-term relationship with men I slept with necessarily, I just needed to know I wasn't only a vagina.

Trystan: *Wish I knew what was going through your head right now.*

I'm thinking how much my feet are killing me in these high heels. I typed out the lie and hit send.

His lips quirked. Trystan: *I bet. Please. Talk to me.* He wasn't buying it. My shoulders dropped, and I decided to be honest.

I woke up in a hotel where I realized all your hookups happen. I felt like I was another one. I didn't like it. I felt manipulated. Like you planned it.

His gaze flew up to mine, and I lifted a shoulder.

Trystan: *God, Emmy. No.*

He scrubbed a hand down his face then straightened from the bar for a second like he was going to come to me.

I stiffened.

Don't I typed.

Suit Monkey: *Do you think we'll ever be able to talk to each other face to face?*

I don't know. I feel like I can tell you anything like this. Like it isn't real.

Suit Monkey: *You don't want this to be real?*

I don't know.

Suit Monkey: *So tell me something you can't say to my face. Because I really like you, Emmy.*

I like you too.

Suit Monkey: *But you think I'm a bad guy.*

No. Yes. Maybe?

Trystan's mouth pressed together.

Suit Monkey: *Because I woke up on top of the world this morning. Even P!nk is starting to grow on me.*

My chest grew tight as my heart felt as if it swelled. This guy was good. *You listening to my music?*

Suit Monkey: *There's a guy behind you who has memorized the shape of your arse. He's about two seconds from building up the nerve to touch you. Now might be a good time to employ those heels.*

I straightened and looked over my shoulder. Sure enough there was guy right behind me, and his face broke into a leery grin, eyes bright with imbibed courage.

"Sorry, I'm not interested," I yelled at him over the music, shaking my head.

He stepped closer, his hand coming around my waist, and my heart leapt to my throat.

Then he wasn't there, having been jerked back by his collar. The guy lost his balance and stumbled, knocking into several people and their drinks, and Trystan who hadn't let go, helped him right himself.

They exchanged words I couldn't hear. Then Trystan was in front of me, and the man was forgotten.

He looked down and pinned me with his intense stare, and my pulse pounded in my throat as I was consumed by it. I remembered the energy that had oozed off him at the airport. This simply wasn't a man anyone could ignore. I wanted to breathe him in, but the sweating humanity of the crowded club made it impossible unless I touched him. He was taller than I remembered.

We were inches away from each other. One bump by the crowd and I'd be plastered against him.

Around us people communicated by getting close and pressing their mouths to each other's ears. I envied their ease. That was too monumental for us.

"Emmy." His mouth formed the word, but I couldn't hear it.

"Thank you," I returned. His eyes watched my mouth.

So many things seemed to pass over his face—concern, questions, happiness . . . hunger. He also looked a little stunned. I guess I understood that feeling. Less than a week ago I didn't know he existed, and now I could barely believe how intense it had gotten between us.

Unsure of what might happen next, I held my breath. I looked down from his shirt and jacket to his jeans.

You're only wearing half a suit, I texted and narrowed my eyes at him, accusing him of not living up to his suit monkey persona. Last night's bare-chested display notwithstanding.

His eyes roamed my bare legs down to Annie's high-heeled lace up shoes.

Suit Monkey: *You're only wearing half a dress*

Then he took a step back from me, and I almost swayed toward him. His eyes didn't miss it.

He typed something into his phone.

Suit Monkey: *I want to touch you.*

Suit Monkey: *But I don't want the first time to be here.*

Suit Monkey: *You should come home to your own bed tonight.*

Will you be in it?

Suit Monkey: *I'd like to be.*

God, I wanted him to be too. I was frozen with indecision. On the one hand, I hadn't had this much chemistry with someone in forever. Or ever. And I didn't mean just the sexual kind, though that had been incendiary. On the other hand . . . one-night stand.

Was this what it would be? Maybe I'd only ever had the wrong kind. Of course, I wasn't dumb enough not to realize that part of me *hoped* it wasn't a one-night stand, and that was the part I had to be most careful of.

Suit Monkey: *We'll always wonder.*

I nodded. *Yes.*

He closed his eyes. Then he typed with a cheeky smirk.

Suit Monkey: *What if I'm too scared of the ghost to stay there alone tonight?*

Nice try.

Suit Monkey: *For what it's worth, I don't think one night would have been enough for us anyway . . .*

Armand chose that moment to materialize, sweaty and out of breath, his hair slicked back.

Trystan shook his hand, and I was jealous of the touch. Then Trystan gave me a long look and held out the phone in his hand.

I looked down at it, then back at him.

He was letting me go.

My breath left me. My stomach clenched, and I bit my lips

between my teeth. God, I suddenly wanted to cry for some reason. Slowly I reached out with my fingertips, careful not to touch his hand, and took my phone.

Then I held out his to him. He took it.

Finally he took his eyes off me, nodded to Armand, and evaporated into the crowd.

TRYSTAN

*T*here's an uncharacteristic chill in the breeze tonight after the muggy heat of the last few days, and I savor it as I exit the cab and walk the cobblestone alleyway. I'm disappointed as I head to Emmy's little home from the club. There's no denying it. But a part of me also recognizes this is my pattern—losing myself in a willing female for a few hours to let go of the day's stressors. It's not every day, I know that. It's not like I have a sexual compulsion, but when Emmy said she'd felt like I'd manipulated her the night before, it hit me hard.

In retrospect, leaving dinner at the Montgomery home and seeking out Emmy was in line with my MO.

Even if it was Armand who asked me to come and sort things out with Emmy, it still doesn't sit comfortably. She'd been right to turn me down. But shit, she was stunning. Watching her dance . . . I almost groan out loud again as I remember. Why had I thought Armand was gay? He said he was meeting a guy the other day and I just assumed. Which was weird for me, and I recognize it must have been wishful thinking back then. A few days ago felt like weeks.

I negotiate the courtyard and unlock the antique front door. I hit all the switches to blaze the place with light and avoid any cats or ghosts sneaking up on me. It strikes me that staying here this last night before I go back to New York feels like the last tie to Emmy. I no longer have her phone, and she doesn't have mine. I hadn't realized what an unspoken connection, a feeling of attachment, that had brought. The idea leaves me with a feeling of emptiness I don't like.

I take off my jacket and hang it on the back of the dining room chair, grab a glass of water, and then reluctantly turn some of the lights off so I can head to bed.

When I get to the top of the stairs I see the cat, sitting with its black and white back to me, tail swishing as it stares at an empty corner of the bedroom.

Oh, fuck no.

I pull out my phone to ask Emmy what she does in these situations but then stop. My hand drops. It's going to seem like I can't take a *no* from a woman. I'm a lot of things, but I'm not a sexually aggressive jerk.

Backing silently down the stairs, I eye the couch. There's a throw draped over the arm and the cushions look all right to sleep on. It's not ideal but it will have to do for now. It's not that I'm scared, I tell myself. But the cat is freaking weird, staring at an empty corner. I've seen the movie *Ghost*, I know the cat freaks out when it sees Patrick Swayze. Who's dead, by the way. Anyone would feel nervous. But I do feel like a bit of an idiot as I unbutton my shirt and take it off. My own phone is loudly silent and devoid of app notifications that I know Emmy disabled, and it doesn't bother me as much as I expect.

Perhaps having Emmy's phone detoxed me somewhat.

Turning on a small lamp, I slip off my shoes and socks and roam over to Emmy's bookshelf. I know she'd mentioned haiku, but I didn't realize what a fan of poetry she is. There's a well-thumbed book by someone named Rupi, so I pick it up. Under it there's a photo wallet. Curiosity gets the better of me and I pick it up. It probably holds a couple dozen four by sixes, though it's not full. I open it and almost laugh out loud at a teenage Emmy, braces and round cheeks. The pictures are faded, but there are some with her and an older couple and some with them and someone who I now assume is David, based on her Instagram. There are no pictures of her as a baby or anything. I turn to the next one and see Emmy at a graduation with the older couple. High school it looks like. Then there's nothing. I put the album down where I found it.

I take the book of poetry to the couch. Within minutes my eyes are heavy. The cat comes slinking silently down the stairs. Either the ghost is gone or the cat got bored.

Something jars me awake. I blink and realize I fell asleep. Reaching for my phone, I see it's after one in the morning. It vibrates in my hand as I look at it.

Suit Monkey: *You awake?*

Who the hell is Suit Monkey?

Who is this?

Suit Monkey: *Emmy.*

I laugh. Then change the contact to Emmy. *You called me suit monkey?*

Emmy: *Sorry. But if the suit fits . . .*

I wish you were here. Immediately I wish I could unsend it. It's my sleepiness that's causing me not to think straight.

There's a knock at the front door and I sit up straight, suddenly wide awake.

Is that you or the ghost?

I head to the front door.

Emmy: *The ghost I guess.*

I swing open the door and Emmy is standing there, her red hair tumbling wildly over a shoulder. Her mouth twitches, and her blue eyes dart nervously to the side and back.

I guess I'm at a loss for words because I stare at her, tracing her from top to toe with my eyes. She's changed into an oversized T-shirt, yoga pants, and silver flip flops. Her toenails are no longer pink like her bikini picture I notice, but turquoise. Not that I expected them to be the same as in the picture.

She drags her eyes away from my chest and then types into her phone, her lower lip nervously pulled between her teeth.

Emmy: *I couldn't sleep.*

My insides have clenched tight, and I have a rock in my throat. Whatever it is I'm feeling, it's unfamiliar, but it's definitely okay. I grin. I think. I can't be sure.

I step back and to the side, silently asking her to come in.

She dips her chin, her gaze lowering as she steps past me. She smells like piney shower wash and not like I imagined from her sheets. She must have showered the sweat off her after the club. That makes me sad for some reason.

Inside, she takes in the couch setup and the book of poetry on the ground. The bang that must have woken me.

Of course, a low rumble starts up as the cat realizes she's home and slinks out of nowhere to noodle around her ankles and purr loudly. She crouches and scratches it between the ears. "Hey, buddy," she croons, and I realize it's the first time I've heard her speak in real life.

"What's his name?" I ask.

"Tuna," she says. "If you ever smell his breath, you'll understand."

"If it's anything like the smell that comes out the other end of him, I do."

She laughs softly.

"Can you ask him if the ghost is gone from upstairs?" I grin.

She stands. "Is that what this was about?" She motions to the couch and blanket with an amused expression.

"He was staring at the corner of your bedroom, by the window."

"It was probably a mosquito. He watches them like Mr. Miyagi watches flies."

"Oh." I reach up and grab a fistful of my hair. I do believe I feel nervous.

She licks her lips and types something into her phone.

Emmy: *Is it okay that I'm here? I can go.*

Shit, no. "Don't leave," I say aloud. I'm not sure what to do though. The tension between us is only going one way, but a part of me doesn't want it to. I want to hold on to this feeling forever. This dance on a knife's edge. A world full of possibility. It's intoxicating.

Emmy's cheeks fill with heightened color.

Emmy: *So do you only talk dirty over the phone or can you do it in real life too?*

I exhale sharply as arousal detonates low and deep, carving its way down through my body and possibly branding me permanently. For a smartish guy it takes me more seconds than it should to penetrate she's propositioning me.

"Get upstairs, Emmy." My voice is low and rough to my own ears. My legs feel weak.

Her face flushes a deeper red and God, I wonder if she flushes all over her skin. She turns slowly and moves to the stairs. I start after her, and she squeaks and starts sprinting, taking the stairs two at a time.

I race after her.

She's stopped, facing the bed. But then she turns, chest heaving, eyes shining with laughter at the chase, and kicks off her flip-flops.

I walk to the window and lower the blinds and then snap the bedside light on, bathing us in a warm glow. God, my heart is pounding so hard, I can hardly breathe. I want, and I don't want this so badly.

"Jesus, Emmy." I run a thumb over my bottom lip. I'm lost. Everything seems so monumental. So confusing. "I'm leaving to go back to New York tomorrow," I say.

She nods though something flickers over her expression.

"I know."

I'm starting to feel like this was a bad idea. That I might start something I can't finish.

Or won't finish.

"You don't want to do this, do you?" she asks, looking disappointed.

I blow out a breath and stuff my fingers in my jeans pockets to keep them from reaching for her. I do. I want it so badly. I'm selfish like that. "Come touch me. Put your hand on my chest, Emmy."

She hesitates, and I wait. Then she steps up close. After a beat, she lifts her palm and lays it right in the middle, touching me for the first time. I want to close my eyes with the relief of it but can't take them off her.

Her hand is soft and cool. I imagine my skin feels heated and feverish to her, my heart beat heavy and loaded.

"Of course, I want this," I manage and revel in the feel of her hand on me. My palms itch to return the gesture. To feel her skin, the texture of it, the weight of her breasts, the tightness of her nipples. "You have freckles," I whisper as I stare down at her perfect skin, and her blue eyes go deep, dark.

"You have gold in your eyes," she says, surprised. "I thought I'd see silver."

"Are you sure about this?" I ask. I want her so much. I want to sink my hands in her hair, to touch her everywhere, taste her everywhere. And I want to not think about tomorrow, about what it will be like between us after we've exorcised days of foreplay.

"We're overthinking it," she says and cocks an eyebrow. "At least, *you* are. Don't." Her palm on my bare chest starts a slow descent. She licks her lips. "I'm sure. Really sure. I promise."

My stomach muscles tense, and I narrow my gaze on her saucy expression. My cock is aching against my jeans. I feel as if I have to remember how to breathe as her hand slips lower.

33

TRYSTAN

*E*mmy in the dim light of her bedroom, her hair wild about her shoulders and eyes bright, is absolutely stunning.

"But you realize I'm staying the whole night, right?" she says.

"What?"

"This is *my* bed, and I'm not giving it up. Can you handle that?"

Her hand makes it to my groin and curves around my erection through my jeans.

"As long as you can handle *that,*" I choke out in a half laugh.

"The general? He feels impressive, I'll admit. But"—she lifts a shoulder—"it's what you do with him that counts. You don't want him to be overshadowed by your massive ego."

I snort with laughter, my shoulders shaking. Then before I overthink it, I sink to my knees.

Emmy catches her breath at my sudden move.

I start at her ankles and run my hands up the outside of her legs, over her yoga pants. My fingers reach her thighs and continue under her oversized T-shirt, and my eyes flick up and hold her gaze as I reach the waistband, my fingers curling in against her warm, soft skin.

Her mouth parts. Her hands slip into my hair and scrape my scalp. "Your hair is so soft," she whispers.

Goosebumps break out across my body.

And I start to pull her stretchy pants down her legs, hoping to hell I've taken her underwear too, if she's wearing any. Closing my eyes, I inhale, getting a mainline hit of her scent. My next breath comes out as a groan, and I yank the pants down over her feet, and she frees one then the other, gripping my hair for balance. In the bunched material I see a scrap of pink. I'm frantic and crazed by the thought of her, the smell of her. My skin feels too tight for my body.

My hands race back up her legs.

"Trystan," she says on a shocked breath as I push her T-shirt up and feast my eyes on her.

"Your natural hair color, you never did confirm it for me," I say on a rush, pressing my nose against her. I risk a flick of my tongue, hitting slick salt and making her gasp. "God, your taste." Then I'm grabbing her around the legs and lifting, tossing her back onto the bed.

"Impatient, are you?" She's laughing but her voice is shaking.

"You have no idea." My voice isn't much better. I grab her ankles and urge her onto her stomach. "Your arse is spectacular." I crawl up her body, my hands skimming, my mouth sliding up to a firm, round butt cheek. I grab and squeeze and can't help the open-mouthed kiss and nip of my teeth.

She squeals.

"God, I love your body." I groan and push her T-shirt impatiently up her back. She helps me and pulls it over her head, though its trapped beneath her. My fingers nimbly unclasp her bra, and I push the straps apart. Suspended on my hands and knees over her, I drop my mouth to her back, running my tongue up her spine, gratified as goosebumps break out. Her skin is salty, and her breathing is hard. I know if I slip my fingers between her legs she'll be soaked. What did she say last night? Warm. Slippery. I groan in remembrance. God, a few flicks of the buttons on my jeans and I could be sinking inside of her. The thought is overwhelming, and I grit my teeth.

But there's something I need to do first.

"Turn over, Emmy." Up on my knees, I slip my arm under her torso to help her, and she turns between my legs, freeing herself from her T-shirt and bra. Her red hair is streaked across her face, and I gently brush it off her flushed cheeks. It's all I can do not to let my eyes drink from the sight of her glorious pale breasts topped with pink nipples. She'd told me they were pink last night, and I'd imagined them, but nothing prepared me for how gorgeous she is. I pull my gaze back up to her face with huge effort. Her eyes are open, honest, dark with arousal, and they look from my eyes to my mouth.

Hands grip my biceps.

Her lips are parted, and I reach up and run my fingertips over her full bottom lip. It's pale pink, matching her nipples, and fitting in with her makeup-free face.

"Your mouth," I whisper. "It's fucking stunning."

I've inhaled her scent, made her come, made her laugh, heard her cry, and had a brief taste. But I've never kissed her mouth. I guess we've done everything backward.

I move slowly, dropping my face closer until our eye contact has to break. It feels monumental to kiss her for the first time. Grazing my lips slowly across hers, I repeat the action, soft, sliding.

Her hands squeeze my arms. Her lips open more, moving over mine in response, beginning to close and open softly, repeatedly, as if tasting me. Deciding. Then firmer like they were always meant to move with mine.

It's a game of parry and retreat, of languidly taking our time, reveling in the sensation of our lips together, and I could play it forever. But I want more, and I lick her pouty bottom lip on my next pass, getting a hint of sweetness and mint. On a sigh, her lips part and her tongue slides against mine.

The action detonates a new, fiercer wave of need through me, causing a desperate sound I've never heard before to rumble through my chest. I open my mouth farther. Dip into hers deeper. I take and taste, my tongue and my lips moving faster, thirstier, one hand holding her jaw, the other keeping my body elevated and at bay when all I want to do is slam myself against her, into her.

But she's taking from me too. Her hands are no longer holding my arms but are on my head, and she's grabbing on to me like I might take my mouth away. I have no intention of ever stopping. Kissing Emmy is delicious and addictive. It's decadent and desperate. Kissing has never been so necessary. A part of me wishes we could do nothing but this.

But every move of our mouths slips us gradually from discovery to greed. Feeding a fire. A hunger without end. And before long I can't keep my body from settling over hers. The feel of her skin against my bare chest is incredible, and we both moan at the contact. Apparently it's not close enough because she presses up against me, her hips moving against my erection.

Aware I'm still in my jeans and could hurt her, I reluctantly slow down, my mouth moves over her jaw and neck, and I bury my nose against her neck and breathe in. The elusive scent of an exotic flower and a hint of vanilla is now my drug of choice, breathing it in is what I do now, I decide. My nose follows it down between her breasts. I inhale, moving over her skin until it's too much for me not to lick a tightly budded peak of her breast.

"Oh God, Trystan, that's so good." She gasps and thrusts her chest forward, needing more. I gladly oblige, nipping, pulling, filling my hands and my mouth, sucking at the stiffening flesh.

Hot hands move over my back and shoulders, and their jerky movements tell me Emmy is as desperate as I feel.

I thought I'd take my time with her, taste more of her, get her ready, but within minutes she's whimpering, begging. "Please, Trystan. God, I need you inside me."

"Thank God." I grin, pinning her with my gaze.

She's flushed and panting hard.

"I want you so damn much. I didn't plan for this to go so fast," I admit. "Actually I didn't plan on it at all."

Her hands move down my sides and push me to roll over so she can reach the button of my jeans. "Me neither." She laughs. "You're like freaking kerosene."

Between the two of us, we manage to get my jeans undone and shoved down my legs. She sits up and uses her feet to push them the last little bit and then tugs on the waistband of my boxer briefs. Rolling onto my back I drink in the sight of her undressing me.

Christ, her tits are spectacular. Perfect. I want to remember this moment forever.

"Thank you," she says, making me realize I've spoken aloud. "Oh, Trystan." She sighs as she reveals my cock. It's stiff, swollen, needy, and it bucks under her hungry gaze. "The general really is impressive." She smirks, and then my eyes slam shut, and I arch as her hot hand closes around me and squeezes.

"Christ." I hiss the word as I feel her hot wet tongue touch the head. I grab her wrist, my other hand gripping her hair. "Don't," I say against every urge and instinct in my body that wants her hot mouth to devour me. "I've never been this ready. It'll be over." A burn of sparks is already shooting down my spine. This is insane.

I urge her to come up my body, and she does, her nipples dragging over my bare chest, which does nothing to calm the rising tide.

"Let's slow down," I manage and can't believe my own words.

She pouts. "I was thinking a quick one now and a slower one later."

Later . . . I wonder if later will even be enough, or if we'll survive the first time without going out in flames. Holding her head, I bring her in and fuse my mouth with hers again and flip her onto her back. She squeals.

My hips settle between her legs, my cock nestled against her, and I feel how wet she is. Hot and cool. I try to talk. "I need"—her hips move and I rock in response, my body closer to its goal—"to suit up the general."

She smiles at my euphemism then bites her lip. "Do you always suit up?"

"Of course. Always." I've never, ever taken a chance of someone using it against me. I control these situations. Always. "You?"

She nods. "Always," she says seriously. "But it's been a while. Obviously," she adds, reminding us of her expired condoms downstairs.

Personally, I fucking love the fact it's been a while for her. The thought of someone else touching her is—nope. Not going there. "I have some in my wash kit, hold on." I hate to break the moment and leave the bed. I should have done it sooner.

"I . . ." She squeezes my arm as I move, making me pause. She swallows. "I'm on the pill. What you said to me last night about . . . c-coming deep inside me. I want that." Her cheeks flush red as she admits it.

"Jesus, Emmy," I moan. I could orgasm right now. "Fuck."

I grab her head, and my mouth finds hers wildly, our bodies straining toward each other.

Her legs open wide, wrapping around my hips, and my cock slips against her hot opening. I heave in a breath like I'm on top of a fucking mountain with no oxygen. There's no way I'll last without a barrier between us. I feel like a teenager. Where's the damn ghost when you need it? I need sports stats. Something. But right now I wouldn't be able to say if someone even needed a bat to play baseball.

The only solution is to get her there with me in case she isn't already. I need access to her body.

I drag my mouth from hers and rise onto my hands. My mouth closes over her nipple, tongue flicking, teeth grazing, mouth sucking.

"Yesss." She's writhing, holding me to her. I've never known breasts to be this responsive. Not that there are any other breasts in the world. Only these. Only Emmy's. "Oh God, yes," she pants, and I switch sides. My mouth works and works the peaks until she's gasping.

Holding her around the waist, I kneel, pushing my legs under her thighs. She is still lying back, her butt raised, her legs spread open for me. I look down. Big mistake. I close my eyes and struggle for control. "God, Emmy, you're fucking gorgeous." Her sweet pussy is winking up at me from beneath the thin smattering of golden red curls. The flesh is pink, moisture sparkling and catching the light. Next to her, my aching flesh looks red, angry, and desperate. I run my fingers down her belly and graze between her legs.

She bucks and whimpers. "More."

"You like that?" I ask, and my fingers slip closer to her opening, bathing in her wetness.

She nods.

My fingers move upward, circling. "Do you like it when I do this?" I ask, and before she answers, her breath catching, my fingers sink lower again and I work one inside her. It's hot. Velvet.

I bring it to my mouth and suck. She's tastes like sweet and salt.

Her eyes are fixed on my hand, her mouth parted, her chest rising and falling rapidly.

I suck two of my fingers and then bring them back to her body.

She's panting, just watching me.

I work in a second finger. Gently, because she's so tight. "Or do you like it when they fuck you?"

Emmy's body is moving against me, against my hand, her mouth is open, her eyes glazed and unfocussed on me, her breath coming in pants. "Don't stop."

My thumb touches her clit.

"All of it," she mumbles. "I like . . . it all."

Her body shudders, I feel it in the muscles of her legs against mine. And I take my hand away.

My mouth is watering so I move my body, holding her open and take a quick taste. A promise. A long swipe of my tongue from the crease of her ass, over the delicious center of her and up over her hard clit, making her cry out and buck.

I'll return here. It will be my new playground.

Then I'm back up, my cock in my fist, positioning myself at her entrance.

We both hold our breath and lock eyes.

"I don't want to come, Trystan. Make it last. Make it last," she begs me. "This place, right here. I want to live here. God, it feels so good. I've never felt this good."

Her words make me feel like a king. And she is my kingdom, my queen, my advisor, my beggar, and every loyal and willing subject. I'll worship at her alter.

My other hand reaches forward, cups her head, and my palm runs to her jaw. My thumb crosses her lips. She leans into the touch and draws my finger into her mouth.

"God, you're beautiful." I sigh and let my hand move down her body until I can grip her hip.

I nudge her with the head of my cock. "Take me in, Emmy," I breathe as I press forward and look down. Her body hotly swallows the tip of me. "Jesus." I squeeze my eyes closed because it's too much. I've never felt this good either. Sweat is freezing on my skin, the prickles racing up and down my body. "God, you feel good," I echo lamely because there are no words to describe what is happening right now.

She's panting, her body still. "You're big," she says.

"You can take it."

"More, give me more."

I sink in farther, and I'm glad I'm bracing my weight on my knees and not my arms because I'm shaking with the effort to stem back the coming rush. My fingers steal over her clit, and I press down, massaging in slow circles.

Emmy lifts her head and comes up on her elbows, her eyes glued to our joining, her chest heaving.

I watch in fascination as a blush comes over her like a tide, and her body starts to shudder.

"No," she moans in shocked fascination. "Not yet. Oh God, it's too much." Her head drops back exposing the skin of her throat, and her body clenches hard and repeatedly, squeezing my cock. Her body twists against my hand on her hip that is trying to hold her still, anchored as the storm buffets through her.

"Trystan." She's sobbing my name, and it's glorious. A symphony. A rhapsody. I've never heard my name sound so beautiful.

Gritting my teeth, I hang on. I'm not even fully inside her, and then I can't anymore. Her body is loosening, grabbing me, pulling me in. With a hoarse sound, I barely register is coming from me, I give in with a hard thrust, forging my way inside.

There's no time to appreciate the tight, snug fit because my orgasm is barreling through me, a racehorse out the gate. "Jesus, Emmy. I'm coming." And all I can do is helplessly ride it, drowning in the beautiful ache and the freefall into euphoria. I work my hips to wring as much of it as I can.

Trying to keep it.

Trying to get as deeply into her as possible.

I want to leave myself there.

I already have.

34

TRYSTAN

*a*s the tide ebbs, and I drop back into my body, it's like dropping back into an empty husk. Like I gave myself completely away. I feel a flicker of alarm but have no energy to analyze it.

Blinking my eyes open, I'm relieved to see Emmy. She is there with me, I wasn't left alone. She's reaching up and pulling my face to hers, her mouth opening to mine. I give another slow thrust, not wanting to leave the snug home, even as I'm softening.

For long moments we say nothing, just panting, waiting for the blood to return the oxygen to our brains.

"How did the general do?" I ask when I think I can talk.

She shakes with silent laughter beneath me. "He was a little trigger happy."

I lean up and kiss her nose. "Um, he wasn't the only one. And anyway, that's because he was unprotected and exposed," I say in his defense. "He wasn't used to it."

"Hmm," she says, eyes sparkling with mirth and hands roaming up my back that's damp and cool with sweat. "But he'd already ascertained it wasn't hostile terrain."

"It was a utopia. But it had to be conquered, nonetheless."

"And it was. Thoroughly. He definitely left his mark." Her mouth nips at mine.

I groan. "I guess he earned a promotion. He's now a four star general."

She scrunches up her nose, and it's cute as fuck. "I need to take a bath."

"Can I watch?" I give her my most hopeful expression.

"You can," she says indulgently like she just gave an ice cream to a toddler. And I adore that she didn't default to self-consciousness. "You can even bathe with me. If you want."

I roll to the side of her, my body instantly missing her warmth, and eye the tub set below the window over my shoulder. "Will we both fit?"

"If we don't, I call first." She leans up on an elbow and purses her lips unapologetically. I can't resist kissing them again. "In fact," she goes on, "can you run it for me while I go to the bathroom?" Then she's shimmying to the edge of the bed and tiptoeing with her legs squeezed together.

I laugh at her and glance at the clock on the side table. "Are you sure you don't want to have a bath in the morning? It's late."

"Ummm. Pretty sure," she answers as I get up and put the plug in the tub and turn on the tap. There's bubble bath on the window sill, and I squeeze a healthy amount into the running water. Yep, I doubt we'd both fit.

Emmy exits the bathroom in a white robe, her hair piled on top of her head. Her cheeks are still flushed.

"I'll make it quick," she says.

"It's fine. No rush." I'm feeling weird suddenly. Out of sorts. I step past her toward the bathroom and try not to notice the small frown line between her eyebrows. "Just going to brush my teeth," I say.

In the bathroom, I shut the door then lean against it and pinch the bridge of my nose. I'm starting to feel claustrophobic. I think. I don't know what I'm feeling. But I no longer have a handle on things. What seemed like a good idea earlier, now seems messy. Complicated. I hate complicated. And I can't leave. I'm here for the night. I guess that's where the feeling of claustrophobia is coming from.

Immediately my brain defaults to figuring out the worst-case scenario so I can mitigate the risk. The problem is I don't know what's on the table. What am I risking? What are the potential gains? What's the guaranteed return on investment?

I splash my face with cold water.

Gains, I have to base on experience: fun, anticipation, sexual release. Laughter. Quite literally the most intense sexual experience of my life.

Risk: She becomes clingy. But she doesn't seem the type, and I negate the thought. Risk that I hurt her? I'd hate that, but somehow I know she'd hide it from me. Protect me from knowing. Something inside my chest flinches at that.

Return on investment: I enjoy my last night and day in Charleston and potentially have a standing arrangement here every time I have to come back. I could more than live with that.

I brush my teeth.

"Trystan?" Emmy's voice calls from the bedroom.

"Yeah?"

"Can you come out here please?"

"One second." I spit and rinse and look at myself. My eyes are bright like I'm drunk. I blink, shake my head, and open the door.

Emmy is standing up and pulling a towel around her, and I feel stupidly disappointed. I missed her in the bath because I had to give myself a fucking pep talk.

"I missed the show," I say and my voice is rough.

She smiles at me, but it seems like she knows I freaked out. "You sure did." Tendrils of her hair are curling from steam, and her skin is shiny and slick from water. She reaches over and grabs her robe, slipping it on before removing the towel wrapped around her body. She's hiding herself from me.

"What did you need?" I ask.

"For you to come out here and realize I'm not going to bite you."

I laugh uncomfortably as I root through my bag for a clean pair of boxers, grateful I used Emmy's washer and dryer earlier. I was definitely on my last set of clean clothes.

"Trystan."

"Yep."

"I know you're kind of freaking out. I'd be an idiot not to realize you don't normally do this."

"Do what?" I say as if I have no idea what she's talking about.

"Spend the night with someone you just slept with."

I'm about to deny it but stop.

"I realized that at the hotel." She lifts a shoulder and bends over to use the towel to dry each of her legs. Then she lifts a foot and balances it on the edge of the bath, turquoise toes curling over the rim. She reaches for a bottle of lotion. "But here's something you may not have realized. I don't do this either."

I laugh humorlessly. "I knew that. Not the same thing."

"Probably not," she says, eyes flashing briefly at my tone, and smooths cream up and down her legs from her ankle up to her thighs and then her butt. I swallow. She changes legs and repeats. The scent of the lotion finally reaches me. It's her signature scent. I inhale deeply, feeling the stirring of arousal, remembering the first time I smelled the concentration in her sheets and heard her lose control. Now I've seen it in person. I know she flushes head to toe, arches her back. I can't remember if she closed her eyes or the exact sound she made. Next time I'll—Christ, that went sideways fast.

"But I'm not sleeping on the couch," she says. "Or going back to Armand's—"

"I'd never—"

She laughs. "I know. You're a good guy. You normally remove *yourself*, don't you?" She somehow manages to finish the contortion of lotioning up her body underneath her robe. "I think we're more alike than you think." She looks at me squarely and lifts an eyebrow in challenge. "But how about you don't sleep on the couch either?"

"It's uncomfortable to sleep on anyway." I rub a thumb over my lip.

"Is not," she argues, offended.

"It is." I turn to climb in the bed.

"What do you think you're doing?" Her question stops me.

"What?"

She rolls her eyes with a long-suffering sigh. "That's *my* side."

I straighten, hands up in surrender. "My bad."

"Scoot." She shoos me past her, and I go around the bed, shaking my head in amusement. I don't know how she does it, but my earlier flight response is nowhere to be found. I'd rather stay here and argue with Emmy Dubois than be anywhere else right now.

"I hope you don't mind if I sleep naked?" Her hand releases the hair tied up on her head so it comes cascading to her shoulders. Then she unbelts the loosely-tied robe and lets it fall to her feet before lifting the duvet and climbing in. "Are you just going to stand there? Tuna will be out of a job, you'll catch all the bugs with that open mouth of yours."

She rolls onto her side away from me and reaches out a long toned arm to the bedside lamp I'd turned on earlier and plunges us into darkness.

I smile in the dark and climb under her covers. I'm probably going to freak out again in the morning, but for now I'll just go with it.

35

EMMY

I stretched, my muscles aching. I danced hard last night. It felt great.

Trystan.

His name, his face and a thousand memories, dark and light, innocent and explicit, were like an explosion in my mind, blanking out everything else. I blinked slowly in the darkness. The heaviness of my body and stickiness of my eyelids told me I'd only been asleep a few hours and could definitely sleep a few more. It was close to dawn.

I turned and made out the outline of Trystan lying on his back. He was breathing deeply, steadily. I wished it was lighter so I could see his face at rest, his beautiful features relaxed, his eyelashes resting against his cheeks.

Last night after we'd slept together was like luring a stray dog inside for a warm meal. Chances were he'd bolt at daybreak.

Besides, he'd already told me he was leaving today. A week ago I had no idea he even existed. Now he was in every crevice of my life. My home. My family. My friends. My mind. My heart.

I never saw him coming, but I knew he had quickly become an addiction that would be impossible to quit. Fortunately, or unfortunately, I acknowledged the choice wouldn't be mine. I'd have to be happy with the time we'd had. I wasn't sure how he'd made it past my defenses. Emotionally I was right in the place I always avoided.

Sighing, I gave in to the longing to be held close, and I slipped up against his warm body, my head nestling into his shoulder. What did I have to lose? He'd either wake up now and leave, or later and . . . leave.

He groaned, and I held my breath. Then his arm lifted and curled around me, warm and tight, and he let out a long sigh before his breathing returned to normal.

I exhaled and closed my eyes, drifting back to sleep.

* * *

A WEIGHT SETTLED on my side. Tuna always liked to perch there. Why? I had no idea. There was light behind my eyelids, and the sounds of a city waking up outside my window. Then I became aware of the heat at my back. It wasn't my cat, it was Trystan spooning me. I bit my lip as arousal spread through me, wondering if he was awake yet.

But then he inhaled against my hair and his body pulled me closer. "You smell so good," he whispered.

"Um, did you bring a broom handle to bed? Or are you happy to see me?"

I felt his body shake with laughter behind me, and he pressed his erection harder against my ass. "It's a broomstick. Yours. You can ride it if you want."

"Are you calling me a witch?" I said, outraged.

He flipped me onto my back.

I was greeted to the sight of "Morning Trystan," gray-blue eyes crinkled with mirth and soft brown hair sticking up all over his head.

I caught my breath.

"Yes." He nodded, eyes on my mouth and settling his weight over me. The duvet and sheet were kind of trapped between us, but what little of his skin I could feel was warm and delicious. "You are a witch. There's no other explanation for why I am still in your bed."

"May as well take advantage of it though." I shrugged with a grin. "You know, since you're here."

He dropped his mouth to mine, and I quickly turned my head with a squeak. "Morning breath!"

"Mine or yours?" he asked with a chuckle.

"Mine, I think. I don't know."

"Give me your mouth, Emmy," he growled.

I turned my face back, and my gaze met his amused one. His eyes watched me until there were two of him, and his lips touched mine.

Wrapping my arms around his head, I closed my eyes and relaxed against his mouth, letting his lips coax mine open. His tongue dipped inside for a quick taste, and my body melted into a pool of heat. "Mmm," I moaned.

"Mmm, indeed." Trystan's mouth left mine and drifted hot wet kisses down my throat and down to my chest, pulling the comforter away as he went. My nipples stiffened and arousal thrummed low in my belly.

He leaned up and drifted his fingertips over the swell of my breasts. "You even have freckles here. I love seeing your skin in the daylight."

I scrunched my nose. I'd never been a big fan of my freckles, but the way Trystan looked at them hungrily and then swiped his tongue across my body like he could taste them, made me gasp and arch for more.

He continued his downward journey, shoving the comforter away as he went, until I was greeted with the shocking sight of all our bare skin draped diagonally across the bed, his tanned against my fair, both contrasted against the white sheets. He settled between my thighs, shoulder nudging my thighs open. I covered my eyes, feeling embarrassed, but I didn't move.

"Couldn't stop thinking about getting back down here," he murmured and kissed one inner thigh followed by the other, his hot breath trailing across me and causing my lower body to jerk and a sound of need to escape from my throat. "Thought about it falling asleep." Kiss. "First thing I thought about when I woke up."

He repeated the action, his breath closer to my wet and needy center.

"Are you teasing me?" I dropped my hand away from my eyes, and I caught his gaze.

"Maybe." His eyebrow was raised cheekily.

Then his hot tongue gave a long lick up the center of me and I gasped loudly in relief, pushing my hips up. "Yes."

Trystan groaned, and his tongue returned. And returned. Long slow delicious swipes until they weren't enough.

Writhing against his mouth and clutching his hair, I hung on as Trystan responded to every one of my needy whimpers, speeding up, slowing down, increasing pressure, slipping fingers inside of me, shocking me at times, and finally succeeding in bringing me crashing to orgasm.

"Holy shit," I finally managed, trying to catch my breath. But no sooner had I spoken than Trystan was crawling up my body. His hard erection brushed against my leg, leaving a thin trail of wetness.

His eyes were wild and feverish as he looked down at me, holding himself up on his arms.

My hands had a life of their own, reaching up and threading through his soft hair. His eyes flickered as I grazed my nails over his scalp. Then I wrapped my legs around his waist and urged him inside of me.

He thrust into me in one strong smooth stroke. "Oh, God," he moaned to match my gasp. "Jesus, Emmy."

Pulling his head down to me, I devoured his mouth with

kisses. His lower body thrust and arched and filled me. His weight on me felt incredible, I could die here.

Eventually we needed too much air to kiss, and I held on tight, my mouth at his ear, panting, urging, begging. Our skin slipped and slid together with the sweat of our exertion.

His breath in my ear felt decadent, delicious. It was laced with words and sounds of need and desire. His pelvic bone pressed hard against me as he moved, and before long, my body was tightening again, liquid fire racing along my veins and swirling in my center.

"Oh, oh my God." The tide of another orgasm was on me so suddenly, it took my words away.

And then Trystan, cursing as soon as my body spasmed, thrust hard once, twice, and came up on an arm, his head arching back.

"Oh shit, Emmy."

I watched his face contort in agonized bliss as he gave a final thrust, and it felt like the most erotic thing I'd ever seen. He was completely given over to the moment, lost in it, lost in me.

And yeah, I had to admit I was lost in him too. Utterly. And not just in the throes of release.

The realization formed a lump in my throat so suddenly I felt I couldn't breathe. I blinked rapidly and dragged his face down to my neck so he couldn't see my expression.

I kissed the side of his jaw, his temple, salty sweat coating my lips. And this was why I shouldn't have one-night stands—I just gave too much of myself. This time I feared I might have given away more than I had to give. And if Trystan freaked out again, which I was pretty certain he would, it was going to crush me.

"Wow." I forced a laugh and tried to keep it light. "You can rent my place anytime." Exactly the wrong thing to say. But it was out there now. And really, it didn't have to mean anything.

Trystan chuckled into my hair, his breathing still exerted. "Does it always come with these perks?"

There was no safe answer, so I strained around with my arm and smacked his naked butt.

He pulled up sharply, looking amused. "You putting spanking on the table?"

"Ha, ha," I returned. God, I wanted him to settle his weight on me forever. "Get up," I complained instead, "I can't breathe."

He frowned slightly and rolled to the side. "You okay?"

I stretched my mouth into a smile. "Never better. Two orgasms to start my day. Can't complain."

"Three counting last night," he said proudly. "It *was* after midnight."

I shifted in the bed, feeling uncomfortable and full of Trystan in more ways than one. "What time are you leaving?" I asked him.

I'd rather get it over with, rip the Band-Aid off, start the new phase of my life—Emmy 2.0—the version who'd now known epic sex and chemistry and massive crushing disappointment. Not that I hadn't known crushing disappointment before, but this felt different.

He laughed. "Trying to get rid of me already?"

"Ha." I looked away.

"Emmy, you sure you're okay?"

"Yep. Stop being so needy. I'm fine."

"Needy. Huh." He sat up and pulled on his jeans and went into the bathroom.

I pulled the comforter up to my shoulders.

The toilet flushed, and I heard the water run as I watched the sunlight through my blinds dapple against the white painted attic eaves. Then he came out. His face was closed. "Gonna run over to Armand's and get us coffees," he said. "How do you take yours?"

"Cream, no sugar," I said, propping up on an elbow. "Thank you."

"Same as me." He pulled on a white T-shirt that hugged the lines of his body. "I'll shower when I get back if that's okay. If you don't need to get rid of me too quickly."

I waited for a grin or a sarcastic smile but got none. And it suddenly occurred to me in my rush to protect myself, I may have offended him. "Sure," I said. "Of course. No rush." I opened my mouth to say more but couldn't.

He gave me a long look then turned and jogged down the stairs.

Shit. I lay back with a sigh. Maybe we were both pretty bad at this.

Ugh. I slipped out of bed and had a quick and thorough shower, then wrapping myself in a towel, went out to the bedroom.

Trystan wasn't back, or perhaps he was downstairs, so I hurriedly applied lotion and pulled on jeans and a long-sleeved T-shirt.

Trystan's suitcase lay open at the end of the bed. I stared at it. How had I invited him so fully into my life? It was against everything I normally did. How did this happen?

I went downstairs.

* * *

TRYSTAN SAT at my dining table with his laptop open. He looked up as I descended and nodded at the paper cup of coffee on the kitchen counter. "Should still be hot."

"Thank you," I said gratefully. "How was Armand this morning?"

"Full of winks and innuendo, considering he knows where you spent the night."

"Ha. I bet. And I'm sure he was tired too, having to get up early to open the shop. He normally has help on the weekend mornings."

"So he's really not gay, huh?" Trystan asked.

I lifted a shoulder and propped my hip against the counter.

"He's bi," I said, smiling as I remembered Trystan's reaction last night.

"Ah."

I popped the lid off my cup so I could blow on the top. "But I enjoyed your reaction."

"I enjoyed your dancing." Trystan looked up at me over the top of his laptop.

"Thank you." I looked away.

He blew out a breath. "So how are you spending your Saturday in this fair city?"

"Aha, you finally admit it's a city?"

"Getting there," he said and leaned back, clasping his hands behind his head.

"Today, I'm going to visit a couple of nursing homes to see about moving David. I have to move him by the end of next month."

"Why so soon?"

"The facility he's at doesn't have adequate dementia care. And after the fiasco this week . . . let's just say they are out of rope to give. He's on Medicaid so options are few and far between. I'm going to go and sweet talk the administrators, or beg and plead, maybe offer a kidney."

Trystan's eyebrows pinched. "To do what?"

"To get him a bed. There's a long waiting list, apparently. So unless you know someone . . ." I shrugged, imagining how I was going to spend the next few weeks. "Or can bribe someone, or just generally beg every day until they get annoyed enough to get you in."

Trystan rocked forward in his chair, intent suddenly on his laptop screen. "What's the name of the place you're going to see?"

"Um." I turned around, looking for my purse and bag that contained the manila folder Penny gave me before belatedly realizing they were still at Armand's. "I don't know. One of them's in

Summerville. That's the one I want to go and see because it would be ideal. Close enough to visit."

"This place?" He swung his screen around.

"I don't know," I said, approaching. "I haven't looked it up yet."

"Well this place is in Summerville and it has dementia care and . . ." He laughed and shook his head incredulously.

"What?" I frowned.

"I'm part-owner. I'd say that was knowing someone, wouldn't you?"

I stared at Trystan. "Are you serious?"

"Yep. But I'm still learning the ropes. I have no idea about the Medicaid situation. Let me put in a call." He picked up his cell phone from the table next to him, and I reached forward and grabbed his wrist.

He stopped.

"Wait," I said. "You can't do that."

"Why not?"

"I—I don't know." I swallowed. "You've already . . . I still owe you so much."

His head bobbed back. "Owe me? What the hell, Emmy?"

I licked my lips.

"I swear to God," Trystan said in a low voice, "you better not have fucking slept with me because you thought you owed me."

"What?" I burst out, let go and pushed back from the table. "No! Ugh!"

He lifted his palms. "Sorry. Just making sure."

"God, Trystan."

"Jesus, Emmy. What am I supposed to think?" He grabbed at his hair. "You've acted really fucking weird since we . . . since we . . ."

"Fucked?" I supplied.

Trystan flinched. "I was going to say made love."

My heart climbed up my chest to my throat. "No, you weren't." God, he wasn't, was he?

He stood and snapped his laptop shut. "Actually, I was. It just took me a damn minute because I've never said that before. But rest assured." He held up a hand. "Temporary insanity."

I closed my mouth. It was dry. My ears rang. My skin felt hot. And pain. God, pain. It was all encompassing. It made me want to claw my skin off. "You should leave," I whispered. I didn't want to be told there was no place for me. Not ever again. This time I controlled my world.

"Check out's at ten a.m., right?" His tone was biting. "I'm sorry I overstayed my welcome."

"I-I'll go to Armand's. You j-just take your time."

He took a step toward me then stopped. But I'd already backed up. An automatic reaction. If I didn't leave right now, I was going to lose my shit right in front of him. Tears were like a salt tide roaring in from the edges of everything I could see, feel, and hear.

I turned and went to the door. Stopping for a moment, I took a breath. "Thank you," I said quietly, my voice wobbling. I couldn't forget he'd helped me, helped David, kept my phone when he could have ditched me high and dry. He was a good person. I knew that. And I knew he probably didn't understand the way I was trying to protect myself. When he realized how close we'd become, it would hurt worse when he pulled away. It was better this way.

"Goddammit, Emmy. Thank you for *what*, exactly?"

I answered by turning the handle on the front door.

"Please," he said, changing tack. "Please don't leave."

"Thank you for your help this week," I finished and opened the door and slipped through it, letting it shut behind me.

"Fuck!" he yelled so loudly it echoed around the outside court-yard, and I winced.

36

EMMY

$\mathcal{I}$ let myself into Armand's empty apartment and curled up on his couch. I wished I could go somewhere else, where Trystan didn't know where I was, but I needn't have worried—he didn't follow me. The tears I'd been afraid of never came. Instead, I felt cold, brittle, and exhausted. I pulled out the manila folder Penny had given me. Sure enough it was the exact place Trystan had shown me. Of course it was. I called and made an appointment to visit them later in the day, then I called a local rent-a-car place out near the Cooper River Bridge.

I grabbed my makeup bag from my suitcase and went to Armand's bathroom and made up my face. I braided my hair to tame it and then called a cab.

My phone was gripped in my fist the whole way to the car rental place and so quiet I actually checked that it still had battery life. I went to my photos, wondering what else Trystan had seen when he went through them. Weirdly, there were a bunch of pictures of food I hadn't taken. Meals Trystan had taken pictures of. Then I went to my messages to let Armand know where I was. I saw messages from Annie earlier in the week. I'd forgotten she'd texted Trystan thinking it was me. The messages were dated from Wednesday. Four days ago.

Annie: *Spill girl! Armand told me about some guy called Trystan.*

Oh? What did he say about him?

Tricky, tricky, Trystan.

Annie: *That he's drop-dead gorgeous. How did you meet him?*

At the airport.

Annie: *Don't be coy! You know I haven't had sex in what feels like a zillionty years and I need to live vicariously. TELL ME MORE!*

Not much more to tell. But . . .

Annie: *But? I'm dying. You are slowly killing me.*

He thinks I'm stunning, and I crack him up.

I inhaled sharply as I read his words pretending to come from me. Trystan had told me I was stunning last night, but seeing him tell someone else days ago was . . . my insides swirled. And he thought I cracked him up? That was good, right? The ability to make someone laugh? Someone who was going through a family funeral and lots of shit needed to laugh.

Annie: *Swoon! Well, it's about time. Yay!*

About time for what?

Annie: *To meet someone.*

I bet that made commitment-phobic Trystan shudder.

How long has it been exactly? Trystan texted from me.

Oh no, he didn't. I winced.

Annie: *Stop it. You were the one who told me you were basically "re-virginized." So if you've finally found a guy you're attracted to then, babe, I'd say this means something. Where does he live?*

I pulled my thumb from my mouth as I heard a sharp crack that told me I'd bitten off a piece of my thumbnail. I hadn't even realized I'd started chewing it. At least Annie didn't answer how long it had been. But re-virginized implied *years*. It had been almost two years. At least. That was an epoch if I thought about how often Trystan probably hooked up. I read on to see what his response was.

He lives in New York. So yeah, definitely nothing serious. Gotta go.
My stomach sank. Of course. Exactly what I knew. God, I was
a mess. I watched the warehouses of East Bay Street pass me by
on my left.

* * *

THE DRIVE out to Summerville in the rental car was easy, and I
found the home without any problem. Magnolia Meadows was
really pretty. Set in a partly rural area, with beautiful landscaping.
Hopefully the staff were as wonderful as they were in Rockaway
because so far, the idea that David could be somewhere this
beautiful seemed too good to be true. And I didn't dare assume
that even with all my begging he might get a bed. Of course I'd
already let my pride get in the way on smoothing his path. I
gritted my teeth and resolutely steered the rental car into visitor
parking.

My meeting with the administrator didn't take long, and she'd
already created a file on David from her call with Penny the day
before. I nodded along with all her explanations about why the
chances of David getting a bed were so slim. Something about
budgets and reimbursements and staff. It was all the things I'd
heard endlessly. She handed me a brochure, and I had to squeeze
my eyes closed hard when I saw the *Montgomery Homes & Facilities* small print along the bottom.

Back in the car, my conversation with Trystan this morning
scrolled on an endless loop through my head. I was so sure he
was getting ready to politely extricate himself from whatever had
happened between us. Had I really misread the situation so
much? Everything I knew about him, especially after his almost
freak-out during the night, told me he wouldn't stick around any
longer than he had to.

But what if I was wrong?

What if Trystan wasn't as relationship averse as he'd

portrayed himself to be?

I thought back to his pictures I'd found in his phone and the ones of him and his "Little Brother" from *Big Brothers Big Sisters*— he wasn't as commitment-phobic either. Relationships like that took a boatload of commitment.

His admissions about his family, and his mother, and everything he was facing this week suddenly felt terribly important— beyond the fact he'd actually shared them with me at all. I had a horrible feeling I had just done what everyone close to Trystan had always done.

Rejected him.

Trystan Montgomery, maybe unbeknownst to himself, was a man in desperate need of a relationship.

The last thing he'd said before I closed the door on him was "Please don't leave."

"Shit," I said aloud and had to steer the car to the side of the highway. I couldn't tell if I was nauseatingly hungry from skipping breakfast and lunch or the thought of hurting Trystan was actually making me sick all by itself. I laid my head on the steering wheel and counted to ten.

"Okay," I said to myself and took a deep breath.

First? I needed food to function and think clearly. *Chic-fil-A* fries and a lemonade. Then counsel from friends while I figured out how to fix this colossal mistake I'd made.

I had to fix it, but I couldn't date him. To start with, we lived in different cities and he'd already broken my trust once by sticking me in his harem hotel and lining me up with all his other women. If I closed my eyes and pictured Trystan Montgomery, he was wearing a crisp, dark suit, arrogant eyes, and a starched white shirt that had my splattered pride all over it. If I didn't walk away from this, he'd likely also end up sponging the mangled remains of my exploded heart off his arctic blue tie.

What I would definitely do, however, after I made him understand my reasons for leaving this morning had more to do with *me* than him, was date more. Even if I had to get on those horrible apps. It could take me a long while to find someone who made my girl parts all swoony like Trystan Montgomery did, but I had to start somewhere and the sooner I got started, the sooner I might find someone.

* * *

"Do I call him?" I asked.

"No!" said Annie.

"Yes, of course," said Armand at the same time.

It was Sunday, and the three of us had driven out to Sullivan's Island to have brunch at The Obstinate Daughter. Annie had left my sweet godson with his daddy, but she kept wincing and pressing her boobs.

"Damn it." She shook her dark curls. "This is like nature's way of trying to make sure you don't abandon your baby. My boobs are about to explode."

"*Por favor* . . ." Armand complained.

"Go pump," I said. "We'll be here." I was currently enjoying a bottomless mimosa on the house as a result of all the social media I'd done for them.

She maneuvered out of the booth with her bag, and then I got the update from Armand about how business was going and his plans for expansion of the café.

"Oh, don't look now," whispered Armand, suddenly agitated. "There's a famous actor behind you."

"Where?" I turned.

"Ugh, I said don't look."

"Sorry." I scanned the area but didn't see anyone. Oh wait, someone looked familiar. "He was in Prometheus." And he kind of reminded me of Trystan. Or maybe Trystan was all I could think about. "The guy who becomes infected and gets his girlfriend pregnant with the alien baby?"

"That's the one. He's *muy caliente.*"

And I had unprotected sex with a self-proclaimed serial dater not once but twice. An alien baby might be a blessing. I was on the pill of course, but . . .

"You are thinking about sex," Armand observed.

My eyes snapped to his, mortified. "How did you know that?"

He shrugged. And waved his fingers in the direction of my face. "You bite your lip and your cheeks go all red. But you didn't look happy. Was it bad sex? Is this why you are all crazy and sad?"

"Ugh. It was good. Amazing."

"And?"

"And I . . . nothing." I picked up the champagne glass and had another sip of orange juice and sparkling wine. "There's nothing."

"Maybe you should let it go then?"

"Exactly what I said." Annie slid back into the booth.

"That was quick," I said.

"Yeah, they were ready if you know what I mean."

Armand shook his head.

Annie smirked at him, always enjoying his discomfort with female workings. "All I'm saying is," she turned back to me, "don't *breadcrumb* the guy if you have no intention of seeing him again."

"Breadcrumb?" asked Armand. "Is this another sexual thing only women know?"

Annie laughed. "No. I mean, if he was hurt by your rejection, let him get over it. Don't message him and call him to make him feel better. It could lead him on again. It's selfish, it's only about making *you* feel better."

"Huh," said Armand. "That makes sense."

"But—" But I wanted to call him. I missed him. Goddamn it, I missed him. How was that even possible? I hadn't known him a week.

"Look, I'm not an expert on relationships," Annie qualified. "I'm only an expert in how to complicate one by getting pregnant."

"She speaks truth." Armand nodded.

"Unless of course, you *want* to see him again?" Annie asked.

I folded my arms. "He lives in New York."

"And will be running a business down here." Annie cocked an eyebrow. "Visiting a lot."

Armand pursed his lips. "Again. She speaks truth."

* * *

I SPENT the rest of Sunday afternoon back in my little cottage, finishing up a few custom drapery orders and then organizing my meeting schedule for the week. I rolled out my yoga mat and went through my workout until I was sweaty and empty-headed.

But my clear mind didn't last long. Despite the fact there was absolutely no evidence Trystan Montgomery had inhabited my life and home the last few days, there he was in my head again. I never asked him how his dinner with his family had gone on Friday night. It must have been hard. And then we'd slept together and I'd bolted. I never asked him what the L stood for in his name. I never—

My phone rang and I startled. I normally turned it to silent when I did yoga; I must have forgotten. I got up and looked at the screen.

D'Andre.

I answered immediately, my first thought being it was something about David.

"What's up, Emmy?"

"I'm good, D'Andre. All okay up there?"

"Good, good. David's good. Talking up a storm today. Got a visitor actually."

"He did?"

"Trystan Montgomery."

My stomach dropped. "God. Really?"

D'Andre chuckled. "Yep, knew you'd be surprised."

"What did he say?"

"I don't know, he just signed in and asked where to find him."

"H—How did David do?" What did they talk about? And why? God, I had so many questions. But also, I was never sure how David would react to new people and new situations. "Was David okay?"

"Good. He was a little scattered, but they chatted for a while. Couldn't stay and eavesdrop. Wish I could have."

"Me too." I breathed deeply. "How weird."

"Yeah, I guess. That's why I thought I should tell you."

"Well, thanks. Let me know if David says anything about it. And how are you?"

"Good, good. Thanks to you, I think Xanderr is going to produce a short piece from me to put on his YouTube channel."

"That's great, D'Andre."

"It really is. Already been gettin' more hits since he talked about going with me to see Logic. Which was awesome, by the way. You missed a great show."

"I bet I did." Instead I'd had phone sex with Trystan.

"All right, girl. I'll let you know if I hear more."

"Thanks, D'Andre."

"Later."

I pressed end and went back to my yoga mat to lie down. Huh.

37

EMMY

*I*t was Tuesday morning. This time last week I'd been on my way to the airport. Now I marched along the sidewalk on my way to work, a cup of Armand's strong Colombian cappuccino in hand, and tried not to think about Trystan.

I actually wished we hadn't slept together. It had been incredible, of course, but if we hadn't, I'd still be texting him. Right now I'd probably send him some kind of one-week anniversary of *losing his phone to a crazy girl* text message. Heck, I might even get really wordy and write him an email. We'd laugh. And flirt. Who knew? We might have even had a few more sexy phone calls. And I would have thought they were mind-blowing because I would be in blissful ignorance of how much more life-altering actually being with him in the flesh was.

But instead my phone was dead silent.

I swallowed a lump in my throat and entered my office.

Steven, my boss, was standing at the railing, looking over the lobby. "Nice of you to make it in."

Looking at the clock on my phone, I noticed I was exactly on time, so I ignored him and nodded to the new receptionist we hired a few weeks after our last one, Trina, lost her job. She handed me a couple of leads who'd called in and pinged our website. Then in an instant I decided something. "Steven, do you have a moment?" I asked, looking up at him. "I'd like to talk to you."

He looked annoyed and checked his own watch. "I think I can spare a few."

"Great." I tossed my empty coffee in the recycling can and trotted up the stairs, heading past him into his office. He had a lovely big window overlooking the old courthouse on East Bay Street. The room was far too big for the little amount of work he actually did.

I took a seat before he could offer. He pulled the door closed and headed around his desk. "Everything all right?" he asked, looking wary.

"Not really." I shook my head and made an unimpressed moue with my mouth. "You see, I've come to the realization I'm pretty indispensable around here. I love my job, and I really enjoy getting to know the clients." I tilted my head to the side. "Their needs, their wants," I listed. "Trying to get them on the map of the Charleston scene within their budget. I live and breathe my job, and I'm good at it."

Steven was quiet.

"Right?" I asked.

"Yes, you are," he allowed. "But, I have to say—"

"And you know I get approached all the time by recruiters from larger holding companies looking for someone to run the face of their hotels and restaurants?"

Steven sat upright but seemed to pretend to be shifting in his chair. He straightened a pen on his desk, and his eyes narrowed almost imperceptibly.

I waited him out to see what he had to say to that. But it looked as if he wasn't going to say anything. My earlier bravado that prompted me to seek this conversation began to fade. Why had I felt strong again? Oh, because I was thinking of my text chats with Trystan and remembering when he said he thought my boss didn't seem to be able to run his company without me.

I swallowed.

But Trystan said a lot of things. And a lot of them were probably simply meant to flatter and flirt.

"Are you resigning?" Steven asked.

Oops. This wasn't the outcome I foresaw at all. What had I done? How could I move David if I'd lost my job? Had I played chicken and lost? I needed to hedge. If I said *yes*, he could accept. *No* and I lost all my power. "Well—"

"Look, Emmaline . . ." Steven scrubbed a hand down his face. "I was waiting to tell you this until after we won the work on Friday, but obviously that didn't happen because the client cancelled. But no matter, you have certainly earned your reputation around here. I wanted to offer you the position of vice president . . . it would come with a pay raise. Modest, but a raise nonetheless."

I thought my mouth dropped open, I wasn't sure. So I made an effort to close it, and it snapped shut. I hadn't even had to ask for a pay raise yet. I'd been busy debating in my head whether this had been a bad idea. Then I thought he was going to usher me out the door with a pat on the back. And now he was offering me a promotion? He was definitely thinking fast.

"I can see that wasn't quite enough." He sighed, looking more disturbed at my silence than I'd ever seen him. "We can't afford to lose you. Your salary was going to increase by five percent. I'll make it ten?"

I sucked my lips between my teeth as I pretended to believe he'd really been planning on giving me a raise.

"Fifteen," Steven said, outbidding himself. He stood up and paced to the window.

His action jerked me into the moment. "Twenty," I said. "And my own office. I can wear what I want and no high heels. And five additional personal days off a year, no questions asked."

Steven crossed his arms as he turned. "Okay."

What? That was easy. "As a company-wide policy," I tacked on, gaining even more confidence. "We *all* need days we don't account for to deal with sick family members or unexpected appointments." Trina, the receptionist, could have done with those.

"Don't push it. *You* can have five extra. Anyone below VP level can have three extra."

Elation was ballooning up inside me, making me want to shout and scream in happiness, but with all my might I tried to keep a straight face. "Deal," I croaked and stood.

Steven's shoulders slumped. "I don't know where I can carve out an office."

"This one could probably be divided into two." I smiled broadly. "I do love the view." I nodded out the window to the courthouse. "Justice and fairness and all that. It's inspiring."

My phone that I still had clutched in my hand began ringing. It was David's facility number in Rockaway. "Sorry, I have to take this," I told Steven hurriedly. "And yes, it's a personal call." I turned and left. "Hello?"

"Emmy, it's Penny from Rockaway Nursing and Rehabilitation." My insides always lurched when I got a call like this, expecting bad news. If it was Penny who called and not D'Andre it usually wasn't good.

"Penny. Hi, is everything okay?"

"It's wonderful," she said. "Have you had a call from the facility in Summerville?"

I frowned. "No?"

"They're making room for David."

"What?" I covered my mouth with my hand. My eyes stung as relief swamped me, making me feel weak. I closed my eyes. "For real?"

"Yes. For real. They may be able to accept him as soon as next week."

"Oh my goodness. How . . .?"

"No idea. But let us know as soon as you speak to them because we'll have to officially stop his Medicaid here in order for you to apply for it there. There's no overlap."

"That's the scary part," I said. But oh my God, I'd just gotten a raise. I might be able to do this.

"Yes," she agreed. "But just think how happy David'll be to see you more often. It'll all work out. I made sure to let the administrator in Summerville know we needed to file the paperwork as quickly as possible."

My phone beeped with an incoming call. A quick check told me it was a South Carolina number. "This might be them on the other line, Penny."

"Okay, honey, call me back later."

"Thank you. Thank you so much." I switched over. "Hello?"

"Miss Dubois? I'm calling from Magnolia Meadows in Summerville."

* * *

To: tmontgomery
  From: edubois
  Subject: L?

Dear Trystan L. Montgomery
  . . .

  . . .

I CLICKED the small red X in the upper corner of the email. A pop-up box appeared. Did I want to delete this message? No. But I didn't know what the hell to say. Asking what the *L* stood for in his name was probably not the most appropriate way to start. I clicked Cancel and tried again.

To: tmontgomery
From: edubois
Subject: Thank you

Dear Trystan
...
...

OH MY GOD. Why was this so hard?

38

TRYSTAN

*N*obody should do anything that feels like base jumping. Ever. It may be exhilarating, an adrenaline rush like no other, but it's the world's most dangerous sport for a reason. Not many people can make a safe landing after that kind of jump.

In contrast to the highs I've woken up with the last couple of mornings, I have definitely miscalculated my landing. When I wake up in my apartment in New York on Sunday morning, alone, I feel hollow. Emotionally I'm lying at the bottom of a cliff.

And to be honest, waking up in my old life feels like waking from a dream where my whole life was thrown into a blender and I'm not sure if I really woke up because I feel so . . . shit.

I have no work to do to keep my mind occupied because my company is selling in four days and every single *i* is dotted and *t* crossed. Montgomery Homes & Facilities. That's something I can focus on.

I get up, make coffee, and shower then pull out all the financials I was given last week. After two hours I'm on the phone to Robert who's on the way out of mass.

"There's a discrepancy. . ." I begin when he answers.

* * *

I THOUGHT MAYBE I made the decision to go out to Rockaway and meet David in person almost to convince myself the previous week hadn't been some elaborate dive into the *Matrix*. *But* then it turned out I needed to anyway.

After finding the discrepancy on our available Medicaid beds and bothering not only Robert, but our two accountants, on a Sunday morning, they somehow miraculously found additional space at the facility in Summerville.

Robert told me the facility needed a personal assessment or recommendation if they were going to make a place for David. I used that as my excuse when I texted Bobby and asked him to drive me out of the city.

* * *

"SHE SEEMS LIKE A LOVELY LADY," Bobby says out of the blue after about twenty minutes.

"I'm sorry. What?"

"Emmy," he says. "You meeting up with Emmy?"

My shoulders lower. "No."

"Oh. My apologies."

"It's fine." I sigh and stare out the window.

When we get to the facility, I step out of the car and stand there for a moment. The building is a squat brick monolith amongst equally nondescript and unappealing buildings. There's a fenced concrete area at the side where a few patients are sitting on benches. There are pots against the wall that probably pass as the gardening activity.

I realize I always thought of nursing homes as happy farms and fields, a place to put ones loved ones out to pasture in the best way possible. Pushing wheelchairs through a garden, enjoying the shady pines and fresh air.

This is not that.

I take a breath, then walk through the front doors.

"Trystan Montgomery to see David Dubois," I tell the security guard.

The receptionist asks for ID and prints a visitor's badge.

"Mr. Montgomery," says a voice to my left. I turn and see a guy in scrubs.

He steps forward. "You were the one who rescued David from his outing. Friend of Emmy's, right?"

I hold out my hand. "Um. Yes."

He takes it. "D'Andre."

Ah. I nod and smile.

D'Andre turns to the receptionist. "It's cool. I'll show him up."

We head to the elevator.

"This is a surprise," he says. "Not sure how much you know about David's condition, but he comes in and out, you know?"

"Actually, I don't know what to expect. But I felt like visiting."

The elevator doors ding open. "Well, here we are." He walks past an empty nurses station. "Lunch hour," he says by way of explanation and continues on to the third door down the hall.

He opens the door and presses it back with an arm, letting me pass. "David. You have a visitor," he calls, and then to me, "I'll be downstairs if you need me."

The smells of ammonia, stale urine, and clean detergent fight over each other. David is sitting in a chair by the window. He's skinnier than the personality I imagined. Frail.

"David," I greet him as he stares at me with concern.

"D-Do I know you?"

"No, it's okay. We've never met."

He breathes out, relaxing slightly.

"I'm Trystan." I approach him and hold out my hand.

He makes to stand up.

"Not on my account." I smile then motion to the window.

"Besides, I think you can see the ocean from here." It's a stretch, but between the buildings, maybe.

"Trystan, you say?"

"Friend of Emmy's." I perch on the end of his bed as there's no other chair.

"Oh yes! I know you. You're her fella."

I swallow, not sure what to say. But he looks ecstatic so I don't correct him.

"Just had a lovely visit with Emmy."

"You did, huh?"

"She came by this morning."

I can't help a bemused laugh. "And how is she doing today?"

"Ah, you know. Always a big smile. She doesn't like me to worry."

"Of course. And I'm sure you don't like her to worry, either."

"Exactly right. I'm feeling good today. So clear about everything. I had to tell her to take some chances. She's scared."

"Of what?"

"Relationships. She was a foster child, you know?"

Inhaling, I purse my lips. "She hasn't told me much. I figured that out, but—"

"Well, she'd been through a bunch of families, but they hadn't worked out for one reason or another, then when she was about eleven she came to live with my sister and her husband."

I feel uncomfortable that David is telling me Emmy's secrets. It should be her telling me, right?

"They were older, of course," David goes on. "But still trying to do what they could since they'd never had kids of their own. She was a good girl. So nervous about getting in trouble and being sent away again."

I swallow, my throat feeling rough. Thinking of Emmy as a nervous little girl, scared she wouldn't be loved or even kept, makes my heart feel jagged in my chest.

"But they loved her," David assures me. "We all did. What's not to love, you know?" He laughs, and I stretch my mouth in a grimace that's nowhere near a smile.

"Anyway, Trystan. I thought you should know she's always single because I don't think she trusts things will last."

I shift. "Why are you telling me this, David?" Did Emmy call him or something?

"Shouldn't I?"

"I don't know." I know nothing anymore. I met a girl less than a week ago and am now getting all up in her business on purpose.

"Ah well. Today my mind actually knows what day of the week it is."

"Huh. Okay. And what day of the week is it?"

"I have no idea." He chuckles. "Every day here is the same as the last, isn't it?"

To: tmontgomery
From: edubois
Subject: Thank you

Dear Trystan,

This morning I found out David got a bed at Magnolia Meadows. I asked the administrator if you had something to do with it. She's either a fabulous actress or you really didn't pull any strings. My heart tells me you did though. So thank you. Again.

Warm regards,

Emmy

P.S. Just a reminder that all the women who texted you while I had your phone are due to show up at your place on Thursday at nine p.m. Sorry about that. But honestly, it was getting a little nauseating.

To: edubois
From: tmontgomery
Subject: Re: Thank you

Emmy ~

You probably won't get this because you won't be able to find it amongst all the junk in your inbox but stop thanking me.

I didn't do it for you. I did it for David. He lives with enough regrets, and at this point in his life he can't change anything. I was in a position to help with that. So I did.

Regards,

Trystan Montgomery

P.S. Thank you for the reminder. I've informed my doorman. I'm sorry my active dating life nauseated you. Luckily you no longer have to deal with it.

Dear Trystan Montgomery,

I heard you visited David. Thank you for taking the day to spend some time with an old man. You made him happy.

Good luck with the sale of your business. You must be so proud of what you built. In spite of your grandfather not reaching out to you, it's clear from his actions he had the utmost respect for you. And he wanted you back with your family. Where you belong. Your family is lucky to have you. And so are all the people who benefit from the business you inherited. They have a hero at the helm.

Regards,

Emmaline Dubois

P.S. You weren't dating. You were hooking up. I hope you start dating instead of hooking up because you deserve so much.

To: edubois
 From: tmontgomery
 Subject: Re: A life of regrets

Dear Emmaline Dubois,

If we are going to talk about value in the workplace, you can do better than having a boss who doesn't appreciate you.

The sale of my business went well yesterday. I sold it to a man (Mac) for whom I have the utmost respect. Over the years he's become friend and mentor.

I'm not sure I "belong" with my family, but it's nice to start getting to know them from a distance again.

Trystan L. Montgomery

P.S. What do I deserve? *Who* do I deserve? Because you made clear it wasn't you.

To: tmontgomery
From: edubois
Subject: Worth

Trystan L. Montgomery,
    Then you'll be pleased to know I put my foot down at work and got a promotion, a pay raise, and more days off.
    Mac sounds like a good person to know and a good judge of character if he counts you amongst his friends.
    Of course you belong with your family. And I'm glad you are getting to know them again. You should move to Charleston.

Emmy

P.S. Please understand, I didn't reject *you*. I rejected being hurt again. Does that make sense?

To: tmontgomery
  From: edubois
  Subject: Re: Worth

Nothing makes sense.

Trystan

39

TRYSTAN

*T*he streets of New York are bleak and gray. Even the heart and beating soul of the city—its people—are fraying my nerves today. The pedestrians are too thoughtless, the cab drivers too loud.

My apartment echoes as I enter the front door, holding the bag of my belongings I picked up from the hotel. Now that I've sold my company, I can no longer include The Chelsea Grand amongst my portfolio. I went by today and closed my account permanently.

My shoes clack along the hardwood floor, and I enter the bedroom and lay my suitcase on the bed. I open it up and pick up the hangers, unfurling my suits. I shake, smooth them out, and then hang them in my closet. Turning back to the bed, I reach for the stack of boxers and pause.

There in the stack is a piece of clothing I don't recognize. It's white with yellow and green pineapples all over it. Unfolding the item, and holding it by an apparent waistband, I see it's a pair of shorts. Women's underwear type shorts. Maybe pajama shorts and most definitely not mine. Emmy's? They must be. The night we—

My stomach tightens. I mash them to my face before I even think and inhale as if they are her. I only smell strong hotel detergent. Of course, the hotel must have found them in the room and laundered them. I'm inexplicably disappointed and sink down to sit on the edge of the bed.

I know Emmy's email this week was her trying to reach out. She was trying to smooth over the jagged edges of our parting. Her postscript about my dating life was meant to amuse. But it cut deep.

She's an appeaser, a smoother of ruffled feathers. Even in the few days I'd known her, she had an uncanny knack of calming my nerves, distracting me, even taking the pressure off my interactions with my family. I know I have to put her out of my mind, but I'm finding it almost impossible. How did someone manage to completely barrel into every single area of my life? Her attempt at a joke pissed me off. I sent her an abrupt postscript of my own. And I've been feeling pretty shitty about it. In retrospect it didn't piss me off, it hurt me.

Working with a realtor in Charleston to find a house, I find myself itching to text Emmy about her opinion a thousand times a day. Even when Mac and I went out for dinner at his club last night to celebrate the closing of our deal, I found myself wanting to reference something she said or tell him about her. I almost took a picture of my fucking food, for God's sake.

And what was there to tell Mac, exactly? Nothing. He was old school. Telling him I had phone sex with a stranger and then met up with her to do it in real life would shock him. And I wouldn't be able to explain how we even got to that stage. How we just . . . clicked, and even though we didn't know each other, for a brief moment we'd had the kind of chemistry that clearly transcended time, place, and physical proximity.

And I wouldn't be able to explain how it ended when I didn't understand it myself.

Earlier in the week I opened a dating app and made an

arrangement to meet up with a girl I'd texted with a few times, then promptly cancelled. The thought of trying to suffer through awkward conversation is bad enough. The thought of being naked with someone who isn't Emmy, flat out leaves me cold. And feeling slightly ill.

But I also know it's not all about Emmy. It's about something that has fundamentally changed inside me, either from spending time with my family in Charleston, selling my business, meeting Emmy, or a combination of all three. I feel completely lost. But also like I found a lost piece of myself. I'm a different person, and I don't know how to fit into my own life.

It could also be that it's Friday in the city, a weekday, and for the first time in ten years, I have no office to go to. What did I used to do on Friday nights? Did I really hook up that much? I had acquaintances, sure. But did I have good friends?

On Friday nights, Emmy goes out dancing. I squeeze my eyes closed. In a few hours, it will be a week since I got to be inside her.

Aaargh. I can't fucking get her out of my head.

Fuck it. I strip and get into my running gear and leave the condo, heading for Central Park. Maybe if I tire myself out enough, I won't think about anything. I can run right through whatever existential crisis I'm having, and maybe it will all be better. I'm supposed to go out tomorrow with some guys I've known since I first moved to New York, and I'd like to be jovial and not a complete sad sack.

I finally slow as I finish my loop. I'm not nearly exhausted enough not to think. I have a hankering to walk the city in search of a place like Armand's. Something small where someone knows me. But the city is massive, and it's no easy task, especially living uptown where I do. I settle for Starbucks and think maybe I'd be happier if I bought a condo in Chelsea. At least it feels like a neighborhood down there, and it has cobbled streets like Charleston.

I should make sure any place I find in Charleston is in a charming historic neighborhood. Though I need to tell my realtor about my allergy to ghosts. Maybe a new building but still in a charming neighborhood?

I pull out my phone as I walk and begin a quick email to the realtor, asking her to narrow down the search to the French Quarter. I lift my thumb off the screen before I hit send. I need to think about this, and I can't type and walk.

Or I could move to Charleston permanently. I have to be there for Montgomery Homes anyway.

But bumping into Emmy would be hard. Maybe for her too.

God. And doesn't that just say it all? David's words about Emmy's growing up came back to me. She's single because she's afraid things won't last.

I stop walking.

Suddenly I'm thrust forward by a blow at my back. My phone and coffee fly out of my hands, and I get my footing just in time —a miracle since my legs are tired from running.

"Geez. Watch it," a man yells. "This is New York! You can't stop dead in the street." He shakes his head and turns away, marching on. "Fucking tourists."

I'm speechless, not able to respond, adrenaline ebbing from the sudden shock, and then he's gone. I lean down and grab my now empty paper coffee cup and step over the milky mess on the sidewalk so I can reach my phone. The screen is smashed.

I think I might need a much-needed break from this city. I came here hungry, scrappy, and ambitious. Now I'm just fucking tired.

"Excuse me?" a female voice says behind me.

I move to the side. "Sorry," I say so she can pass.

"No, I wanted to tell you that you have something stuck to the back of your shorts."

She's a pretty brunette in a skirt suit and heels.

"What?"

"Turn around," she says, laughing. I smile, bemused, and do what she says. "Okay. Look."

I look back to see her dangling a pale pink scrap of elastic, silk, and lace. Frowning, I bob my head back.

"You're embarrassed. Sorry. But it happens all the time. Static cling from the dryer."

"Those aren't mine." I'm so confused.

She laughs again and presses them into my hand. "You don't seem like you wear women's underwear. Though who knows? But they belong to someone special, I hope?"

I used Emmy's washer and dryer . . . wore these exact running shorts in Charleston. "Yes, someone special," I echo.

"She's probably been wondering where they are. Have a good day."

She strolls off. And I'm left holding an empty coffee cup, a smashed phone, and yet another pair of Emmy's undergarments. Twice in one day.

What in the actual fuck is this life?

To: edubois
From: tmontgomery
Subject: Haunted

I'm being haunted by your underwear.

Regards,
Trystan L. Montgomery

On Saturday, I visit the smart phone store and buy a new phone. Thank God I have everything backed up, I think, and have a brief understanding of what Emmy must have felt like to have lost her phone and have nothing backed up. It's incredible how much we depend on these things.

But I'm grateful.

Without one, I'd never have met her.

I re-download all my apps. Well, not all of them. I don't replace all my dating apps, except one. Then I go through my recovered texts from the days Emmy had my phone and save D'Andre's number, her friend Annie's number that I'd forwarded to her, and begin to make plans.

40

EMMY

"*I*'m not doing it!" I stressed to Annie and Armand as we hung out in his empty café on Monday after work. Armand was chopping and prepping for the next morning. Annie and I nursed a huge slice of gluten-free carrot cake.

"Why?" asked Annie. "You told me you were ready to start putting yourself out there again. This was *your* idea."

"Yeah, well, I changed my mind."

Annie and Armand glanced at each other.

"What?" I asked them.

"Can I see?" asked Annie, looking at my phone.

I handed it to her. "Be my guest. I thought we were getting together to celebrate your return to work and my promotion. Now it feels like an intervention."

She opened up the Whirl app I'd downloaded. I'd seen it on Trystan's phone but never tried it myself. It seemed like the least obscene of all the dating apps though. At Annie's insistence, I'd gone ahead and put my profile up over my lunch break.

"You have a notification," she said.

"Already?" I asked, surprised.

"She does?" Armand came around from the kitchen area.

I frowned. "That was quick. God, don't open it," I squeaked and leaned across to try and grab my phone.

Annie held it out of reach. "Why?"

I swallowed. "I don't know. Just—I'm not ready."

"*Aye, Madre.* You will never be ready," Armand grumbled.

"Too late," Annie sang. "Oh, he's close by too."

"Wait, how do you know that? I thought this wasn't supposed to be like Tinder?"

She shrugged. "Oh, there's a location setting you can turn on. I turned it on."

"Oh my God," I moaned. "If I get kidnapped or killed, it's on your hands."

"Oh. Wow." Annie's mouth dropped open.

"What?" I lunged for the phone. Annie stood, abruptly moving it out of reach as Armand joined her.

"Yes," Armand said and smiled at me. "It is just as I hoped."

Annie pressed her hand to her cheek. "Holy shit, he's hot." Then she looked to Armand, who nodded and pursed his lips as if to say, "See?"

"Dammit," I said loudly. "Can I at least look at my own phone?"

Annie grinned at me. "So you want to see him now, huh?"

"No. Fine. Yes."

"Let . . . me . . . just . . ." She did something on the screen. "Confirm the match. There." She handed me my phone.

"Wait. What did you do?" I looked down and my heart stopped.

Trystan Montgomery? He filled my screen.

Forget stopped, my heart *hurt.*

Why would they do this to me? "What the hell is this?" I asked. "Is this a joke?" God, he looked good. He was in a suit, holding . . . wait. Was that a cat? Was that Tuna? "He's holding my cat!" I looked up at my two friends' smug faces.

"I took the picture," Armand said, looking pleased, then seeing my face sobered somewhat. "Sorry. I thought it was funny."

"Just read his profile," Annie begged. "Please?"

My skin throbbed with heat and betrayal. I felt like I was in some elaborate joke. I stood. "No."

"No?"

"What is this?" I asked, my voice beginning to shake. "Do you think it's some kind of joke to put me in this position with him?"

"He asked us to. He asked for help." Annie chewed her lip, her eyes large as she realized how upset I was.

"He did? Why?"

Armand came and put his arm around me. "Emmy. He likes you. He really likes you."

"But . . . I can't be with him."

"Why not?" Annie touched the top of my hand.

"Because Trystan doesn't do relationships."

"He wants one with you," she said.

I swallowed, my tongue feeling like it might slip down and choke me. I was lightheaded. Probably from shock at being railroaded by my supposed two best friends.

"Yeah, well why is he putting himself on a dating app, then? And to do it Charleston and right under my nose? What the hell? How is that supposed to make me see him as relationship material?"

"Could you just look at his profile, already?" Annie whined.

I squeezed my eyes closed. "I don't want to. I thought we were going to hang out here, then I was going to get an early night because I have to get to the airport and meet D'Andre and David tomorrow morning. It's a big day for me. I can't do this right now. I love you guys. I'm sure Trystan made it sound like a great idea. And I'm sure you didn't mean to hurt me." My eyes stung with unshed tears. "But I can't do this."

Armand looked stricken, Annie confused.

I stood up.

I double clicked the home button on my phone and swiped

up, effectively closing the app and closing the door on Trystan.
"Bye," I managed to my two friends and grabbed my purse.

I burst out of the café into the muggy evening. It was still light. Taking a deep breath, I secured my purse on my shoulder, turned for home, and stopped dead.

Trystan stood outside the gate to my cottage, leaning against the wall in sneakers, dark jeans, and a light gray T-shirt that molded to his upper body. He pushed up when he saw me. His face was open, hopeful. His eyes in the evening light caught the color of his shirt and almost took my breath away.

Great. I had been set up completely and then caught in mid run by the very guy I was running from.

Whatever he saw on my face made his expression turn serious. He raked the fingers of one hand through his brown hair and grabbed the back of his neck.

"It didn't go well in there." I nodded behind me to indicate the café. My tone was somewhat accusing. I wasn't good at being blindsided.

"I'm gathering that." He grimaced. "I'm sorry, Emmy."

We stared at each other. It felt like the first time when we stared at each other over the phone screen, finally getting to see the person we'd imagined in our minds from our brief meeting and through pictures.

"Please, can we talk?" he asked.

I walked closer and dug in my purse for my keys. "Why didn't you come and talk to me if you needed to. Why did you enlist my friends? I hate feeling manipulated. You know that."

"I wasn't manipulating. I wanted to show you something. To tell you something."

"And that was?" I asked as I unlocked the gate. A cool breeze blew, making me feel underdressed in my blue and white sundress.

"Can we talk inside?"

I exhaled, my shoulders lowering. "Trystan—"

"Please, Emmy."

"Fine." I pushed open the gate, and he held it over my shoulder as I went in then followed me. Dammit, the smell of him like pine trees and waterfalls made me feel high.

I unlocked my front door, my heart pounding with nerves, entered, and dumped my purse on a kitchen chair. "So you talked to my friends and came up with some stupid idea of meeting me on a dating app? I can't think of what else it was. What in the hell kind of idea is that?" I turned with my arms crossed over my chest.

Trystan closed the door and looked around. Then he stuffed his fingers in his jeans. "Apparently not the best one. I wanted you to know something before I came and tried to talk to you in person. So Annie suggested it."

"And what was it you needed me to know? That you're thirty-one?" I started counting on my fingers. "You no longer go by Jeff? Good job not lying. That you love cats now instead of dogs? That you look sexy as shit in a suit? I already know that. That you may be open to hooking up with someone in Charleston too, instead of just in Manhattan?" Ugh. "Lucky me," I added with a sarcastic tone.

"No. That I'm all in, Emmy. Whatever this is between you and me, I'm all in. That's what I wanted you to know."

I closed my eyes, too afraid to let myself believe his words. My palms felt sweaty.

"And you thought I'd get that from a dating profile?" I stalked over to the fridge and pulled out a bottle of white wine I'd opened a few days ago. Pulling the cork out, I took down a wine glass from the upper cabinet and poured a hefty serving. Then I left it sitting on the counter as I turned to face him.

"Well, you didn't read it, so I guess not."

"You know what?" I asked.

"What?"

"We did better when we were separated by eight hundred fifty miles and just had a cell phone connection."

Trystan folded his arms across his chest, his T-shirt stretched around his biceps, the muscles in his forearms flexed. He set his jaw. "Is that right?"

The way he wore those broken-in jeans, the soft T-shirt, and stood there all hot and annoyed was . . .

I grabbed the glass of wine and took a swig. "That's right."

Trystan approached slowly until he was a few feet away. "Because the way you sobbed my name in ecstasy upstairs the last time I was here would say otherwise."

Heat flashed through me, and I caught my breath. "That's not fair," I whispered.

"Not fair? What's not fair is you not even giving me a chance."

"A chance to break me?"

"A chance to love you."

I swallowed. Hard. With a shaking hand, I set down my glass before I spilled it all over myself. "Why would you even say that? You don't."

His mouth opened. Closed. His jaw ticked and his eyes flickered.

Then his lips hardened. "I could," he said.

"You . . . could? Wow. I'm flattered."

"Emmy."

"It's fine, Trystan. Lovely. But it's not certain. We've known each other for less than two weeks. And I . . . I . . ."

"Nothing is certain, Emmy. God knows I learned that the hard way too." He unfolded his arms and caged me in against the counter, looking down at me.

I lowered my face and closed my eyes. God, he smelled good.

"Emmy, look at us. We're both products of really fucked up upbringings. You clung to family. I shoved it away. But now when it comes to us, to the chance of us being something, you're the one shoving it away, and I'm the one hanging on and hoping like hell. How is that sane, or fair?"

I shook my head. "How we met was crazy. Accidental. It was a twist of fate. We were caught up in it. But it's not real."

Trystan grabbed my face in his hands, tilting me to look at him. His hands were hot. His eyes were ice and fire, angry and hungry all at the same time. They roamed my face and settled on my mouth.

Before I could even process that I wanted him to kiss me, his lips were on me.

He crushed his mouth to mine, sending a missile of arousal through me like a lightning bolt.

Whereas the first time he'd kissed me had been slow and searching, building to a fever, this started on the edge of desperation.

I was instantly overwhelmed with the feel and taste of him. His hard body against mine, pinning me to the counter, and the heat of his tongue as it swept into my mouth. Fire raced along my skin, and my hands were wrapped around his head before I could even think.

Anger and fear had my lips and tongue working to punish him. To take what I wanted while I had it. But it pierced my awareness I was kissing him like I wanted to consume him, like I never, ever wanted to stop. I couldn't stop. God, it was so good. Why couldn't I stop? He tasted like summer and rain, cold beer and hot sex.

Trystan's hands swept down my sides, up my back, fisted in my hair, and then I was lifted onto the counter and my body closed around his—legs and arms gripping tightly, his body in my embrace, and it felt incredible.

He pulled back, and I made some sound of desperation to get him back.

"God, Emmy." His words were an aching whisper against my mouth before his lips were on mine again.

My hands left his hair and roamed over his T-shirt-covered muscled shoulders then down his back, and I had to feel his hot

skin once. Our desperation had slowed slightly, but every movement seemed deeper, harder, more deliberate.

He grunted against my mouth as my fingers met skin. His
hips rocked slow and hard against me, his own hand hauling my
lower body tight and close. His tongue dipped deeply against
mine before retreating. God, he was making love to my mouth.
He was making love to *me* fully clothed. His lips left mine and
slid toward my ear, his hot breath searing goosebumps over my
skin like a blowtorch. "We're not imagining this. Please don't
push me away."

"This feels good."

"So good."

"But this isn't enough." I set my hands on his chest and pushed
gently.

He let up.

My body throbbed with need. With unexpended passion.
Trystan . . ." my voice wobbled. "Chemistry is great. Yes, I admit
it. But—"

"You think I'm shallow? Is that it? That I can't or won't take us
seriously? You're not just a hookup, Emmy. What do I need to do
to prove to you I'm willing to give this a shot?"

"I don't know." I blew out a breath and pushed at him so I
could hop off the counter.

He didn't budge, one hand was on my bare knee, the other
scorching a brand on my thigh. "Let me just stand here. I won't
kiss you, I promise."

I didn't want that promise. I ached and throbbed between my
thighs. I wanted to flick open his jeans and pull him out, and . . .
Emmy, keep your wits.

"Fine." I leaned back on two hands, working hard not to show
how much I wanted him inside me. His eyes dropped to my chest
that my position had thrust forward, then returned to mine.

He swallowed heavily. "You think you're the only one afraid
of this?"

I sighed. "Trystan. I know I was wrong. I labeled you wrong from the start. You aren't a shallow, serial dater. At least, you don't mean to be. You were afraid of being rejected. So you stayed in control the only way you knew how—by never getting close."

"You know I'm afraid of being rejected. Yet here I fucking stand."

I winced. "But I labeled myself wrong too," I continued, trying to say my piece while I had the courage. "I never realized how afraid I was of being vulnerable again. And I was with you. I *am* with you. So vulnerable. You've blown through layers of me to a core I've spent since childhood protecting. And it happened before I even realized you did it."

Trystan touched my chin, asking me to look at him. But I had to look away from the intensity in his eyes, suddenly feeling like I'd admitted too much. "I've learned the hard way," I continued with difficulty, "that just because someone makes you feel happy, or safe and secure, or protected, doesn't mean you are." I swallowed. "I'm sorry. I I don't think I'm ready to trust those things. It took meeting you to realize I have major issues."

"Take a chance, Emmy. Please."

I lowered my chin, refusing to look at him. With my eyes closed I could focus on his delicious woodsy smell and the feel of his hands on the skin of my legs. "I'm scared," I admitted. "Because God, I want to take a chance so badly."

"Me too."

I sighed. "I know. And I'm sorry."

"Emmy—"

When I heard him cut himself off, I looked up automatically. He bit his teeth together and then breathed in through his nose deeply.

Eventually he squeezed his eyes closed for long moments. When they opened and found me, he seemed calm.

He cleared his throat. "Can we be scared together?"

41

EMMY

*T*rystan dropped his forehead to rest against mine, and I looped my arms around his tense shoulders.

"Yes," I said finally. "Okay. Let's be scared together." I lifted my face.

"Thank Christ, Emmy." He breathed the words against my lips.

"But—" I started.

"I know," Trystan said. "Slow."

I pulled back, bemused. "How did you know that's what I was going to say?"

His shoulders lifted slightly. "We've done everything backward."

I tap my finger on my chin. "What comes first? Kissing? Let's do more of it. Right now, if possible."

He chuckled. "I was thinking more of you inviting me in for a drink so we can get to know each other more."

"You're already in. For someone who doesn't date, you seem to have a pretty set idea of how it's supposed to go."

He let go of me and slapped a hand to his forehead. "And I still got it wrong. We have to have the date first before you invite me in."

"Good point."

His brow furrowed. "So when can I see you?"

I glanced around the room. "Now?"

"Maybe tomorrow?" he asked.

"Are you sure you're feeling okay?" I pressed my palm to his forehead.

"Hey, I can go slow. If I have to."

"That's not slow, it's glacial." I huffed with disappointment. "And you don't have to go *that* slow."

"Actually, I was thinking I could take you to the airport to get David."

I licked my lips. "That . . . that might be really nice. Not your typical date though."

"But there's nothing typical about us. And I'm thinking it's a pretty big day. I'd like to be there for you. But also, it might be good for me to see what the transition is like and be a fly on the wall at one of the facilities I own."

"Spy on them, you mean?" I arch an eyebrow.

His lips quirked. "Sort of."

"How romantic."

"Right? I thought it was the most brilliant idea I've ever had."

I punched his arm softly, laughing. "Jerk."

"I can buy you an airport coffee."

"You just keep coming up with winners."

Trystan's lips settled on mine for another round of soft and slow kisses.

"They are going to be insufferable, by the way," I muttered when we broke apart again.

"Who?"

"Armand and Annie. They'll take full responsibility for us."

He squeezed my knee. The soft lighting made his hair and eyes darker. "Us. I like that. And I don't care."

I couldn't look away from him. I couldn't believe I was

jumping into this with him. "Me too," I said, grinning. "And since you *are* already in, can I offer you a drink? I may have a couple of those beers left if you didn't drink them all."

"Sure. That'd be good."

He stepped back, and I hopped off the counter and got him a cold beer. Grabbing my glass of wine, we went to sit on the couch. I curled up on one end, expecting him to go to the other.

"This is . . ."

"Weird," he said.

"Yeah."

"Come here." He helped me up and settled in my spot then gently pulled me down next to him.

I melted against his warm, solid frame, and curled my legs up next to me.

"Emmy?"

"Yeah."

"How did you crack the code to my phone?"

"Ah, so that's what this is about. You want to know my secrets."

"I do," he said then brought his mouth to my ear, causing a flight of goosebumps to flutter down my body. "I want to know them all. Especially what's in your bedside drawer."

I swallowed down a flood of embarrassed laughter. "You have to pick. How I cracked the code to your phone, or what's in my bedside drawer."

"Aww, come on."

I shook my head.

"Tell me both, and I'll tell you what the L stands for," he offered.

"That's one secret for two, what kind of businessman are you?"

"One who always gets two for the price of one." He chuckled.

"Ha. Not from me you don't."

"Okay, how about you tell me about growing up?"

I tensed.

"You don't have to, of course, and David's told me a few things, but—"

"What do you want to know?"

"Whatever you want to tell me?"

I glanced sideways at him. "Does it really matter?"

"It matters to me."

"Well, I was never abused if that's what you're thinking. And I don't know much about what the situation was that got me into the foster system. But I never found a forever home until the Dubois family took me in. God, I sound like a stray cat."

"You were." He smiled, but it was a sad smile.

"Don't feel sorry for me, Trystan. I'm happy. I got a good family in the end. My foster father had a weak heart and my foster mom died of breast cancer, but you can't predict those things. They gave me the years they had left. And when they were gone, I had David. I was grateful for every moment they wanted to keep me around."

Trystan took a sip of his beer with his free hand. "You have an amazing outlook on life."

"There's no point in being any other way." I shrugged and sipped my own drink.

"Yes, but I get it now. Why you're having a hard time giving us a chance." He leaned forward and removed his arm from my shoulder, dislodging me from his side.

I made a sound of distress at the loss of his warmth.

He set down his beer and moved off the couch to sit on the coffee table facing me, his legs spread.

"I want to keep you around," he said with intensity.

"Good," I smiled. "I want to keep you around too."

"I mean it. I want to keep you."

"Okay." I narrowed my eyes still grinning. "Weirdo."

He leaned forward and pressed his lips to mine. "Thanks for the drink, but I think I'm going to go."

"Wait. What?" My stomach sank.

"Taking it slow, remember?"

I pouted. "Where are you staying?"

"At my grandmother's if you can believe it. For now. But I'm going to move to Charleston permanently."

My sinking stomach suddenly lurched right back up my insides in happiness. "You are?" I couldn't help the grin that spread, even as I tried to bite my lips to keep it in.

"I take it that's a good thing."

I nodded. "Very."

He smirked and leaned forward again. Taking my face in his, he kissed my mouth softly then my forehead. "Emmy, I . . ."

"What?"

He let out a breath. "Nothing. I'll see you in the morning."

* * *

I WOKE IN MY BED, sunlight streaming through the cracks in the blinds. Stretching across my empty bed, I reached for my phone on the nightstand. It was early. Early enough to enjoy lying in bed for a few minutes.

Silently, I apologized to my morning *Skimm* email with the latest things I had to know in the world, and instead I pulled up the dating app Armand and Annie had tried to get me to look at last night.

Trystan's image filled the screen again, and I took a moment to really look. My gaze traced his hair that caught the sunlight and the curves and hard lines of his face. His eyes. The crinkles near his eyes, though he wasn't smiling exactly. It was more of a candid shot. His lips. I wanted to kiss those again. Soon. His suit. And then . . .

I turned and looked at my cat, Tuna, who lay next to me and stared through slitted eyes. "Traitor," I whispered.

Tuna let out a sound like a half meow as if he couldn't quite muster up the energy for a response, then lapsed into a deep purr.

I scrolled down:

97% match.

Trystan

31 years old.

0.6 miles away.

Charleston, SC

LOOKING FOR: Only redheads (real ones). Cats not dogs (can be persuaded. I mean . . . dogs). Sense of humor. Girls who read poetry. Take pictures of food. Sew. Freckles. Cream no sugar. Must be 28. Live in French Quarter. Must have ability to dance to Latin beats. Gluten free. Better with no makeup. Great at job but dislike boss. Must have French sounding name. And love dirty talk. Also don't mean to be creepy, but have no blood relatives they consider family. Someone to build a life with.

I SMILED STUPIDLY. Reading this first would certainly have primed me to see Trystan in a more positive light when he showed up last night. It was a silly move. A silly gesture. But I could see the heartfelt nature of it. And I could certainly see Annie's fingerprints all over it. My phone vibrated as I held it.

TRYSTAN: *Good morning.*

MORNING.

I PRESSED my lips together to control my smile and stop the butterflies flying from my stomach up my throat.

I'M CONCERNED *about the 3%.*

TRYSTAN: *What? 3%? This is Trystan. You did save my number in your phone, right? You didn't delete it?*

LOL. Our dating profile says we are a 97% match. I'm concerned about the 3%.

TRYSTAN: *Oh. About that. I think it's sexual compatibility.*

I SNORTED A LAUGH.

WHAT?

TRYSTAN: *You know? In the bedroom?*

I KNOW WHAT IT MEANS. *But it makes no sense.*

TRYSTAN: *You said it, not me.*

HA.

TRYSTAN: *But you know . . . maybe there are a couple things you wouldn't try. Not assuming, just suggesting.*

NOT LIKELY.

TRYSTAN: *Oh Emmy, be careful.*

A THRILL of giddiness went through me. My insides felt warm and gooey. I was glad he left last night after we spoke though. I think we both needed to get some distance and perspective on our feelings. Spoiler, they hadn't changed. He still made me all sorts of terrified, but it was mixed with the most exquisite and exhilarating joy.

PROMISES. Promises. I text back, biting my lip to contain my smile.

TRYSTAN: *Looking forward to our first date. (He says, trying to change the subject and keep his dirty, dirty mind in check)*

IT'S AN INTERESTING FIRST DATE, that's for sure.

TRYSTAN: *Picking you up to take you to the airport so you can meet another man? Sure.*

NOT MAN. Men! David AND D'Andre.

TRYSTAN: *Yep. Men. I'm taking you to meet two other men.*

AND BUYING ME COFFEE.

TRYSTAN: *You still in bed?*

YES.

TRYSTAN: *Me too . . .*

OH NO YOU DON'T.

TRYSTAN: *Aww. Come on. What r u wearing?*

NOTHING.

TRYSTAN: *:: Groan :: Fantastic. And what is your hand doing?*

HOLDING THE PHONE.

TRYSTAN: *Your other hand?*

STROKING my pussy

I CHUCKLED AND TEXTED AGAIN.

PUSSY CAT.

TUNA.

TRYSTAN: *I didn't get your last two messages.*

HA HA.

TRYSTAN: *Whhhyyyy won't you tell me how you bypassed the security code on my phone?*

WHY WON'T you tell me what the L in your name stands for?

TRYSTAN: *Not even my shrink knows that.*

YOU DON'T HAVE A SHRINK.

TRYSTAN: *Do you remember how you said that when we texted you felt like you could tell me anything?*

YEAH . . .

TRYSTAN: *Be my shrink then. Can I tell you something? Something I backed off telling you last night?*

I LICKED my lips nervously and shifted in the bed.

WHY COULDN'T you tell me?

TRYSTAN: *I was worried you wouldn't believe me. Or you'd run away again. It was thiiiiiiiis close last night.*

I FROWNED.

WHY TELL me this morning then? What changed?

TRYSTAN: *I'm taking a chance.*

OKAY, shoot.

TRYSTAN: *Do you promise to accept it on face value?*

FACE VALUE?

TRYSTAN: *Like . . . it is what it is.*

YOU'RE PUTTING it in writing. So it has to stand.

TRYSTAN: *It does.*

I WAITED, biting my lip and scowling at my phone.

TRYSTAN: *Here goes . . .*

TRYSTAN: *I think we should try anal.*

OH MY GOD.

TRYSTAN: *Just kidding.*

TRYSTAN: *What I wanted to say was . . .*

TRYSTAN: *I fell for you before I ever touched you. But I didn't think you'd believe me. Or you'd be too shocked and reject it. But I'm pretty sure about it. I've never felt the way I do about you, ever. And now this doesn't seem so shocking after the anal comment does it?*

OH MY GOD. You. Are. A. Psycho.

TRYSTAN: *Nah. Just a little fucked in the head.*

MY HEART BEAT SO HARD, I sat up in bed dislodging the cat and causing him to give a disgruntled mewl.

PICK *me up in thirty minutes. I need time to process . . .*

HOLY SHIT, did I ever need time to process. Thirty minutes might not cut it. But it would have to do since I didn't want to be late to get to the airport to meet David and D'Andre, who was so kindly escorting him to South Carolina.

My feelings for Trystan had shocked me too. They'd made me completely freak out after sleeping with him. Knowing he'd been feeling the same way . . . I sighed and couldn't help the stupid grin on my face. God, we were like two newborn calves trying to walk. It probably wasn't going to be easy, but if he was willing to take a chance, I guess I was too.

TRYSTAN: *Your processing time is freaking me out. Why I decided to text you and not tell you to your face is beyond me. I need to see you right now.*

RELAX. *Texting is what we do best :)*

TRYSTAN: *Not true. We do other things extremely well. Texting is like . . . third.*

GUESS WHAT?

TRYSTAN: *What?*

IT'S TUESDAY.

TRYSTAN: *And?*

AND?!?! It's our anniversary. *The anniversary of our accidental meeting.*

TRYSTAN: *So it is.*

I LOVE TUESDAYS.

AND YOU.

Thank you for reading Emmy and Trystan's Story

Beau's story
INCONVENIENT WIFE
Coming Soon

Join my reader group so you never miss a release:
http://eepurl.com/dk9N75

Or text NATASHABOYD to 31996 from a US based cellphone

Have you read my romance EVERSEA?
Would you like a free copy?
Go here to claim your free book

ACKNOWLEDGMENTS

Thank you so much for joining me on this journey with Emmy and Trystan. You, dear readers, are the reason I do this. If my books can help anyone smile, laugh, cry or get out of their own heads for even few minutes in this crazy world, I consider that a success. Please consider leaving an honest review, no matter how short. I'm not exaggerating when I say it's the most wonderful gift you can give an author after buying their book. Many times retailers and other advertisers only offer us promotional opportunities when we have reviews, so we depend on them to grow our careers. It also helps other readers discover our work.

Thank you to my husband for his continuing and uplifting support of me and my career. Honey, I love you so much. I could never do this without you. Thank you to my sons for tolerating my hours spent typing.

Julie of hearttocover.com, thank you for working with me on my vision of the pink vintage UK chick-lit covers! Julie and Lisa, and Karina, my dear friends and beta readers, I appreciate you so much. Karina, I don't know how I'd live without our WhatsApp voice-memo friendship! It keeps me sane. Tech historians of the future will have a gold mine if they ever get a hold of our threads.

Thank you, Karen Lawson, for your eagle eyes.

Judy, (Judy-roth.com) thank you for your amazing editing services. I can't ever imagine publishing a book without your eyes and input on my work.

ALSO BY NATASHA BOYD

The Butler Cove Novels
Eversea (Eversea #1)
Forever, Jack (Eversea #2)
My Star, My Love (An Eversea Christmas Novella)
All That Jazz
Beach Wedding (Eversea #3)

and

Deep Blue Eternity
(*A standalone contemporary romance*)
and
Accidental Tryst (*March 2018*)
(*A Romantic Comedy*)
Inconvenient Wife (*Coming Soon*)

ALSO : Ever wished your favorite romance author would write a "bookclub" type book? Well, I did! *The Indigo Girl* a historical fiction (or should I say, *herstorical* fiction?) novel is available now in hardcover, ebook and audio. It's based on a true story and it's a woman's story you don't want to miss.

Inconvenient Wife coming 2018

All Beau Montgomery, one of Charleston's most eligible bachelors, wants to do is build boats. He has no interest in marriage whatsoever ... until it means he might not get his inheritance and he can kiss his boat building dreams goodbye. But the hungry hordes of Charleston debutantes looking to score a Montgomery scare him sh*tless. Luckily, his best girlfriend Gwen has found him the perfect out. Marry a member of the armed services by proxy! He'll never have to even meet the girl! Though her emails are starting to become highly addictive.

Gwen has loved Beau Montgomery since she used to run barefoot around the marina as scrappy preteen tomboy. Knowing she'll never fit into his high society family, she decided long ago that she'd become his indispensable best friend rather than not be in his life at all. When he tells her he needs to marry in order to fulfill his dreams, she panics that he might actually meet someone and she'll lose him forever. So she hatches the perfect plan. A marriage by proxy! But when her chosen target proves unreliable and impossible to pin down, Gwen writes Beau a few emails just to keep the connection going before the big day. I mean Beau is never going to even meet this woman in real life so what does does it matter if the words are hers ...

COMING SOON

Add it to your Goodreads

ABOUT THE AUTHOR

Natasha Boyd holds a Bachelor of Science in Psychology. She has lived in Spain, South Africa, Belgium, England and wrote most of the Butler Cove novels while residing with her husband and two boys on Hilton Head Island, SC, USA—complete with Spanish moss, alligators and mosquitos the size of tiny birds. She now splits her time between the "Lowcountry" and Atlanta, GA.
Text NATASHABOYD to 31996